ERLE STANLEY GARDNER

- Cited by the Guinness Book of World Records as the #1 best-selling writer of all time!

- Author of more than 150 clever, authentic, and sophisticated mystery novels!

- Creator of the amazing Perry Mason, the savvy Della Street, and dynamite detective Paul Drake!

- **THE ONLY AUTHOR WHO OUT-SELLS AGATHA CHRISTIE, HAROLD ROBBINS, BARBARA CARTLAND, AND LOUIS L'AMOUR *COMBINED!***

Why?

Because he writes the best, most fascinating whodunits of all!

You'll want to read every one of them,
from
BALLANTINE BOOKS

D0908062

The Case of the
Dangerous
Dowager

Erle Stanley Gardner

BALLANTINE BOOKS • NEW YORK

ISBN 0-345-33192-3

This edition published by arrangement with William Morrow and
Company

Manufactured in the United States of America

First Ballantine Books Edition: August 1986

CAST OF CHARACTERS

and PERRY MASON

1

PERRY MASON studied the white-haired woman with
that interest which new clients always aroused. She returned the lawyer's gaze with bright gray eyes in which a
hard glitter gradually softened to a twinkle.

"No," she said, "I haven't killed anyone—not yet, I
haven't. But don't think I'm a peaceful old lady who sits
by the fire and knits, because I'm not. I'm a hard-bitten
old hellion."

The lawyer laughed. "Perhaps," he said, "this gambling
girl you wanted to see me about may be overshadowed
by a . . ."

"Dowager," she said, as he hesitated. "Go on and say
it—a dangerous dowager. I saw you in court when you
were trying that howling dog case, Mr. Mason. I liked you
because you fought every inch of the way. I'm something of a fighter myself."

Della Street, catching Mason's eye, said to the woman,
"I'd like to have your name, age, and address for our office records."

"The name's Matilda Benson," the dowager said.
"The address is 1090 Wedgewood Drive. The age is none
of your business."

"How long have you been smoking cigars?" Mason
asked curiously.

Her eyes flicked back to his. "Ever since I kicked loose
from the conventional traces."

"When was that?"

"After my husband died and I realized what spineless

hypocrites my relatives were . . . do you have to go into all that?"

Mason said, "I'd like to know something about your background. Go ahead. You're doing fine— So you kicked over the traces?"

"Yes. And I'm getting worse every year. My husband's relatives think I'm a brand for the burning—and I don't give a damn what they think! You hear a lot about people who are afraid to die. Well, they're nothing compared to the ones who are afraid to live—people who go through life just making motions—and conventional motions at that. My relatives think I've started Sylvia on the downward path and . . ."

"Who's Sylvia?" Mason interrupted.

"My granddaughter."

"Married?"

"Yes. To Frank Oxman. And they have a daughter, Virginia. She's six now."

"So," Mason said, "you're a great-grandmother?"

She puffed contentedly at the big cigar. "Yes," she admitted, "I'm a great-grandmother."

"Tell me some more about your husband's relatives," the lawyer invited. "Have you been fighting with them?"

"Not particularly. I got fed up with them, with what they stood for. I just revolted, that's all."

"Revolted at what?"

She frowned impatiently, "Why worry so much about my ideas of life?"

"Because they're interesting. I want to get your mental background before I decide whether I can take your case."

"Well," she said, "I'm making up some of my lost life. I was brought up according to rigid, puritanic standards. None of the people around me took time out to enjoy life. They couldn't enjoy youth because they were preparing to take a part in life. They couldn't enjoy themselves after that because they were saving money for their

2

old age. And they put in their old age making peace with God. I was brought up on that philosophy. Then my husband died and I was left alone. There was some insurance money. I invested that and did well with it. I started to travel, looked around me, and decided I might as well enjoy life. I was past sixty and I'd never really lived.

"Now I drink, swear, smoke cigars, and do as I damn please. I'm tired of living a treadmill existence. I have enough money to allow me to do things the way I want."

"And you need a lawyer?" Mason asked.

She nodded, suddenly serious.

"Why? Are you in some trouble?"

"Not yet."

"But you expect to be?"

She pursed her lips thoughtfully, regarded the tip of her cigar, flicked the ash from it with a deftly expert little finger, and said, "I hope it won't come to that."

"Exactly what is it," Mason asked, "that you want me to do?"

"Do you know a man by the name of Sam Grieb?"

"No. Who is he?"

"He's a gambler. He and a man by the name of Duncan run *The Horn of Plenty*. That's the gambling ship that's anchored out beyond the twelve-mile limit."

"What about Grieb?" Mason asked.

"He's put Sylvia in a spot."

"How?"

"He has her I O U's."

"For how much?"

"Somewhere around seven thousand dollars."

"What were they given for?" Mason asked.

"Gambling debts."

"And you want me to get those without paying . . ."

"Certainly not," she interrupted. "I want you to pay every cent that's due on them. But I *don't* want to be held up for a bonus. I'll pay debts, but I won't pay blackmail."

"Do you mean to say," Mason asked, puzzled, "that Grieb won't surrender the I O U's for their face value? Why, he'd have to. He'd be . . ."

"Don't jump at conclusions, young man," she snapped. "There's a lot more to this than you know about. There's a lot more to it than I'm going to tell you. But Grieb has heard in a roundabout way that Sylvia's husband, Frank Oxman, might be willing to pay more than face value for those I O U's."

"Why?" Mason asked.

"Evidence," she snapped.

"Evidence of what?"

"Evidence that Sylvia is a chronic gambler and can't be trusted with money."

"Why does Frank want to get evidence of that?"

"Because he does."

"Why does he?"

"I don't think," she said, "I'm going into that right now. All I want you to do is get those I O U's. I'll give you the money to take them up. If you have to pay a bonus, pay a bonus, but don't pay a big one. I hate blackmail and I hate blackmailers."

"But," Mason objected, "you don't need me. Simply give your granddaughter the money and tell her to go to the gambling ship and take up the I O U's. They'd have to surrender them if she offered to redeem them."

Matilda Benson shook her head. "I don't want to make it that easy for her. I'm going to teach my granddaughter a lesson by scaring hell out of her. I want *you* to get those I O U's and give them to *me* as soon as you get them. I don't care how you get them."

"I'm afraid," Mason said, "I wouldn't care to handle it. After all, this isn't a legal matter. It's something a detective can handle to better advantage. Now, Paul Drake, of the Drake Detective Agency, handles my work. He's thoroughly competent and trustworthy. I'll put you in touch with him and . . ."

4

"I don't *want* a detective," she interrupted. "I want you."

"But if you hired me," Mason protested, "I'd turn around and hire Drake. He does all my leg work."

"I don't care *what* you do, nor *whom* you hire," Matilda Benson said. "That's up to you. And don't think this is going to be an easy job. You're going up against a crook who is smart as a steel trap and absolutely ruthless."

Mason said, "I'm afraid you're making a mountain out of a molehill."

"No," she said, "you're the one who's making a molehill out of a mountain. I'll pay you a retainer of twenty-five hundred dollars. I'll pay you another twenty-five hundred when you get those I O U's, if you can get them in such a way that my name doesn't figure in it. And I'll pay all your expenses, including whatever you have to pay out for detectives and whatever you have to pay to get those I O U's. That's fair, isn't it?"

Mason watched her with a puzzled frown.

"Could I," he asked, "go out to call on Grieb and tell him I was acting as Sylvia's attorney and . . ."

"No, because he'd tell Sylvia, and Sylvia mustn't know anything about it."

"And you don't want Grieb to know that *you're* interested in it?"

"No. Aside from that, the sky's the limit. You can work any scheme on him you want to. But don't let him know you're willing to pay a bonus, because the minute you do he'll stall you off until he can get to Frank Oxman for a bigger bid and start playing you, one against the other."

"That," Mason admitted, "complicates matters."

"Of course it complicates matters. I haven't the faintest idea how you're going about it. But I do know that if anyone can handle those two crooks, you're the one to do it."

5

"You don't think they've approached Oxman yet?"

"Not yet."

Mason stared thoughtfully at the carpet for a moment, then raised his eyes and said smilingly, "Let's go."

Matilda Benson pulled a sheaf of hundred-dollar bills from her handbag. "This," she said, "is the money you can use in taking up the I O U's. You'll have to pay cash. The balance will apply on your fees and expenses."

Mason took the money. "My secretary will give you a receipt, Mrs. Benson, and . . ."

"I don't want a receipt," she said.

The lawyer regarded her quizzically.

"You see," she said, "I know all about the person with whom *I'm* dealing. And," she added with a chuckle, "that's more than you can say, Mr. Perry Mason. Good day!"

2

■

PERRY MASON, thumbs hooked through the armholes of his vest, paced his office, glancing impatiently at his wristwatch. "You left word for Paul Drake to come in as soon as he came to his office?" he asked.

Della Street nodded. "How are you going about it, Chief?" she asked.

"I've got a scheme," he told her, "that may work. We'll lay a trap and see if Sam Grieb walks into it."

"Suppose he doesn't?"

Mason grinned and said, "Then we'll think up another scheme."

"I don't suppose," she said, her eyes wistful, "that it would do any good to ask you to be careful?"

"None whatever."

"Why can't you let Paul Drake handle those gamblers?"

"Because my client doesn't want Paul, she wants *me*. I collected the fee and I take the responsibility."

"Most generals," she pointed out, "don't go into the front-line trenches."

"And thereby miss all the fun," he told her.

She nodded slowly. "Yes," she agreed, "life in this office never lacks for excitement."

"Like it, Della?"

"Of course I like it."

"Then why adopt that hang-your-clothes-on-a-hickory-limb-but-don't-go-near-the-water attitude?"

"Just my maternal instinct, Chief."

"You're too young to have maternal instincts."

"You'd be surprised. There's Paul Drake at the door, now." Della Street crossed the office, opened a door and nodded to the tall man who grinned down at her.

Drake's mouth twisted into a carp-like grin as he closed the door behind him and said, "My God, Perry, don't tell me you're starting a new case. Or did you want to conduct a postmortem on that other one?"

Mason said, "The other one's finished, Paul. This is a new one. Do you own any evening clothes?"

The detective chuckled. "Sure, I list them in my office inventory as a disguise. Why?"

"Know a man by the name of Sam Grieb?"

"You mean the gambler?"

"Yes."

"Know *of* him. I don't know him personally. He runs this gambling ship, *The Horn of Plenty,* which is anchored out beyond the twelve-mile limit. Every once in a while they try to control him by passing ordinances about the speed boats that run out there, but they don't get very far with it."

"What's his reputation, Paul?" Mason asked.

"Hard as steel and cold as concrete," the detective said. "He's a good business man, and he's reported to be making money. I can find out *all* about him within twenty-four hours if you want."

"No," Mason said, "that isn't going to be necessary, Paul. Here's the sketch. A married woman, name of Sylvia Oxman, has left I O U's with Grieb. These I O U's amount to somewhere around seven thousand dollars. She hasn't the money to take them up right now. And her husband's willing to pay a bonus to get his hands on them. That's all anyone has *told* me, and that's all I'm *telling* you. *I* did a little thinking. You can do the same."

"Well," Drake said, "if Grieb wants to peddle those I O U's to the husband, there isn't any way we can stop him, is there? . . . Unless the woman went out there and paid off the I O U's and demanded possession of them."

Mason grinned. "Looking at it from a purely ethical and legal standpoint, Paul, you may be right."

The detective crossed his fingers. "I suppose you've hatched out some scheme by which we'll just scrape past the walls of State's Prison, if we're lucky, and be corpses or convicts if we're not. Well, Perry, count me out. I've had enough."

Mason said, "Now, listen, Paul, there's no law against a man taking any name he wants to, provided he doesn't do it for the purpose of defrauding some other person. Now I want you to go down to a bank where you're not personally known and deposit one thousand dollars in the name of Frank Oxman. Register your signature as Frank Oxman and get a book of blank checks."

Drake straightened to rigid attention and said suspiciously, "Then what?"

"Then," Mason said, "we go out aboard the gambling ship and you lose a couple hundred bucks gambling. You make out a check for five hundred dollars, sign it 'Frank Oxman' and ask the croupier if he'll accept it. The croupier will send the check in to Sam Grieb for an okay. Grieb will figure Frank Oxman has come aboard and that it'll be a swell chance to sell him the I O U's at a bonus. He'll ask you to step into the office to be identified and start asking you questions. You can pretend that you're afraid he's trying to trap you, and deny that you're the Frank Oxman he thinks you are; but you'll do it in such a way that it will convince Grieb you're lying. Then Grieb will make us an offer on Sylvia Oxman's I O U's.

"Now get this sketch, Paul. If Oxman himself isn't willing to pay a premium for those I O U's, no one is. So when Grieb suggests that you take them up, you show a big lack of enthusiasm. Finally offer him a five-hundred-dollar or a thousand-dollar bonus and say that's as high as you'll go. We'll go another five hundred if we have to."

"Wait a minute," Drake protested, "ain't that getting pretty close to the line, Perry? I don't want to get hooked."

"Bosh," Mason said. "I'll be with you all the time. You'll tell him repeatedly that you're not the man he thinks you are, but that you *might* be interested in buying those I O U's."

Drake slowly shook his head. "No dice, Perry."

Mason said, "Okay, *I'll* do the talking. I'll be along with you as your friend, and I'll do all the talking."

"I still don't like it," Drake said.

"You'd like five hundred dollars, wouldn't you?"

"Yes."

"Okay," Mason told him, "we'll leave here about five-thirty. I'll pick you up in my car."

"You're sure we won't get in trouble over this?" Drake asked.

"Nothing we can't get out of," Mason said. "After all, we sometimes have to fight the devil with fire."

Drake said, without enthusiasm, *"You* fight him with an acetylene torch. Some day, Perry, you're going to get your fingers burnt."

9

The lawyer nodded. "That's what makes life interesting. Go home and doll up in your soup and fish, Paul, and wipe that worried look off your map. Tonight we gamble."

Drake started for the door. "I'll say we do," he said.

3

LIGHTS FROM the amusement concessions reddened the heavens and reflected in shimmering beams from the water. Beneath the piles of the pier the surf boomed into foam, to run hissing up on the beach. Out at the end of the wharf a man sold tickets to "excursion" trips via speed boat. Perry Mason and Paul Drake, attired in full dress, wearing overcoats and scarfs, passed through the gate and down a flight of stairs to a float which was creaking on the long swells. Tied to this float was a long, narrow speed boat, containing some half dozen passengers.

Drake said, "I sure as hell *feel* disguised. I hope none of the gang from headquarters sees me."

Mason chuckled. "If you don't smell too strong of moth balls you'll get by all right, Paul. You look like a rich playboy."

They took seats in the speed boat. A man blew a whistle, and the motor, which had been idling, roared into a staccato song of power, rattling out explosions which drowned all other sounds. The man on the float jerked loose a line, and Mason's head shot back with the thrust which swept the speed boat out of the lighted area into the dark waters. White-bordered waves curled up just back of the bow. Drops of spray peppered the windshield in front of the lawyer's face as though they had been buckshot. The small craft vibrated into greater speed, then raised its bow to skim over the long swells. Mason grinned at Paul Drake and yelled, "More fun than I've had for a month." His words were blown from his mouth.

The lawyer settled back against the cushions, turned to look back at the diminishing lights of the amusement pier, at the frosty glitter of the city lights, then peered ahead into the darkness. His nostrils dilated; he breathed deeply of the night air as his lips parted in a smile of sheer enjoyment.

The detective sat huddled in his overcoat, his face wearing the lugubrious expression of one who is submitting to a disagreeable experience which he has been unable to avoid.

At length, out of the darkness ahead, loomed the glitter of the gambling ship. The speed boat swept in a long circle. The motors slowed, and the nose of the frail craft seemed to be pulled into the water by some giant hand. A man standing on a grated landing-stage surveyed the boat with disinterested appraisal, looped a rope around a bitt and yelled, "All aboard."

The passengers made the landing an occasion for much merriment. Women in evening dress held their long skirts well above their knees as they jumped. Two girls in sports outfits leapt unassisted to the landing and ran up the stairway. Mason and Drake were among the last to disembark. They climbed the swaying stairway to find a group of eight or ten persons held back from the steep incline by a taut rope between two stanchions. When the last of the incoming passengers had left the stairway, a man jerked the rope to one side and called out, "All aboard for the shore trip. Please don't crowd. There's plenty of room."

Mason led the way along the deck and into a lighted salon, from which came the sound of voices, the rattle of chips and the whir of roulette wheels. "Okay, Paul," he said, "do your stuff."

"You going to buck the tiger?" the detective asked.

"I think I'll watch for the time being," Mason said. "You start plunging. Try to attract plenty of attention."

Drake pushed his way toward a crowded roulette wheel, while Mason, strolling aimlessly about, sized up the general layout, lost a few dollars on roulette, recouped his losses playing the field numbers in a crap game, turned to the wheel of fortune and killed time by placing several small bets. He felt a touch on his elbow and Drake said, grinning, "I'm three hundred dollars to the good, Perry. What if I break the bank? Would I have to credit our expense account?"

"You won't break it, Paul."

"How about salting these winnings? I hate to credit a client with winnings."

"Okay, go to another table. Try your luck there. Keep drifting around. Don't keep much money in front of you. As soon as you run into a losing streak, buck the game hard. Then write a check. Soon as you do that, give me the high-sign and I'll come over."

Drake moved to a nearby table. The lawyer watched him quietly. Steady winnings augmented the stack of chips at first, then Drake started to lose. He increased the size of his bets, scattered money recklessly around the table. The croupier watched him with appraising eyes. It was from men who became angry as they lost that the gambling tables made the biggest winnings.

When the pile of chips disappeared, Drake emptied one of his trousers pockets of crumpled bills and silver. He gambled first with the silver, then changed the bills and flung them around the board. He stepped back from the table, pulled a checkbook from his pocket and scrawled out a check to "Cash" in the amount of five hundred dollars. He signed the check "Frank Oxman" and passed it across to the croupier. "How about this," he asked.

The croupier looked at the check. Drake caught Mason's eye and nodded. The croupier held up the check in his right hand. A man in a dinner jacket glided to his side. The croupier whispered in his ear. The man nodded, took the check and vanished.

Drake said, "How about it?"

"Just a minute, Mr. Oxman," the croupier replied suavely. "There'll be a few minutes' delay." He put the ball into play and devoted his entire attention to the table.

Mason strolled over to Drake's side. Two or three minutes passed while Drake fidgeted uneasily and Mason maintained the casual interest of a detached spectator. Then the man who had taken the check approached Drake. "Would you mind stepping this way a moment, Mr. Oxman?" he asked.

The detective hesitated, glanced at Perry Mason.

Mason said, "Okay, I'll go with you."

The man in the tuxedo favored Mason with an appraising stare from uncordial eyes.

"I'm with this gentleman," Mason explained. "Go ahead and lead the way." The man turned, crossed the gambling room to a door, in front of which lounged a guard in blue uniform, a gun ostentatiously strapped to his hip. A silver badge on his vest bore the words SPECIAL OFFICER.

The guide nodded to the officer, held open the swinging door and said, "This way, please." They followed him down a passageway which made an abrupt turn at right angles, to disclose an open door. The three went through this door and entered a reception room. Their guide crossed the room and stood expectantly in front of a heavy mahogany door.

A peephole slid back in the door. A bolt shot back and a man's voice said, "Okay."

The man in the dinner jacket held the door open for Mason and Drake. Mason, taking the lead, entered a sumptuously furnished office. A short, stocky man with a pasty face twisted his fat lips into an amiable smile. His eyes seemed as pale as the starched front of his shirt—and as hard and expressionless.

"This is Mr. Grieb," their guide said, and pulled the big mahogany door shut behind him as he stepped into the outer office. Mason heard the click of a spring lock. Grieb said, "Pardon me." He stepped to the door, pushed a lever which shot iron bars into place, then crossed the office and seated himself in a swivel chair behind a huge, glass-topped desk.

The desk was devoid of any papers save the check Drake had just written. It lay on a brown blotter, encased in a leather backer. Aside from this check, the blotter and the leather backer, there was nothing whatever on the glass-topped surface.

"Which one of you is Oxman?" the man behind the desk asked.

Drake glanced helplessly at the lawyer.

Mason stepped forward and said, "*My* name's Mason."

Grieb nodded. "Glad to know you, Mr. Mason," he said, and shifted his pale eyes to Paul Drake. "You wanted a check cashed, Mr. Oxman, and it's customary to ask a few questions to establish credit. Is this your first visit to the ship?"

Drake nodded.

"Know anyone out here?" Grieb asked.

"No," Drake said.

"Would you mind giving me your residence address, your occupation, and your telephone number, both at your residence and at your office?"

Mason said, "I think we can save you all this trouble, Mr. Grieb."

Grieb raised his eyebrows, and in a flat, toneless voice said, "How do *you* figure in this, Mr. Mason?"

"I'm with this gentleman," Mason explained, indicating Drake with a nod of his head.

"Friend of his?"

"I'm his lawyer."

Grieb interlaced fat hands across his stomach. Huge diamonds on his fingers caught the light and glittered scintillating accompaniment to the motion. "A lawyer, eh?" he said, almost musingly.

Mason nodded, moving closer to the edge of the desk.

"And just how did you propose to save us all this trouble?" Grieb asked, still in that same flat voice.

Mason, smiling amiably, suddenly reached across the desk and picked up the check from the blotter. "You won't have to cash it," he said.

Grieb sat bolt-upright in his chair. His diamonds made a glittering streak of motion as he started to reach for the check, then caught himself, and sat with his finger-tips resting on the edge of the blotter. "What's the idea?" he asked.

Mason said, "My client isn't a very good gambler. He's rather a hard loser. He started to place a few casual bets, then won a little money, got into the spirit of the thing, and was swept off his feet. He's come down to earth now. He doesn't want any more money. He's finished gambling."

Grieb's eyes focused on Mason's face. "This little business matter," he said coldly, "is between Oxman and me."

Mason handed the check across to Drake. "Better tear it up," he said.

Drake tore it into pieces and shoved the pieces down deep into his trousers pocket. Grieb got to his feet. Mason moved so that he was standing between Drake and the gambler. "My client made a mistake in giving you this check," he said, by way of explanation.

"You mean there aren't any funds in the bank to cover it?" Grieb asked ominously.

"Of course there are," Mason said. "Telephone the

bank tomorrow if that's what's bothering you. What I meant was that I don't want my client to have one of his checks cashed through this gambling ship. You see, we didn't come out here to gamble."

Grieb slowly sat down, eyed the two men for a moment, then indicated chairs with a glittering gesture of his right hand. "Sit down, gentlemen," he said. "I want to talk with you."

Drake looked to Mason for instructions. Mason nodded and seated himself on Grieb's left. Drake rather ostentatiously moved over to a chair nearer the door, farther from Grieb. The gambler still sat very erect, his fingertips resting on the edge of the blotter. "That check's good?" he asked.

Mason laughed. "I'll guarantee this gentleman's checks up to any amount he wants to write them."

"With that signature and on that bank?" Grieb persisted.

Mason nodded and said, apparently as an afterthought, "Or with any other signature."

Grieb's eyes studied Paul Drake, who, obviously ill at ease, returned the stare. Grieb shifted his eyes to Perry Mason and surveyed the granite-hard face of the lawyer. "So your name's Mason and you're a lawyer?"

Mason nodded.

"Tell me more about you."

"Why?" Mason asked.

"Because I want to know," Grieb said.

"I think," Mason told him, "our little business transaction is entirely concluded, isn't it, Mr. Grieb?"

Grieb shook his head. Suddenly a puzzled frown crossed his forehead. He said, "Say, wait a minute, you're not Perry Mason, are you?"

Mason nodded. Grieb swung half around in the swivel chair and put his right elbow on the blotter. "That," he said, "is different. Suppose we talk business, gentlemen."

Mason raised his eyebrows and said, "Business?"

16

Grieb nodded, turned suddenly to Drake and said, "If you didn't come out here to gamble, what *did* you come out here for, Mr. Oxman?"

Drake sucked in a quick breath, as though about to answer, then glanced at Mason and became silent.

Mason said easily, "Let me do the talking." He turned to the gambler and said, "I don't want any misunderstandings, Mr. Grieb. You don't know this man. He's offered you a check signed 'Frank Oxman.' That check's good as gold, but that doesn't mean this man is really Frank Oxman. It only means he has a banking account under that name. And if you should ever say that Frank Oxman won or lost a dime on your ship, you might get yourself into serious trouble. My client came out here, not for the purpose of gambling, but for the purpose of looking the place over."

"Why did he want to look it over?" Grieb asked.

"He wanted to find out something about the general background, what it looked like, and things of that sort."

"So now you claim he *isn't* Frank Oxman, eh?" Grieb asked.

Mason smiled affably. "No," he said, "I haven't made that claim."

"Then he *is* Frank Oxman."

"I won't even admit that," Mason said, smiling.

Grieb said slowly, "You two came out here to try and collect evidence."

Mason remained silent.

"You thought you could look the joint over, maybe strike up an acquaintance with one of the croupiers, stick around until the tables closed, get one of the men in conversation, and find out something you wanted to know," Grieb charged.

Mason took a cigarette case from his pocket, extracted a cigarette, and lit it. "After all," he said, "does it make any difference why we came out here?"

Grieb said, "You're damn right it does."

Mason exhaled cigarette smoke as he slipped the compact cigarette case back into his pocket. "Just how does it make a difference?" he asked.

Grieb said, "I have some business to talk over with your client."

"You haven't anything to talk over with my client," Mason said. "My client, from now on, is deaf, dumb and blind."

"All right, then, I have some business to talk over with you."

"Right now," Mason said, crossing his long legs and blowing smoke at the ceiling, "I'm not in a mood to talk. . . . Nice offices you have here, Grieb."

Grieb nodded casually. "I'd like to have you boys meet my partner," he said, and shifted his position slightly, raising one side of his body as though pressing with his right foot. A moment later an electric buzzer sounded, and Grieb, pushing back the swivel chair, said, "Excuse me a minute."

The lawyer and Drake exchanged glances as Grieb walked to the heavy mahogany door, slid back the peephole, then pulled back the lever which controlled the bolts, opened the door and said to the special officer who stood on the threshold, "Arthur, get hold of Charlie Duncan for me. Tell him I want him in here at once."

The guard glanced curiously at the two visitors. "Charlie went ashore to telephone," he said. "He's coming right back. I'll tell him as soon as he comes aboard."

Grieb pushed the door shut, slammed the bolts into position, and waddled back to the desk. "How about a drink, boys?"

Mason shook his head. "Any reason why we can't go ashore?" he asked.

"I'd prefer to have you wait a little while."

"Wait for what?"

Grieb said slowly, "You came out here to get some evidence."

18

Mason's face lost its smile as he said, "I don't think I care to discuss why we came out here. You're running a public place. It's open to anyone who wants to come aboard."

Grieb's voice was soothing. "Now wait a minute, Mr. Mason," he said. "Let's not argue."

"I'm not arguing, I'm telling you."

"All right," Grieb grinned, "then you're telling me, and that's that. . . . How'd you boys like to look the ship over?"

Mason shook his head. Grieb said irritably, "Look here. My time's just as valuable as yours. I've got something to say to you, but I want to wait until Charlie gets here. Charlie Duncan's my partner."

Mason glanced at Paul Drake. The detective shook his head. Mason said, "I don't think we'd care to wait."

Grieb lowered his voice. "Suppose I could give you the evidence you were looking for?"

"You don't know what evidence we're after," Mason said.

Grieb laughed. "Don't play me for a damn fool, Mason. Your client is Frank Oxman. His wife is Sylvia Oxman. He wanted to find some evidence which would help him in a divorce action."

Mason, avoiding Drake's eyes, said, after a moment, "I'm not saying anything. You're talking. I'm listening. . . ."

"I've said all I'm going to," Grieb went on, his pale eyes studying Mason.

"How long do you think it'll be before your partner gets here?"

"Not over fifteen minutes."

Mason shifted his position, making himself comfortable in the chair. "Fifteen minutes isn't long," he said. "Nice place you have here."

"I like it," Grieb admitted. "I designed it and picked out the furniture myself."

"That a vault over there?" Mason asked, jerking his head toward a steel door.

"Yes, we turned an adjoining cabin into a vault. It's lined with concrete. Like to take a look at it?"

Grieb crossed over to the steel door of the vault and flung it open, disclosing a commodious, lighted interior. In the back of the vault was a cannonball safe.

"Keep your cash in that safe?" Mason asked, following Grieb into the cold interior of the vault.

"Our cash," Grieb said, staring at him steadily, "and our *evidences of indebtedness.*"

"Meaning I O U's?" Mason asked.

"Meaning I O U's," Grieb said, regarding the lawyer with steady eyes.

"I'm commencing to be interested," Mason said.

"I thought you would," Grieb told him. "Over here in these plush-lined receptacles, we keep the wheels, where no one can tamper with them. You see, we're out beyond the twelve-mile limit and that puts us beyond police protection. We're on the high seas."

"You must keep quite a bit of cash on hand, then."

"We do."

"What's to keep a mob from boarding the ship, taking possession of it and cleaning you out?"

"That'd be piracy," Grieb said.

"So what?" Mason asked, laughing.

Grieb said, "We've figured all that out, Mr. Mason."

"How?"

"Well, in the first place, it's impossible to get into these offices except by coming down that corridor with the right-angle turn in it. When a man comes down that corridor, he has to walk over a wired section of flooring. His weight causes a contact and rings a buzzer here in the office. The door to this office is *always* kept locked. It's covered with wood on both sides, but the center is steel. It would take a long while to smash that door down. There are signals planted all over the office.

I can sound an alarm from any part of the office, and without moving my hands.

"Moreover, there's an armed guard who's always somewhere around. He's as handy with his fists as he is with the .45 automatic he carries."

Mason nodded. "I saw him when we came in. I notice he has a badge which reads SPECIAL OFFICER. What does that mean? If you're out beyond the twelve-mile limit he can't be a deputy sheriff."

Grieb laughed. "The badge," he said, "is just for its psychological effect. The blue uniform the same way. The real authority comes from the gun. Remember, you're on the high seas now and *I'm* in supreme command."

"Suppose a mob dropped in some foggy night?" Mason asked.

"They wouldn't get anywhere."

"Your guard wouldn't last long."

"You think he wouldn't."

"You admit you keep a lot of cash here," Mason said.

"Sure."

"Banks keep cash. Banks have guards, and banks get stuck up regularly."

Grieb said, "Well, *we* don't get stuck up. It's not generally known, but in case you're interested, there's a balcony in back of that gambling casino. The front wall is of bullet-proof steel. There's an inch-and-a-half slit in the wall, and two guards are on duty up there. They have machine guns and tear gas bombs."

"That," Mason admitted, "is different."

"Don't ever worry about us," Grieb said. "We . . ."

He broke off as the electric buzzer sounded its warning.

"Someone's coming," he said. "It's probably Charlie. Let's go back into the office."

He led the way through the steel door of the vault, into the private office, walked to the communicating door and slid back the panel. As he did so, a speed launch pulled away from the side of the ship on its return trip to the shore, and the roar of its exhaust, sounding through the open portholes back of Grieb's desk, completely drowned out all other sounds, including a swift exchange of words between Grieb and the man on the other side of the door.

Grieb jerked back the lever which freed the bars from their sockets, twisted the knob of the spring lock, and opened the door as the roar of the speed boat died to a throbbing undertone of pulsating power. A bald-headed man of forty-five, with perpetual smile-wrinkles about his eyes, and calipers stretching between nose and mouth, stood on the threshold. He was wearing a gray-checkered suit, and his lips, twisting back in an affable smile, showed three gleaming gold teeth.

Grieb said, "Gentlemen, shake hands with my partner, Charlie Duncan. Duncan, this is Perry Mason, the lawyer. And the other man . . ."

"If it's all the same to you," Mason said, extending his hand, "the other gentleman will be nameless."

Duncan, pushing forward his right hand, suddenly froze into immobility. The gold teeth vanished as his lips came together. His eyes shifted for a quick moment to his partner and he said, "What is this, Sam?"

"It's okay, Charlie," Grieb said hastily.

Duncan's hands gripped Mason's. "Glad to know you, Mr. Mason," he said. His eyes shifted to study Paul Drake in cold appraisal.

"Come on over and sit down, Charlie," Grieb invited. "We're going to talk some business. I wanted you to be here."

"We're not doing any talking," Mason said.

"No," Grieb told him, speaking with nervous haste. "No one's asking you to. You can listen."

"All right," Mason agreed. "We'll listen."

They seated themselves, and Grieb turned to Duncan. "Charlie," he said, "this guy"—indicating Drake with a nod of his head—"started bucking the game. He was playing easy at first. Then he got hot and started raking

22

'em in. When things didn't go so well, he started plunging. When he went broke, he wanted to cash a check. Jimmy brought the check in and I took a look at the signature. That check was signed 'Frank Oxman.' "

"That doesn't mean anything," Mason interrupted. "I wish you boys would forget about that check."

"I'm just telling my partner what happened," Grieb said. "You don't have to say anything if you don't want to."

"All right," Mason told him, "I don't want to."

Duncan's face was completely without expression. "Go on, Sammy. Tell me the rest of it."

"I told Jimmy to bring him in. When he came in, Mason came with him. Mason did a little talking, then reached over, grabbed the check, and gave it to his friend to tear up."

Duncan's eyes partially closed. "Like that, eh?" he asked. "I don't think we're going to like that, Sammy."

Grieb said hastily, "Now, don't get this wrong, Charlie. I'm just telling you, see? Naturally, at first I was a little peeved. But then, I got the sketch. Mason didn't want me to know Oxman was aboard the ship. He didn't want anyone to know Oxman had been gambling out here. He didn't want us to have one of Oxman's checks. Get the sketch?"

"I think what I *said* was," Mason observed, "that my client had changed his mind about requiring any money. I think I also told you that if you should say Frank Oxman had been out here gambling you might put yourself in rather an embarrassing position. I pointed out very clearly to you, Grieb, that my client didn't come out here for the *purpose* of gambling."

"Sure, sure, I know," Grieb said affably. "We understand your position perfectly, Mason."

Duncan settled back in his chair. The gold teeth gradually came into evidence as his lips relaxed into his habitual smile.

"Talk any business, Sammy?" he asked.

"Not yet," Grieb said. "I was waiting for you to come aboard."

Duncan fished a cigar from his pocket, clipped off the end with a penknife, scraped a match across his shoe and said, "Okay, Sammy, I'm here."

"You want to do the talking?" Grieb asked.

"No, Sammy, you do it."

Grieb faced Mason. "Sylvia Oxman's been giving us quite a play lately. We looked her up and found her husband's name was Frank Oxman. A little bird told us Frank Oxman was maybe going to file a divorce action and would like to get some evidence that his wife had been squandering her time and money gambling, and therefore wasn't a fit person to have the custody of their child and couldn't be trusted with money in a guardianship proceeding. Would you know anything about that?"

Mason said cautiously, "No, I wouldn't *know* anything about that."

"Well, your client would."

"Let's leave my client out of it, *please.*"

"Well," Grieb said, "we always like to co-operate. Now, you came out here looking for evidence. Perhaps we could help you out a little bit."

"In what way?" Mason asked.

"By giving you some evidence."

"On what terms?"

"Well," Grieb said, flashing a swift glance at his partner, "we'd have to discuss the terms."

"Your idea of evidence might not be my idea of evidence," Mason said.

"The evidence is all right," Grieb rejoined. "It's just a question of what you boys would be willing to do."

"We'd want to see the evidence," Mason said.

Grieb looked at Duncan significantly and jerked his head toward the vault. Duncan, his face still wearing a set smile, crossed to the vault and stepped inside. The

24

three men in the room sat in tense silence. After a few seconds there was the peculiar *whooshing* sound made by air escaping as the door of the cannonball safe was slammed shut. Duncan emerged from the vault carrying three oblongs of paper which he slid across the glass top of the big desk.

Grieb's diamonds again made glittering streaks as he scooped up the oblongs of paper and said, "Three demand notes, signed by Sylvia Oxman, and totaling seven thousand five hundred dollars."

Mason frowned. "We hadn't figured on anything like this," he said.

Grieb's voice was harsh with greed. "Figure on it now, then."

Mason pursed his lips. "I suppose," he ventured, "you boys want something."

Grieb moved impatiently. "Don't be so God damn cagey. You've drawn cards in this game but we hold all the aces. Quit stalling. You're going to have to come across—and *like* it."

Duncan said chidingly, "Now, Sammy!"

Mason said, "I'd want to inspect these."

Grieb spread them out on the desk, holding them flat against the glass, his extended fingers pressing firmly against the upper edges. "Look 'em over," he invited grimly.

Mason objected. "That's not what I'd call inspecting them."

"That's what *I* call inspecting them," Grieb said.

Duncan said soothingly, "Now, Sammy. Now, Sammy. Take it easy."

"I'm taking it easy," Grieb said. "There was a check on this desk and he picked it up to 'inspect' it. Now it's torn in pieces and is in this guy's pocket."

"The check was different," Mason said.

"Well, I didn't like the way you did it," Grieb told him.

Mason's eyes were cold. "No one asked you to," he said shortly.

Duncan interposed. "Now, wait a minute, boys. This isn't getting us anywhere."

Grieb's face darkened with rage. He picked up the oblongs of paper and said irritably, "That's the way he's been ever since he came in. You'd think he was God and I was some sort of a crook. To hell with him!"

Duncan moved over to the desk, extended his hands for the notes. His face still smiling, but his eyes were hard. "This is a business deal, Sammy," he said.

"It isn't with me," Grieb told him. "As far as I'm concerned, there's no dice. We're handing these guys a lawsuit on a silver platter and they're trying to make us come all the way. To hell with it."

Duncan said nothing, but stood by the desk, his hand extended. And after a moment, Grieb handed him the slips of paper and said, "All right, *you* do it, if you know so much about it."

Duncan handed one of the notes to the lawyer. "The other two," he said, "are like this."

"I'd want to see them all," Mason said, without reaching for the note.

"You can look them over one at a time," Duncan told him.

Drake said, "That's fair, Perry. We'll look them over one at a time."

Mason slowly extended his hand and took the oblong of paper. He and Drake studied it carefully while Duncan watched them with cold eyes over smiling lips. Grieb opened the left-hand drawer of the desk and dropped his hand casually into the interior.

The note was on a printed form such as might have been readily obtained in any stationery store. It was in an amount of twenty-five hundred dollars, signed "Sylvia Oxman," and in the blank left for the name of the payee had been filled in, in the same feminine handwriting, the letters, "I O U." The date showed that the note was sixty days old.

Mason handed it back to Duncan. Duncan handed him another one and said, "This one was made a month earlier," and as Mason finished his inspection and returned it, handed him the third, saying, "This is the first one."

As Mason returned the I O U to Duncan, Grieb removed his hand from the desk drawer and slammed it shut. Mason said softly, "So what?"

"Well," Duncan said, "you're a lawyer. You don't need me to tell you what those things are."

Grieb said, *"We* know what those things are worth."

Duncan's voice was soothing. "With those in your hand, Mr. Mason," he said, "you'd hold all the trumps. A court would never let a woman handle a kid's money if she was a fiend for gambling. Suppose you make us an offer."

"Offer, hell," Grieb interrupted. *"We'll* set the price on those, Charlie. This means a lot to Oxman. It's just what he's been looking for, and he can't get to first base without them. They've been snooping around, trying to get some of our men to talk. You know as well as I do how much chance they stand of doing that. We hold the cards and we'll call the trumps." Mason got to his feet.

"Now, wait a minute," Duncan said. "Don't be like that, Mason. My partner's hot-headed, that's all."

"He's not hot-headed, he's cold-hearted."

"Well, after all, it's a matter of business," Duncan pointed out.

Mason nodded. "Sure it is, but *you're* the ones who don't know it. Sylvia hasn't any money right now. She can't even pay the face of those notes. You *think* they're worth a lot to me and you think you can hold me up. That's where you're making a mistake. There isn't any competitive market. No one else gives a damn about them."

27

"Let's put 'em back in the safe, Duncan," Grieb said, "I don't like to do business with pikers."

"And," Mason told him steadily, "I don't like to do business with crooks."

Grieb got to his feet so violently that the swivel chair shot back on its rollers to crash against the wall. His pasty face mottled into bluish patches.

Charlie Duncan, tilting his chair back against the wall, thrust his thumbs through the armholes of his vest and said chidingly, "Now, boys, don't be like that."

Mason walked across to the desk to stare steadily at Grieb. "Now," he said, *"I'll* tell *you* something about where *you* get off. You're out beyond the twelve-mile limit, which means out of the state. I can serve a *subpœna duces tecum* on you, have a commission appointed to take your deposition, come out here and make you swear under oath that you haven't got those I O U's, or else make you produce them. In that way I won't have to pay so much as a thin dime."

Charlie Duncan laughed softly. "Sammy's memory's awfully bad at times, Mason."

"Well, mine isn't," Mason snapped. "I'd ask you about those I O U's. If you made false answers I'd do things to you in a federal court. You're outside the state, but you're in United States territory as long as your ship is registered under the American flag.

"Now then, the only chance you stand of getting one cent above the face of those I O U's is to sell them to *me*. I'll offer you a bonus of one thousand dollars. That doesn't grow on bushes. You can take it or leave it. I'm going to give you thirty seconds to say yes or no, and then I'm going to walk out."

Grieb was breathing heavily. "Keep on walking, as far as I'm concerned," he said. "The answer is no."

Duncan didn't bother to look at Grieb. His eyes were appraising Mason. They were hard and merciless, but his gold teeth still glittered through grinning lips. *"I've got* something to say about this, Sammy, keep your shirt on. Now, Mr. Mason, you know as well as I do that these notes are worth a lot more than a thousand dollars above their face."

"Not to me they aren't," Mason said.

Grieb snorted. "Throw the piker off the ship, Charlie."

"Take it easy, Sammy," Duncan said, still looking at Mason. "Take your weight off your feet and shut up. *I'm* handling this."

"I guess *I* have something to say about it," Grieb protested. "I don't know who the hell you think *you* are. You're gumming the works. These notes are worth ten thousand dollars above their face, and I won't let them go until I get my share."

Duncan, still tilted back in his chair, said, "You see how my partner feels, Mason. Suppose we compromise on five grand."

"I don't give a damn how your partner feels," Mason said. "I've offered you a thousand dollars and that's my limit. If you suckers keep on holding those notes, you'll find yourselves holding the sack. By the time the smoke blows away, Sylvia isn't going to be able to pay even the face of those notes."

"That's a bluff," Grieb said.

"Now, Sammy, keep your shirt on," Duncan told him.

Grieb started toward Duncan. "Listen, Charlie," he shouted. "I'm running the office end of this business. You haven't invested anything here except a lot of conversation. I know what those I O U's are worth, and you ain't going to make a cheapskate out of me."

Duncan turned to look at him then, and his gold teeth vanished. "Sit down, you damn fool," he said, "and shut up. If Frank Oxman doesn't buy these notes, who's going to?"

"Sylvia will take them up."

"When?"

"Pretty soon."

"For how much?"

"Well, if she knew we had a chance to sell them ..."

Duncan's coldly contemptuous gaze silenced his partner. He turned to Mason, "Suppose you boys go out in the other room for a little while," he said, "and let me talk to my partner. I want to be reasonable, but I agree with him a thousand dollars is altogether too small a sum to ..."

"Then," Mason interrupted, "there's no need of our waiting. I've offered you a thousand dollars, and that's final. Take it or leave it. Don't ever forget I can put you two birds on the witness stand and find out everything I want to know without its costing me a damn cent. Anytime a ..."

"Now, take it easy," Duncan interrupted soothingly. "This isn't going to get us anywhere, Mason. It's a business proposition. You two boys go out in the other room and wait a few minutes." He walked over to the heavy door, jerked the lever which pulled the bolts back, twisted the knurled knob of the spring lock and held the door open. "Make yourselves at home, boys. There's some magazines right over there. We won't be over five minutes."

"If you're as long as five minutes," Mason said, "you won't find us here when you come out."

Grieb yelled, "Go ahead and go, you damn piker, and see who cares!"

Duncan, still smiling, closed the door on Mason and the detective. The spring lock clicked into position. A half second later the iron bars shot home.

Drake turned to Mason and said, "Why not boost it to fifteen hundred, Perry? They'd take that. It would give Grieb a chance to save his face."

Mason said, "To hell with Grieb, and his face too. I don't like his damned blackmailing hide."

Drake shrugged his shoulders. "It's your funeral, Perry."

Mason slowly grinned and said, "No, it isn't. Duncan's nobody's fool. That talk I gave him about taking their depositions scared hell out of him. It's just a question of how long it'll take him to whip Grieb into line. . . . Evidently there's friction between them."

"That's going to make it all the harder for us," Drake said.

Mason shook his head. "No, it isn't, Paul, it's going to make it easier."

"Why?"

"Because this partnership isn't going to last very much longer. They're fighting. Duncan is a shrewd thinker. Grieb flies off the handle. Now then, figure it out. If this partnership is going to bust up, it's a lot better to have eighty-five hundred dollars in cash to divide than seventy-five hundred in I O U's to try and collect."

Drake said, "That's so, Perry. I hadn't figured on that."

"Duncan's figuring on it," Mason said.

They were silent for a moment. Quick, nervous steps sounded in the passageway outside of the office. The two men listened while the steps swung around the right-angle turn in the corridor and approached the door of the reception office. Iron bars were jerked back on the other side of the door from the inner office. A knob twisted. The door opened explosively and Duncan, carrying the I O U's, said to Mason, "Okay. Pay over the money. It'll have to be cash."

"How about your partner?" Mason asked.

"Pay over the cash," Duncan said. "I have the I O U's here. That's all *you* want . . ."

The door from the hallway opened. A woman in her middle twenties, her trim figure clad in a dark, tailored suit, stared at them with black, disinterested eyes, then turned to Duncan and said, "I want to see Sam."

Duncan crumpled the oblongs of paper in his right hand and pushed them down into his coat pocket. His gold teeth came into evidence. "Sure, sure," he said.

"Sam's right inside." But he continued to stand in the doorway, blocking her passage.

Once more she flashed her eyes in quick appraisal of the two men, then stepped forward until she was standing within two feet of Duncan, who kept his left hand on the knob of the partially opened door. "Well?" she asked, smiling. "Do I go in?"

Duncan shifted his eyes to study Mason and Drake, and she, following the direction of his gaze, glanced at them for the third time. Duncan's smile expanded into a grin. "Sure," he said, his eyes focused on Drake's face, "go right on in." He shoved the door open, stepped to one side, raised his voice and said, "Don't you two talk any business until I get there."

She swept through the door and Duncan, still grinning, pulled it shut behind her.

"Well, boys," he said, "it's too bad your little scheme didn't work. I'll see a lawyer tomorrow, Mason, and see if we can't pin something on you. We may have something to take before the D.A. In the meantime, don't forget the ship, boys. It's a nice place to gamble. We give you a good run for your money."

Mason said, "No, Duncan, we won't forget the ship."

"And," Duncan assured him, *"we* won't forget *you."* He escorted them down the corridor until the uniformed guard had opened the outer door. "Well, good night, boys," he said. "Come back any time."

He turned and retraced his steps down the corridor. Mason took the detective's arm and led him toward the gangway where departing patrons caught the speed boat.

"Was that Sylvia Oxman?" Drake asked.

"It must have been," Mason said, "and when she failed to recognize you and you gave her a dead pan, Duncan saw the play. Remember, you're supposed to be the lady's husband."

"Doesn't that leave us in something of a spot," Drake

asked anxiously, "having tried to pick up the lady's notes and pulled all this hocus-pocus?"

"That depends on the breaks," Mason said gloomily. "Evidently it isn't our night to gamble."

Drake pushed his fingers down inside his collar, ran them around the neckband of his shirt, and said, "Let's beat it. If we're going to be pinched, I sure as hell don't want to go to jail in *this* outfit."

4

MASON LOOKED across his desk at Matilda Benson and said, "I sent for you because I'm going to ask you a lot of questions."

"May I ask you some first?" she inquired.

He nodded.

"You saw Grieb?"

"Yes."

"Get anywhere?"

Mason shook his head and said, "Not yet. The breaks went against me."

She eyed him in shrewd appraisal. "I suppose you don't go in much for alibis and explanations."

Mason shook his head and was silent.

"Do you want to tell me about it?"

"No."

"Well, then, what's the next move?" she asked.

Mason said, "I'm going to try him again—this time from another angle. Before I do, I want to know more of what I'm up against."

She opened her purse, took out her cigar case and selected a cigar. While she was cutting off the end, Mason scratched a match and held it across the desk to her. She regarded him with twinkling eyes through the first white puffs of cigar smoke and said, "All right, go ahead. Ask your questions."

"What do you know about Grieb?"

"Nothing much. Just what my granddaughter tells me. He's hard and ruthless. I warned you he wouldn't be easy."

"Know anything about Duncan?"

"Sylvia says he doesn't count. He's sort of a yes-man."

"I think your granddaughter is fooled," Mason said.

"I wouldn't doubt it. She's too young to know much about men of that type. She can size up the sheiks all right, tell just about when they're going to start getting ambitious and what their line's going to be, but she can't size up gamblers."

"Her husband wants to get a divorce?"

"Yes."

"Why?"

"Why do men usually want to get divorces?"

Mason shook his head impatiently and said, "You'll have to play fair with me, Mrs. Benson. What's behind all this?"

She smoked in silence for a few seconds and said, "When my granddaughter is twenty-six, which'll be next year, she gets one-half of a trust fund, and her daughter, Virginia, who's six, gets the other half, unless a judge should decide Sylvia isn't a fit person to have the custody of Virginia. In that case, Virginia gets all of it."

"And with a situation like that brewing," Mason said incredulously, "she's given I O U's to a couple of gamblers?"

Matilda Benson nodded. "Sylvia's always done pretty much as she pleased. That's why the property was left in trust and not given to her outright."

"So her husband's trying to get some evidence which'll give him a divorce and cause Sylvia to lose her share of the trust funds?"

"Yes."

"Why?"

"So his daughter will have twice as much money, and so he can have the handling of that money. If he ever finds out about those I O U's, he'll get them and use them to show Sylvia can't be trusted with money. He has other evidence, too, but, right now, he wants to show she can't be trusted with money. You'll have to work fast. I want those I O U's before Sam Grieb finds out how important they are."

Mason said slowly, "I think Grieb already knows."

"Then we're licked before we start."

"No, we're not licked, but I begin to see why you wanted a lawyer. How much is the trust fund?"

"Half a million in all. If Frank Oxman ever gets the custody of Virginia and gets his hands on the money it'll be like signing the kid's death warrant."

"Surely not that bad," Mason said.

"That man's like a rattlesnake."

"He'd be under the control and supervision of the courts," Mason pointed out.

She laughed mirthlessly. "You don't know Frank Oxman. Sylvia isn't any match for him. As long as I'm here I'll fight him, but I'm almost seventy. I'm not going to be here forever."

"But look here," Mason said, "a court wouldn't deprive Sylvia of the custody of her child simply because she'd been gambling."

"There are other things," Matilda Benson said grimly.

"How about Frank Oxman, does he have any money?"

"He has a little to gamble with."

"What sort of gambling?"

"The stock market mostly. That's considered respectable. Sylvia plays roulette, and that's considered immoral. People make me sick. They're hypocrites."

"What I'm trying to find out," Mason said, "is how Oxman is going to get the money to take up those I O U's."

"Don't worry, he'll raise that all right."

"How?"

"There's a ring that will put up money for things like that," she said. "Occasionally Frank is able to fix a prize fight or a horse race or something of that sort. He can always raise the necessary money to make a killing then."

"Sylvia will pay off those I O U's if she gets that money from the trust fund?"

"Of course."

"No matter who has the I O U's?"

Matilda Benson nodded.

"It would help a lot," Mason said slowly, "if she wouldn't."

"What do you mean?"

"If Frank Oxman is going to buy those I O U's he'd have to offer cash for them. He'd have to offer the amount of the notes plus a bonus. If he's borrowing the money, he'd have to put up the I O U's as collateral. If the people who were loaning the money thought the collateral wasn't good, they'd refuse to put up the money."

"No," she said slowly, "that won't work. Sylvia would never go back on her word."

Mason said, "I have an idea. I don't know how good it is, but I think it may work. From what I saw last night, I think there's friction between Grieb and Duncan. I have an idea that friction may be sufficiently intensified to throw them into a court of equity. A court wouldn't consider the gambling business an equitable asset. But there's quite a lot of money invested in furniture and fixtures, and the partnership must have that gambling ship under lease. Now, if I could start the pair fighting, and one of the partners should drag the other into court and have a receiver appointed to wind up the partnership

36

business, they couldn't transfer those notes. And if I pointed out to a federal court that the notes had been given to secure a gambling debt, it would probably refuse to consider them as assets."

Matilda Benson leaned forward. "Listen," she said, "I don't want to be held up by a couple of crooked gamblers. But if you can pull something like this, the sky's the limit so far as expenses are concerned."

"Which brings us," Mason said casually, "to the question of why *you're* so anxious to get those I O U's. If you make Sylvia a present of them, the effect is just the same as though you'd given her the money to go and pay them off. And that wouldn't take any premium. Therefore . . ."

Della Street gently opened the door from the outer office and said in a low voice, "Charles Duncan is in the outer office, Chief. He says he wants to see you personally and that it's important."

Matilda Benson's gray eyes stared significantly at the lawyer. "That means," she said, "they've already approached Oxman, and Duncan is going to play one bidder against the other."

Mason shook his head, his forehead furrowed into a puzzled frown. "I don't think so," he told her. "I have detectives on Oxman, Duncan and Grieb. This certainly isn't a matter they'd discuss over the telephone, and if there'd been a personal meeting I'd have known of it."

"Then what *does* he want to see you about?"

Mason said, "The best way to find out is by talking with him." She nodded. He turned to his secretary and said, "Della, take Mrs. Benson into the law library. Tell Mr. Duncan to come in. . . . Does Duncan know you, Mrs. Benson?"

"No, he never saw me in his life."

"All right, you wait in the law library. I think Duncan is going to make some proposition. It may prove interesting."

Della Street said, "This way, please," escorted Matilda

Benson into the law library, and then brought Charlie Duncan into Mason's private office.

Duncan's face was twisted into his customary cordial grin, prominently displaying the burnished gold teeth in his upper jaw. "No hard feelings because of last night?" he asked.

"No hard feelings," Mason said.

"You played a pretty smart game," Duncan went on. "If it hadn't been that the breaks went against you, you'd have had us licked."

Mason said nothing.

Duncan said, "Oh, well, we can't always win, you know."

Mason indicated a chair and said, "Sit down."

Ducan took a cigar case from his pocket and extended it to Mason.

"No," Mason told him, "I only smoke cigarettes."

Duncan sniffed and then indicated Matilda Benson's leather cigar case which she had left on the desk.

"Looks like some client must have left a cigar case here, then."

Mason frowned and said, "My law clerk." He pressed a button which summoned Della Street, handed her the leather cigar case and said, "Take this out to Jackson and tell him he left his cigars in here."

Della Street nodded, a twinkle showing in her eyes. "Yes," she said demurely, "Jackson will be missing his cigars."

She took the cigar case and left the room. Duncan grinned and said, "So the grandmother's your client, eh?"

Mason raised his eyebrows. Duncan laughed and said, "Don't think we're quite such damn fools as you made us seem last night, Mason. Naturally we tried to figure out how you fitted into the picture. We didn't think you were representing Oxman, or you wouldn't have tried to run a ringer on us. You certainly weren't representing

Sylvia. But Sylvia has a grandmother who smokes cigars. That was a woman's cigar case."

"Are you asking me or telling me?" Mason asked.

"I'm telling you."

"Nice of you," the lawyer remarked, yawning. "And that's all you wanted to see me about?"

"No."

"What did you want to see me about?"

"About those I O U's."

"What about them?"

Duncan crossed his knees, said, "Now listen, Mr. Mason, I want you to get me straight. I like the way you played the game last night. Checking back on the conversation you had with Sam, we found we couldn't pin anything on you. You never claimed the man with you was Frank Oxman. You had him try to cash a check, and Sam did all the leading from there on. And the damn fool led with his chin. We thought we might have you on that check business because Sam remembered the name of the bank. But we did a little snooping around and found you'd plugged up that loophole. If we could have found a weak point in your play, we'd have been mean about it. But we couldn't find any. It was a slick piece of work."

"And you dropped in to tell me that?" Mason asked.

Duncan shook his head and said, "I dropped in to tell you how you could get those I O U's."

"How?"

"I'd want you to do something for me. You're smart. I need a smart lawyer."

Mason stared steadily at the gambler and said, "Get me straight on this, Duncan: I'm interested in those I O U's. I'm not interested for myself, but for a client. Now, I don't know what you have in mind, but I don't want you to tell me anything you wouldn't want repeated to my client. In other words, you and I are dealing at arm's length. If you tell me anything, I'm not going to keep the conversation confidential. If I can capitalize on what you tell me, I'm going to do it. A lawyer can't serve two masters.

"Now then, with that understanding, if you want to talk about those I O U's, go ahead. I'd advise you not to."

Duncan's gold teeth flashed into prominence. "Well," he said, waving his cigar in a little gesture, "I can't say you didn't warn me."

Mason sat silent.

"Listen," Duncan went on, "I've been a gambler all my life. I'm going to take a chance on you. I have a proposition I think will look good to you."

Mason said slowly, "I'm going to tell you once more, Duncan. I'm not in this business for my health. Whenever I do something it's because some client is paying me money to do it. That means I've already been employed by some client whose interests are adverse to yours. If you don't tell me anything, you won't have anything to regret later on."

"Spoken like a gentleman," Duncan said.

"No," Mason corrected, "spoken like a lawyer."

"Okay," Duncan said, "you've told me—not only once, but twice. If I put my head in a noose it's my own funeral. Is that it?"

"That's it," Mason said.

"All right, now suppose you listen to me for a while. I need a smart lawyer. I need you. You've been employed to get those I O U's. That's the limit of your interest in my affairs, at present. All right, I'll see that you get the I O U's. I'll give them to you. In return, I want you to do something for me.

"I want to get rid of Sam. He's hard to get along with. He thinks he's the whole show. I don't like it. Now then, is it true that when a partnership is organized for an unspecified term either partner can dissolve the partnership at any time he wants to?"

Mason said, "Supposing that's the law, then what?"

"I want to dissolve that partnership."

"You don't need a smart lawyer to do that," Mason pointed out.

"I need a smart lawyer to do it the way I want to do it."

"Aren't you two doing a pretty good business out there?"

"A land-office business."

"The minute you dissolve the partnership," Mason said, "you'll knock that business into a cocked hat."

"No, we won't," Duncan said. "Let me tell you something; I'm pretty smart, myself. Grieb had some money and a fine opinion of himself. He wanted to open a gambling ship, but good hulls that can be made into gambling ships aren't so easy to find. I happened to know a man who had one. The man didn't know Grieb. He knew me. He gave us a lease, and in that lease there's a clause that any time the partnership of Grieb and Duncan is dissolved, the lease is automatically terminated."

"So what?" Mason asked, his eyes staring steadily in level-lidded scrutiny.

"So," Duncan said, "I'm going to terminate the partnership. That'll terminate the lease. We'll wind up the partnership business. It isn't worth a damn without a place to carry on. The furniture and fixtures won't bring ten cents on the dollar at a forced sale. I'll see there's a forced sale, and I'll bid the stuff in through a dummy. Ten minutes after I have title to it, the owner of the ship will execute a new lease with me. That'll show Mr. Sam Grieb just how smart *he* is.

"He struts around that place ten inches taller than God, telling me what I can do and what I can't do, trying to give me orders, bossing me around, countermanding my instructions, bullying the employees, and being a general pain in the neck.

"Now then, you can go ahead and represent me in this

thing. Part of the partnership assets are those I O U's. I'll get all the partnership assets. I'll turn the I O U's over to you as your fee. I don't care what you do with them afterwards. You can collect as big a bonus as you want. I didn't know the grandmother was interested in 'em, but if she is, you've got her on the one hand and Frank Oxman on the other. You can run the price up and sell out to the best bidder."

"That's not my way of doing business," Mason said.

"Well, you know your way of doing business," Duncan told him, "and I know mine. You know what I want. You know what you'll get. Now then, do we shoot or not?"

"We don't," Mason said unhesitatingly.

"Why not?"

"Because I don't like the way you're going about it, Duncan. I don't want to represent you. I'm representing interests adverse to you. I'm fighting you."

Duncan said affably, "Better think it over, Mason. I'm giving you an out. It's the only out you have. You've tipped your hand on those I O U's. If you don't play ball with me I'll play it both ends against the middle, the grandmother on one side and Frank Oxman on the other, and Sylvia in between. The one who pays the most money gets the I O U's. Oxman'll want 'em for evidence, and the grandmother will want to keep 'em from coming into court. We don't care which side comes out on top. What we're after is money."

Mason shook his head.

Duncan got to his feet. "And to think I thought you were smart!" he said. "That shows what a sucker *I* was. . . . How do I get out of here?"

"Through that door into the corridor."

Duncan strode across the office, jerked the door open and slammed it shut behind him.

Mason picked up the receiver on his desk telephone and said, "Ring the law library. Tell Della to bring Mrs. Benson back in here, and get Paul Drake on the line for me right away." He dropped the receiver back into place and stared moodily at the blotter on his desk. Just as the door from the law library opened, the telephone rang and Mason, again picking up the receiver, heard Paul Drake's voice say, "Okay, Perry. What is it?"

"Duncan was just in my office," Mason told him.

"You aren't telling me anything, Perry. I've had two men on him ever since he came ashore from the gambling ship."

"I want to know just where he goes and just what he does," Mason said. "No matter what happens, don't lose sight of him. If necessary, put more men on the job."

"Okay, Perry," Drake replied. "Don't worry. He'll never lose the two shadows who are tailing him now."

"Just wanted to make sure," Mason said, "because he's going to be important. I'll tell you about it later." He dropped the receiver into position, smiled up at Matilda Benson and said, "Well, we're getting the breaks."

"What are they?" she asked.

"Duncan," Mason said, "has been playing Sam Grieb for a sucker. Now he's ready to spring the trap. He's got Grieb's money in the business and is now going to throw the whole thing into a receivership so he can take advantage of a joker in the lease."

Matilda Benson relaxed comfortably in the big overstuffed leather chair and said, "I thought Duncan was just a yes-man."

"Well, you're going to have one more think coming. He's smart."

"Can he make it stick?" she asked.

"Yes," Mason said slowly, "I think he can. I think he's got Grieb. Grieb was trying to put Duncan on the spot in some way, but Duncan beat him to it by putting a joker in the lease, and now Duncan is ready to clamp down on Grieb. It's a case of two crooks, each trying to outsmart the other, with Duncan holding more trumps."

"Why did Duncan tell you all this?"

"He wanted me to act as his lawyer."

"Why you? What I mean is, he must know you're hostile to him and . . ."

"That was the bait he held out," Mason said. "He told me he'd let me have those I O U's as my fee."

"Could he do that?"

"Probably."

"Why didn't you do it?"

"Because, in the first place, I don't like Duncan. In the second place, I don't like business of that sort. And in the third place, we don't have to do it. They're playing directly into our hands. Just because I wouldn't represent him doesn't mean Duncan isn't going ahead. He's ready to shoot now. He'll get some other lawyer. They'll strike out of a clear sky. Duncan will dissolve the partnership and file an action asking to have a receiver appointed. The court will issue an order requiring Grieb to appear and show cause why a receiver shouldn't be appointed. That order will probably be served sometime tonight. I'll arrange to be aboard the gambling ship when the service is made. There'll be a lot of fur flying out there, and what I'll say won't make matters any better. By the time I've finished, I'll have those I O U's."

Matilda Benson got to her feet, ground out the end of her cigar in an ash tray on the desk, smiled at Mason and said, "I like your methods very much, Mr. Mason. The affair is entirely in your hands."

When she had gone, Della Street came over to stand at Mason's side, her right hand resting lightly on his left shoulder. "Listen, Chief," she said, "I wish you wouldn't do it."

"Do what?"

"Go out to that gambling ship tonight."

"Why?"

"There's going to be trouble out there. Those men are going to get nasty."

"I can be nasty myself, on occasion," he told her.

44

"But you're out on their ship. You'll be out of the jurisdiction of all state laws. You're surrounded by their men who will do exactly what they're told."

"They're rats," Mason said. "I don't like either of them. I'm particularly sore at Grieb. It'll do me a lot of good to point out to Grieb just where he stands and show Duncan where he's overreached himself."

"And then what'll they do?" she said.

"When I get finished they'll turn over the I O U's to me at their face value, or perhaps for a few hundred dollars bonus," Mason said.

She smiled down at him as his arm circled her waist and drew her close. "Well," she told him, "there's nothing like being optimistic."

5

■

BEADS OF MOISTURE glinted on the upturned collar of Perry Mason's gray overcoat as he stood in the telephone booth of the beach-town drugstore. His brown felt hat was also covered with glistening particles. From time to time, he snapped his left arm into position to consult his wristwatch. The telephone in the pay station suddenly shattered the silence. Mason jerked the receiver from its hook almost as soon as the bell started to ring. A feminine voice said, "Mr. Perry Mason, please."

"Yes, this is Mr. Mason."

"Go ahead, please."

Mason heard Drake's voice saying, "Okay, Perry. Duncan's filed his lawsuit. He's had a summons and an order to show cause issued and is on his way down to the beach with a deputy marshal who's going to serve the papers. He'll go right to the gambling ship."

Mason said, "Thanks, Paul. When your shadows call in next, tell them not to follow Duncan any farther than the pier."

"Right," the detective said. "Now listen, Perry, here's something else: Frank Oxman is headed for the beach. The operative who's shadowing him telephoned in the report."

"How long ago?" Mason asked.

"About half an hour ago."

"Then Oxman will get aboard the ship before Duncan gets there?"

"It looks that way."

"That," Mason said, "may complicate things. Grieb's evidently . . ."

"Wait a minute," Drake cut in, "you haven't heard anything yet. Sylvia Oxman's been out somewhere and my men couldn't pick up her trail. I've had operatives shadowing her apartment, and just to be on the safe side, I assigned a man to shadow her maid. Now, the maid went out a little while ago wearing one of Sylvia's Oxman's fur coats. The shadow tailed along, handling it just as a routine assignment; but he drew the lucky number. The maid contacted Sylvia, and my man had a chance to telephone in for instructions. Of course, I told him to drop the maid and pick up Sylvia."

"Know where she was going?" Mason asked. "It's foggy as the devil down here now, Paul, and that fur coat may mean that *she's* heading for the gambling ship."

"That's what I'm afraid of," Drake said. "Here's a peculiar coincidence, Perry. I had to put so many men on this case that I didn't have a chance to check them over carefully. I've just discovered that the man who's tailing Sylvia knows Duncan and Grieb personally. Will that make any difference?"

"It may. Do they know he's a detective?"

"No, I don't think they do. From all I can learn, this chap, whose name's Belgrade, had some sort of a partnership with Duncan and Grieb and they froze him out. I think he dropped a few thousand. It was all the money he had in the world and he had to go to work. He'd been a detective before, and when he struck me for a job I liked his looks and gave him a trial. He seemed to do all right, so I kept giving him little jobs."

Mason said slowly, "I don't think you'd better let him go aboard the gambling ship, if that's the case, Paul. It might complicate matters."

"That's the way I figured," Drake said. "Of course, shadowing the maid was just a routine job, but after this man contacted Sylvia I remembered something about his having been mixed up with gamblers and looked up his history. Incidentally, Perry, he claims that Duncan is the more crooked and the more dangerous of the two, but that they're both a couple of crooks."

"Well," Mason said, "you'd better jerk him off before he gets out on the ship."

"Yeah, I'm rushing a man down to the wharf to relieve Belgrade. Staples is his name. You'll probably remember him. He worked on that Dalton murder case. Of course, I don't *know* that Sylvia's headed for the ship. If she is, the relief will take over."

"Okay," Mason said. "Anything else?"

"That's all, Perry, but listen: I don't like the way things are shaping up. You're playing with dynamite. These gamblers are bad actors, and if Grieb gets the idea you encouraged Duncan to play foxy, it may not be so hot. When you get aboard that ship you'll be on the high seas and the men who are working as a crew are pretty tough citizens."

"Forget it," Mason told him. "I'll be all right."

"Well," Drake said, "remember that if Sylvia Oxman goes aboard that ship I'll have Staples shadowing her. Staples knows you. If you should have any trouble you can count on him. He's packing a .38 automatic and knows how to use it. If it comes to a showdown, remember he'll stand back of you."

Mason laughed into the transmitter and said, "You're doing too much worrying, Paul."

"Well, watch your step, Perry."

"Okay," the lawyer said, and hung up. His face was granite-grim as he left the drugstore and went out to his car.

Fog hung over the beach town in a thick, white pall which muffled sounds and blanketed the street lights with reddish, circular auras. Mason drove slowly, his windshield wiper beating monotonously. He speeded up as he came to the better-lighted business district, drove to the amusement pier, parked his car, and walked down the lighted pathway between the concessions.

Here the bright blaze of lights dispersed the gloom of the fog, but a few feet above the tops of the concessions the moisture closed in as a curtain, reflecting the illumination below as a crimson glare.

A man was selling tickets at the steps which led down to the float, where a speed boat was waiting. "Here you are," he said, "three boats running constantly. Take a cruise out to the high seas. Out beyond the twelve-mile limit. Who's next?"

Mason bought a ticket, went down the slippery steps, his gloved hands sliding along the rope rail. Two men came just behind him, and Mason heard the ticket seller say, "That's all for this load. There'll be another boat in, in just a few minutes."

The water was like black oil. The glossy surface barely moved to a long lazy swell which gently rocked the waiting speed boat. Moisture dripped from the wharf to the water; and in the fog-muffled silence could be heard the gentle lapping of waves against the piles of the wharf, the sound of the idling motor in the speed boat.

Mason took his place in a rear seat. A line thudded

to the float. The speed boat roared into motion. Moisture from the fog whipped over Mason's face. Behind him, the amusement concessions glowed for a few minutes as a yellow blob of light, then were swallowed into the fog. A horn, operated by compressed air, sent forth mournful warnings as the speed boat hissed through the darkness. The red and green running lights stained the reflecting fog in colored blotches.

By the time the speed boat pulled alongside the gambling ship, Mason was wet and chilled. The crowd which clambered stiffly from the boat to the landing stage showed none of the joyous spontaneity which had characterized those who had disembarked on Mason's previous visit. They climbed the swaying stairway, for the most part, in silence, a black, somber line of people who would presently cluster about the bar in an attempt to warm their blood.

There were some half dozen people waiting at the head of the landing-stairs to go back on the speed boat. Mason walked down the deck toward the bar entrance, and heard the staccato exhaust of the launch ripping the silence of the night as it swung away toward land. He ordered a Tom-and-Jerry, sipped it in leisurely appreciation, responding to the genial warmth and the glittering lights which so brilliantly illuminated the interior of the bar. He checked his hat and coat, and heard the exhaust of another speed boat as it arrived and departed.

Mason strolled into the main gambling room and turned toward the passageway which led to the offices. There were perhaps eighty or a hundred players clustered around the various gambling tables. He saw nothing of the uniformed guard who had previously been stationed near the entrance to the offices, so marched unannounced down the echoing wooden passageway, made the right-angle turn, and pushed open the door of the reception office.

At first glance Mason thought the office was empty;

then, in a corner, away from the door, he caught sight of a woman, dressed in a blue suit, an orange blouse giving it a splash of color, her face concealed by a magazine she was reading. A stretch of shapely leg showing beneath the skirt caught Mason's eye. Apparently absorbed in the magazine, she didn't look up as the lawyer entered the room. A blue leather handbag lay on her lap.

Mason stepped to the door which led to the inner office and knocked. There was no answer.

The woman in the far corner of the office looked up and said, "I don't think anyone's in there. I knocked several times and got no answer."

Mason stared at the ribbon of light which showed along the side of the door. "The door isn't even latched," he said. "I thought they always kept it locked."

The woman said nothing. The lawyer crossed the office, seated himself in a chair separated from hers by only a few feet, and turned casual eyes to her profile. He recognized her then as the woman he had seen on his last visit to the gambling ship—Sylvia Oxman—whose inopportune arrival had upset his plans.

Mason studied the toe of his shoe for a moment in frowning concentration, then turned to her and said, "You'll pardon me, but do you have an appointment with Mr. Grieb?"

"No," she said, "no appointment. I just wanted to see him."

"I," Mason told her, "have a very definite appointment, and it's for this hour. I don't like to inconvenience you, but it's important that I see him as soon as he comes in. *My* business will take about twenty minutes. Perhaps it would inconvenience you less if you went out and returned then."

She got swiftly to her feet. "Thank you very much for telling me," she said. And Mason thought there was relief in her voice, as though he had said something she had been hopefully anticipating.

"I'm sorry it's impossible for me to postpone the appointment in your favor," Mason said, smiling affably. "I think I'll wait for him in his private office."

Mason pushed open the heavy door as Sylvia Oxman tossed her magazine on the table and started for the passageway.

Sam Grieb's body, seated in the swivel chair, lay slumped over the huge desk. One shoulder was propped against the side of the desk. The head lolled at a grotesque angle, showing a red bullet hole in the left temple. A shaded lamp, which flooded illumination over the discolored face, was reflected from the glassy surfaces of open, staring eyes. The diamonds on his right hand sent out scintillating brilliance. His left hand was out of sight, under the desk.

Mason whirled back toward the outer office. Sylvia Oxman was just stepping into the corridor. "Sylvia!" he said sharply.

She paused at the sound of his voice, stood uncertainly in the doorway, then turned, dark eyes luminous with some emotion.

"Come here," Mason ordered.

"Just who are you?" she asked. "What do you want? What do you mean by speaking to me in . . ."

Mason reached her side in three swift steps, clamped strong fingers about her left arm just above the elbow. "Take a look," he ordered.

She hung back for a moment, then tried to shake herself free. Mason circled her swiftly with his arm and swung her through the door of the private office. She turned toward him indignantly, said, "How dare you . . ." and then broke off as she caught sight of the huddled figure at the desk. She opened her mouth to scream. Mason clamped his hand over her lips. "Steady now," he warned.

He waited until she struggled for breath, then released his hand and asked, "How long had you been waiting in the reception office before I came?"

"Just a minute or two," she said in a low, barely audible voice. She caught her breath. Her eyes, wild and staring, turned away from the desk, then, as though drawn by some overpowering fascination, drifted back.

"Can you prove it?"

"What do you mean?"

"Did anyone see you come in?"

"I don't know. I don't think so. I can't tell. . . . Who . . . who are you? I've seen you here before. You know my name."

Mason nodded and said, "My name's Mason. I'm a lawyer. Now listen, cut out this acting. Either you did this, or . . ."

He broke off as his eyes stared down at several oblongs of paper on the blotter. He reached forward and gingerly picked them up.

Sylvia Oxman gasped, "My I O U's! I came to pay up on them."

"Seventy-five hundred," Mason said. "Is that right?"

"Yes."

"You wanted to give Grieb the money for these?"

"Yes."

"That's why you came here tonight?"

"Yes."

"All right," Mason told her grimly, "let's see the money."

"What money?"

"Quit stalling. The seventy-five hundred bucks you were going to give Grieb in return for the I O U's."

"Why should I show it to you?"

Mason made a grab for her handbag. She avoided him, jumped back and stood staring at him with wide, frightened eyes. Mason said, "You haven't got seventy-five hundred dollars."

She said nothing, her rapid breathing slightly distending her nostrils.

"Did you kill him?" Mason asked.

"No . . . of course not. . . . I didn't know he was in here."

"Do you know who did?" She slowly shook her head.

Mason said, "Listen. I'm going to give you a break. Get out through that door, try to avoid being seen when you leave the passageway. Start gambling at one of the roulette tables. Wait for me. I'll talk with you out there, and you'll tell me the truth. Remember that, Sylvia, no lies."

She hesitated a moment, then said, "Why should *you* do this for *me?*"

Mason laughed grimly. "I'll bite, why should I? Just a foolish loyalty I have for my clients. I protect them, even when they lie to me—which most of them do—or try to double-cross me—which *has* been done."

Her dark, luminous eyes studied the rugged determination of his face. She was suddenly cool and self-possessed. "Thanks," she said, "but *I'm* not your client, you know."

"Well," he told her, "you're the next thing to it. And *I'm* damned if I can figure you as being guilty of murder. But you've got to do a lot of explaining before you can convince anyone else. Go ahead, now, get out."

"My I O U's," she said. "If my husband ever . . ."

"Forget it," Mason interrupted. "Have confidence in me for a change. I'm having plenty in you."

She studied him for a moment thoughtfully, then stepped to the door, her eyes avoiding the desk. "Those I O U's," she said, "are . . ."

"Beat it," he interrupted, "and don't close the door. Leave it ajar, just as it was."

She slipped through the door, and a moment later the electric signal announced she had rounded the turn in the corridor.

Mason pulled a wallet from his pocket, counted out seventy-five hundred dollars in bills, opened a drawer of the desk with the toe of his shoe, and dropped the bills into the drawer. He kicked the drawer shut, held the I O U's clamped between thumb and forefinger, struck a match, and held the flame to the paper. By the time the flame had burnt down to his hand, the I O U's had withered into dark, charred oblongs, traced with a glowing perimeter which gradually ate its way into the darker centers.

Abruptly, the electric buzzer burst into noise, announcing that someone was coming down the corridor toward the office. A split-second later it zipped into noise once more—two people were approaching.

The lawyer crumpled the bits of burned ash in his hand, thrust the corners which had been unconsumed into his mouth, and stepped swiftly into the reception office, pulling shut the door to the inner office by catching the knob with his elbow. He wiped his darkened hands on the sides of his trousers, threw himself into a chair, opened a magazine, and was unwrapping a stick of chewing gum when the door of the reception office opened, to disclose Duncan, accompanied by a tall man with watery blue eyes, dressed in a tweed suit. Both men wore overcoats, and fog particles glistened from the surfaces of the coats.

Duncan jerked to a dead stop, stared at Mason and said, "What the hell are *you* doing here?"

Mason casually fed the stick of chewing gum into his mouth, rolled the wrapper into a ball, dropped it into an ash tray, munched the chewing gum into a wad and said, "I *was* waiting for Sam Grieb because I wanted to talk to him. Now that you're here, I can talk to both of you."

"Where's Sam?"

"I don't know. I knocked on the door, but got no answer, so I decided I'd wait—not having anything else to do. . . . It's a wonder you wouldn't get some up-to-date magazines here. You'd think this was a dentist's office."

Duncan said irritably, "Sam's here. He's *got* to be here.

Whenever the tables are in operation one or the other of us has to be in this office."

Mason shrugged his shoulders, let his eyebrows show mild surprise. "Indeed," he said. "Any way in except through this room?"

"No."

"Well," Mason said, "suppose I talk with *you* while we're waiting. I understand you've filed your case."

"Of course I've filed it," Duncan said irritably. "You aren't the only attorney in the country. If you're too damned dumb to take good business when it's offered you, there are others who aren't so finicky."

Mason said politely, "How about a stick of gum?"

"No. I don't chew it."

"Of course," Mason said, "now that you've dragged your difficulties into court, you've submitted yourself to the jurisdiction of a court of equity. That throws your assets into court."

"Well, what if it does?"

"Those I O U's," Mason pointed out, "are part of your assets. They were given for a gambling debt. A court of equity wouldn't permit itself to be used as a collection agency for a gambling debt."

"We're on the high seas," Duncan said. "There's no law against gambling here."

"*You* may be on the high seas," Mason told him, "but your *assets* are in a court of equity. It's an equitable rule that all gambling contracts are void as being against public policy, whether there's a law against gambling or not. Those I O U's aren't worth the paper they're written on. You've been just a little too smart, Duncan, you've turned seventy-five hundred dollars worth of assets into scrap paper."

"Sylvia would never raise the point," Duncan said.

"*I'll* raise it," Mason told him.

Duncan studied him with blue, glittering eyes, "So *that's* why you wouldn't represent me, eh?"

"That's one of the reasons," Mason admitted.

Duncan pulled a leather key container from his pocket, started to fit a key in the lock of the door to the inner office. "If Sam hasn't the door barred from the inside, I'll open it," he said to the man in tweeds, then suddenly turned again to the lawyer. "What's your best offer, Mason?"

"I'll give you the face value of the I O U's."

"How about the thousand-dollar bonus?"

"Nothing doing."

"You made that offer yesterday," Duncan remonstrated.

"That was yesterday," Mason told him. "A lot's happened since yesterday."

Duncan twisted the key, clicked back the spring lock, and flung the door open. "Well," he said, "you sit down and wait a few minutes, and . . . Good God! What's this!"

He jumped backward, stared at the desk, then whirled to Mason and yelled, "Say, what are you trying to cover up here? Don't tell me you didn't know about this."

Mason pushed forward, saying, "What the hell are you talking about? I told you . . ." He became abruptly silent.

The man in tweeds said, "Don't touch anything. This is a job for the homicide squad. . . . Gosh, I don't know who *is* supposed to take charge. Probably the marshal . . ."

"Listen," Duncan said, speaking rapidly, "we come in and find this guy perched in the outer office, chewing gum and reading a three-months-old magazine. It looks fishy to me. Sam's been shot."

"Suicide, perhaps," Mason suggested.

"We'll take a look around," Duncan said, "and see if it's suicide."

"Don't touch anything," the man in tweeds warned.

"Don't be a sap," Duncan said. "How long have you been here, Mason?"

"Oh, I don't know. Four or five minutes."

"Hear anything suspicious?"

Mason shook his head.

The man in tweeds bent over the desk and said, "There's no sign of a gun. And it's an awkward place for a man to have hit himself with a bullet, if it's suicide."

"Look under the desk," Mason suggested. "The gun might have dropped from his hand."

The man in tweeds kept his attention concentrated on the body. "He'd have had to hold the gun in his left hand to do it himself," he said slowly. "He wasn't left-handed, was he, Duncan?"

Duncan, his blue eyes wide and startled, stood with his back against the vault door, his mouth sagging open. "It's murder!" he said, and gulped. "For God's sake, turn off that desk light! It gives me the willies to see his open eyes staring into that light!"

The man in tweeds said, "No you don't! Don't touch a thing."

Mason, standing in the doorway between the two rooms, taking care not to enter the room which contained the body, said, "Let's make sure there isn't a gun down there on the floor. After all, you know, it's going to make a lot of difference whether this is murder or suicide. I, for one, would like to know before we send out a report. He *could* have dropped a gun . . ."

Duncan stepped forward, bent over the body, peered down under the desk and said, "No, there's no gun here."

The man in tweeds asked, "Can you see? I'll get a light and . . ."

"Sure I can see," Duncan exclaimed irritably. "There's no gun here. You keep your eyes on this guy, Perkins. He's trying to get us both looking for something so he can pull a fast one. He's talked too damn much about a gun being down there."

Mason said ominously, "Watch your lip, Duncan!"

The tall man nodded. "I'd be careful what I said, Mr.

57

Duncan. You haven't any proof, you know. This man might make trouble."

"To hell with him," Duncan snapped. "There's seven thousand five hundred dollars in I O U's somewhere around here, and Mason wants them. I'm going to take a look in the vault. You keep your eye on Mason."

Duncan crossed over to the vault, his back turned to the men as he faced the vault door, rattled the handle, then started spinning the combination. "I don't like the looks of things," he called out over his shoulder. "This guy Mason is smart, too damn smart."

The tall man said, "I wouldn't touch anything, Mr. Duncan. If I were you, I wouldn't open that vault."

Duncan straightened up and turned to face Perkins. "I've *got* to find out about those I O U's," he said indignantly. "After all, I own a half interest in this place."

"Just the same," Perkins persisted, "I wouldn't open that vault."

Mason, from the doorway between the rooms, said, "And you're leaving a lot of fingerprints on things, Duncan. The police aren't going to like that."

Duncan's face darkened with rage. "A hell of a slick guy, ain't you," he shouted, "standing there and telling us to look for a gun, and to do this and do that until you've got us leaving fingerprints all over things, and *then* telling us about it!

"To hell with you! You ain't in the clear on this thing —particularly if those I O U's are missing. You could have done the whole job here—easy! Sammy would have let you in, and you could have given him the works, and then gone back out, pulled the door shut, and been waiting here . . . Perkins, you're an officer. Search him. Let's see if he's got those I O U's. And he may have the murder gun in his pocket. Let's not let him talk us out of anything."

Mason said, "Listen, Duncan, *I'm* not going to be the goat in this thing."

Duncan faced him with blazing eyes. "The hell you're not! We come in here and find you sitting next to a murdered man, and you have the nerve to try and tell us what you're going to do and what you're not going to do!

"You're going to take it and like it, and you're going to be searched before you have a chance to ditch anything that you might have taken from this room. You know and I know there's something here you want, and want damn bad."

"So I came in and murdered Grieb to get it; is that right?" Mason asked.

The man in tweeds said, "Better be careful, Mr. Duncan, I think he's laying a trap for you. Don't accuse him of anything."

"I'm not afraid of him," Duncan said, "but I sure want to know a lot more about this thing before I let him go wandering off the ship."

"Well," Mason said, "suppose you search me now. I'll dump everything out of my pockets here, and you can both check the stuff."

"That's a good idea," the man in tweeds said. "I'd like to have someone check up on . . ."

"Take him into my bedroom," Duncan said. "That's through the door marked 'Private,' at the end of the bar. You go down a corridor, and my room's the second door on the left. Take him in there and wait until I come."

"When'll *that* be?" Mason asked.

"That'll be just as soon as I can get Arthur Manning in here. Manning's the one to handle this business. He's a special deputy. He's around the casino somewhere. You try and find him, Perkins. You'll know him when you see him. He's wearing a blue uniform with a badge on it that says SPECIAL OFFICER."

"You want me to parade around with this guy until I locate this deputy?"

"No—wait a minute—I'll signal him from here."

Duncan stepped behind the desk, reached down past

Grieb's body and pressed a concealed button. The man in tweeds said, "I don't know what my legal rights are, but if I'm going to act under your orders, you're going to take *all* the responsibility. Is that understood?"

"Of course it is," Duncan said impatiently, "but watch Mason. Don't let him pull any fast ones, and don't let him ditch anything."

Mason drawled, "If you feel that way about it, Duncan, in justice to myself, I demand that I be handcuffed."

"*You're* asking for it?" Perkins inquired. Mason nodded.

Perkins heaved a sigh of relief and said, "You heard him say that, Duncan."

Duncan said, "Sure I did. Don't be so damn technical. Put the bracelets on him."

Mason held out his wrists. Perkins slipped the handcuffs on them and said, "Come on, let's go."

"The second door on the left after you go through the door marked 'Private,' at the end of the bar," Duncan instructed.

The man in tweeds slipped his right arm through Mason's left arm and said, "Put your wrists down, buddy. Then your coat sleeves will conceal the handcuffs. I'll hold my hand here and we can walk through the bar without making a lot of commotion."

Mason, still casually chewing gum, permitted himself to be escorted along the passageway, through the bar, through the door marked "Private," and into Duncan's bedroom.

Perkins closed the door behind them and said, "You understand I haven't any hard feelings."

Mason nodded.

"And I'm just following Duncan's orders. He's the one who's responsible, in case you feel like making any trouble."

"I don't feel like making any trouble," Mason said, "unless you put me in a position where I have to. You're in enough trouble already."

"What do you mean?"

"Leaving Duncan alone in that room."

"Somebody has to stay there until the authorities show up."

Mason shrugged his shoulders as though dismissing the subject. "The name's Perkins?" he asked.

"Yes."

"All right, Perkins, Duncan wants you to search me, and I want to be searched. You can start with the wallet in my inside coat pocket. You'll find some money in there and some business cards, a driving license, and a lodge card."

Perkins pulled the wallet from the inner pocket of Mason's coat, opened it, looked hastily through the wallet, then pushed it back in Mason's pocket. He patted Mason's pockets in search of a gun, then inserted the key in the handcuffs with fumbling fingers and said, "I hope you aren't going to be sore about this, Mr. Mason, I . . ."

As the handcuffs clicked open, Mason said, "Now wait a minute, Perkins. Let's go at this thing right. I'm doing this for my own protection. Now let's make a good job of it."

Mason walked to the dresser and emptied his pockets, then unfastened his collar.

"What are you doing?" Perkins asked.

"I'm stripping," Mason told him, "and you're going to search every inch of me and every stitch of clothes I've got on. Later on, you're going to get on the witness stand and swear that I didn't take anything out of that room, that I haven't any weapon on me and that you've listed absolutely everything which was in my possession."

Perkins nodded and said, "That suits me swell."

Mason had just taken off his shirt when the door opened and Duncan entered the room.

"What's coming off here?" Duncan asked.

Mason grinned and said, "Everything. I'm going to get a clean bill of health out of this."

"You don't need to go *that* far," Duncan said, his voice conciliatory.

"Well, I'm *going* that far," Mason told him.

"But that's absurd. I'm not accusing you of murder or of robbery, but you're a lawyer and I don't know just what your client's up to. I thought perhaps you *might* have picked up a gun in there, or perhaps there was some evidence you didn't want to have the officers find and . . ."

"Exactly," Mason said, "so we're going to settle this business right now and right here."

"Just search him for a gun, Perkins," Duncan ordered. "This business of taking off all of his clothes is absurd."

Perkins frowned. "A little while ago," he said, "you wanted him turned inside out. Now you . . ."

Mason, unbuckling his belt and slipping off his trousers, interrupted him. "Can't you see what he's doing, Perkins? He realizes *now* that it would have been a lot better for him if he'd let me go out without being searched. Then if anything was missing he could blame it on me. He'd like to have you make just a casual search now, and then, later on, he could claim there was something you didn't find."

"You talk as though you knew all about what I was thinking," Duncan said sarcastically.

Mason kicked off his shoes, pulled off his undershirt, stepped out of his shorts and stooped to unfasten his garters. "Perhaps I do," he said grimly. "Now, Perkins, go through my clothes and make a list of everything you find. As you finish with my clothes, hand them back to me and I'll put them on."

Duncan shoved a cigar into his mouth, took from his pocket a card of matches bearing the imprint of the gambling ship, started to say something, then checked himself and stood, matches in hand, chewing the cigar thoughtfully and watching Perkins go through Mason's clothes and toss them back to the lawyer.

While Mason was dressing, Perkins made a laborious inventory of the articles on the dresser which Mason had taken from his pockets.

Mason turned to Duncan and said, "Light your cigar, Duncan, you make me nervous. Did you lock up the offices?"

Duncan nodded, absently pulled a key from his pocket and held it out to Perkins.

"Any other keys to the door?" Mason asked.

"Only the one Grieb has," Duncan said, "and Arthur Manning's on guard in front of the door, with instructions not to let anyone in. I've sent word by one of the speed boats to telephone the police and have them come out and take charge."

"I suppose," Mason said, "you've stopped anyone from leaving the ship?"

Duncan shook his head. "I haven't any authority to do that. They could sue me for damages. People come and go, and I've got no right to . . ." As he talked, his voice gradually lost its assurance, first became a mumbling monotone, then faded into dubious silence.

Perkins looked up from making his inventory and said, "Hell, Duncan, they shouldn't be allowed to leave. The police won't like that. The officers will want to interview everyone aboard the ship at the time. Letting people leave is the worst thing you can do." As he spoke, the ripping exhaust of a speed boat gave unmistakable evidence that the launches were continuing their regular trips.

Duncan stepped out into the corridor, pushed open the door to the bar and yelled, "Jimmy, come in here." He returned to the bedroom while Perkins was counting the money in Mason's wallet.

He left the door open, and the bald-headed bartender, wearing his white apron, a genial smile turning up his fat lips, entered the room and let the smile fade into frowning concentration as he surveyed the three men. His eyes grew hard and watchful. "What is it?" he asked.

Duncan said, "We've had some trouble aboard, Jimmy."

The bartender, taking a cautious step toward Perkins and Mason, held his left shoulder slightly forward, his weight on the balls of his feet, his right fist doubled. "What trouble?" he asked ominously.

"Not here," Duncan said hastily, "it's in the other office. Something's happened to Sam Grieb."

"What?" the bartender asked, his eyes still watching Mason and Perkins.

"He was murdered."

"Who did it?"

"We don't know."

"Okay," the bartender said, "what do I do with these guys?"

"Nothing. I want you to stop the launches," Duncan said. "Don't let anyone leave until the police get here."

"Have you sent word to the police?"

"Yes."

The bartender slowly turned away from Mason and Perkins, to stare at Duncan.

"Just how do you want me to go about it?"

"Put a couple of boys at the head of the landing stairs and on the platform. Don't let anyone come aboard or get off."

"You taking charge here?" the bartender asked.

"Yes, of course."

"If you want a suggestion," the bartender said, "why not just pull up the landing-stage for emergency repairs? If we try to stop people coming and going, we've got to make explanations, and we'll have a panic here."

"That's a good idea, Jimmy," Duncan agreed. "I'm leaving it to you."

"Okay," the bartender said as he turned and strode from the room.

Perkins finished counting the money in Mason's wallet

64

and said to the lawyer, "This is the way I've made the inventory. You'd better look it over."

"All right, I will," Mason said. "How about any other entrance to that room, Duncan?"

"There isn't any."

"Are you certain?"

"Of course I'm certain. This ship was completely refinished inside, in accordance with our specifications. It'd been a fishing barge, and the owner turned it into a gambling ship for us. We furnished the wheels and the layout, but he did the rest of it. We designed that office on purpose so people couldn't come busting in from two or three different doors. There's only one way into that private office, and that's through the reception room, and there's only one way into that reception room and that's through the right-angled corridor. We didn't know but what we might have trouble with the boys from some of the other ships; and when we laid the thing out we did it so muscle men couldn't come busting in, pull any rough stuff and get out. There's a bell button on the underside of the desk which calls the officer on duty, and then there's an emergency alarm which is a peach. If a suspicious-looking guy ever came into the office, Sam could press his foot on a little square plate beneath the desk. As soon as he pressed that, it made a contact, and then as long as his foot kept pressing it, nothing happened. But, if he took his foot away, without first throwing a switch, an emergency-alarm signal rang bells all over the ship and even down on the landing-stage. We've never had to use those bells, but if any guys had ever tried to muscle in and take us for a ride, we could have sewed them up. Once those bells rang, the men up in the watch room wouldn't let anyone out of Grieb's office. No one could get off the ship. And the crew had been drilled to grab guns and stand by."

"Then," Mason said, "whoever killed Grieb was someone who entered the office on legitimate business and

65

shot Grieb before Grieb had any idea what was going to happen."

Duncan nodded and said, *"You* came here on legitimate business, I suppose."

"What do you mean by that crack?" Mason asked.

Duncan said, "I'm not making any cracks. I'm just telling you that the bird who bumped Sam off was someone he'd expected to see on business, someone who was able to walk into the office and pull a rod before Sammy had any idea what was going to happen.

"Sammy opened the door and let him in. Then Sammy went back to his desk, sat down and started talking. While he was in the middle of saying something, this guy, who was probably sitting on the other side of the desk, slipped a gun out of his pocket where Sammy couldn't see it, and all of a sudden pulled up the rod and let Sammy have it right through the head at short range. Then this guy walked out, pulled the door shut behind him and perhaps went on deck to toss the gun overboard, or he *might* have sat down in the other office for a while, reading magazines."

"Or," Mason said dryly, "might have taken a speed boat and gone ashore, for all you know."

"Well, whatever he did, it isn't my fault. I couldn't have sewed the ship up. Sammy was dead before *I* came aboard. We don't even know when he was killed. There might have been a dozen boats leave before I discovered it, and then again . . ."

Duncan glanced meaningly at Perry Mason.

"Then again, what?" Mason asked.

Duncan grinned, and his gold teeth once more flashed into evidence. "Nope," he said, "I'm not making any guesses. That's up to the officers."

Mason said, "There's no need for me to stick around. You've got an inventory of everything that was on me, Perkins. I'm going up on deck and see if anyone's particularly worried about not being able to leave."

Duncan nodded, started for the door, then stopped, frowned thoughtfully and said, "You're pretty smart, ain't you?"

"What do you mean?" Mason asked.

"I mean that you were damned anxious to be searched."

"Of course I was."

"I think *I'll* be searched," Duncan said. "After all, I was in that room for a minute or two before Manning showed up, and it might be a good idea to be able to prove I didn't take anything away with me."

Mason's laugh was sarcastic. "You might just as well spare yourself the trouble, Duncan. You've had an opportunity to take anything you wanted out of that room, toss it overboard or hide it in any one of a hundred different places. Being searched *now* isn't going to help you any."

Duncan said, "I don't like the way you say that."

Mason grinned. "I'm *so* sorry. You could have left the room at the same time we did, Duncan, and then there wouldn't have been any necessity for searching you."

"Yes," Duncan sneered, "and left the place wide open for an accomplice of yours to have come back and . . ."

"Accomplice of *mine?*" Mason asked, raising his eyebrows.

"I didn't mean it that way," Duncan admitted. "I meant a client of yours, or an accomplice of the murderer."

Mason yawned. "Personally, I don't like the air in here. It's stuffy. I think I'll mingle around."

"You're sure you made a list of *everything* he had on him?" Duncan asked Perkins.

Perkins nodded.

"The lining of his coat?"

"You bet," Perkins said. "I used to be a jailer. I know something about where a man hides things. I looked in his shoes, in the lining of his coat."

"Did you look under the collar of his coat?"

Perkins laughed and said, "Don't be silly. Of course I looked under the collar of his coat and in the cuffs of his pants. I went over every inch of cloth with my fingers."

"How much money did he have in that wallet?"

"Twenty-five hundred dollars in hundreds and fifties, and three hundred and twenty dollars in twenties, and then he had four fives, three ones and some silver, six quarters, ten dimes, four nickels and six pennies."

Mason grinned and said, "When you make an inventory, you make a good one, don't you, Perkins?"

"I wasn't a jailer for nothing," Perkins admitted. "Lots of times guys would swear they had a lot more money than they did."

Duncan stared at Mason with narrowed eyes. There was no trace of a smile either on his lips or in his eyes.

"Twenty-five hundred in fifties and hundreds, eh?" he asked.

Perkins said, "That's right."

"Were you," Mason asked, "thinking of something, Duncan?"

"Yes," Duncan said, "I was just thinking that seventy-five hundred dollars from ten thousand would leave twenty-five hundred."

Perkins looked puzzled. Mason's grin was affable. "Quite right, Duncan," he said, "and ten thousand from twelve thousand five hundred would leave twenty-five hundred; and twenty-five thousand from twenty-seven thousand five hundred would still leave twenty-five hundred."

Duncan's face darkened. He said to Perkins, "Could he have folded or wadded up any papers and concealed them on him somewhere?"

Perkins said, with some show of impatience, "Not a chance. I know what to look for, and I know where to look. I've been searching guys for years. Some of 'em used to try putting a flexible saw around the inside of their collars or down the stiffening in the front of their coats. But they didn't get away with it. I'm telling you I *searched* this guy. He asked for it and he got it."

Duncan jerked the door open and pounded out into the outer corridor. Mason grinned at Perkins. "Did you inventory the chewing gum, Perkins?"

"Sure. Three sticks of Wrigley's Double-Mint. And I even looked at the wrappers to make certain *they* hadn't been tampered with."

"Well, how about having a stick?" Mason asked. "I think I'll put in another stick to freshen this one."

Perkins said, "No, I don't chew gum, thanks."

Mason paused with the stick of gum half in his mouth and said, "Wait a minute, Perkins. You didn't look *in* my mouth. Perhaps you'd better do that, just in case there's some question. Duncan, you know, might fight dirty if he had a chance."

"I was thinking of that," Perkins admitted, "—about looking in your mouth, I mean—when Duncan was making all those cracks, but I didn't want to say anything."

Mason moistened his thumb and the tip of his forefinger, pulled out the wad of chewing gum and said, "Well, you'd better take a look now."

Perkins turned Mason's head so that the light showed in his mouth. "Okay," he said, "now raise up your tongue."

Mason raised his tongue. Perkins grinned, nodded, and said, "I'm giving you a clean bill of health. I'll bet fifty bucks you haven't got anything on you except what I inventoried."

Mason slapped Perkins on the shoulder and said, "Let's mingle around and see what Duncan's doing. You can follow his mental processes. First he was damned anxious to have me searched, and then he *didn't* want me searched. Then, when he realized you were going to search me anyway, he wanted me gone over with a microscope. He figures that something's missing. He's not sure I have it; but if I haven't, he'd like to make me a fall guy, anyhow."

"Well," Perkins said, "so far as I'm concerned, this trip's a bust. I came out here to serve some papers. The man I was to serve them on is dead."

"By the way," Mason said, "how long have you been with Duncan?"

"What do you mean?"

"If it came to a question of an alibi," Mason asked, "how far could you go with Duncan?"

"He picked me up in Los Angeles at ten minutes to five," Perkins said, "—or right around there. It might have been quarter to five, or it might have been around five minutes to five."

"But it was before five o'clock?" Mason asked.

"Yes, I know it was before five o'clock, because he bought me a cocktail and I noticed the clock over the bar. It said five o'clock."

"Then what did you do?"

"We went to dinner; and Duncan explained to me what papers I was to serve and just how I was to go about doing it. He said he wanted to catch Grieb when the place was running full tilt. So I waited around with him until he said okay."

"Did he say why?"

"No, but I gathered it was something about Grieb keeping all the books and the cash. Duncan wanted to serve the papers when the cash was all on the tables and have me go around and make some sort of an inventory, I think."

"Did you have any authority to do that?" Mason asked.

"No, not unless Grieb consented to it, but that would have been the smart thing for Grieb to do."

Mason stepped to the porthole and casually tossed out the wad of gum he had been chewing. "Well, let's go out and see what's happening. Duncan's going to have a

70

job on his hands with these people if he isn't careful. It'll be an hour or so before the officers can get out here."

"When you come right down to it," Perkins said, "this ship's on the high seas, and no one's got any authority here except a representative of the United States Marshal's office."

"Or the Captain," Mason suggested.

"Well, yes, the Captain's entitled to give orders. I suppose they have someone here who rates as a captain, but of course he's just a figurehead. Duncan and Grieb are the big shots. Now Grieb's dead, Duncan's the whole squeeze."

"Yes," Mason said, "and if you wanted to be cold-blooded about it, you could say that Grieb's death hadn't been the worst thing in the world for Charlie Duncan."

"Uh-huh," Perkins grunted noncommittally.

Mason went on, "Duncan, as the surviving partner, will have the job of winding up the partnership affairs. You know, Perkins, if I were you, seeing you have sort of an official status here, I'd stick around to make certain Duncan didn't go back into that room, perhaps long enough to open the vault and start prowling around. You know Manning, who's standing guard, is in the employ of the ship, and, now that Grieb's dead, he's dependent on Duncan for his bread and butter."

Perkins nodded. "I guess that's not a bad idea. The officers may figure I should take charge. I'm a deputy United States Marshal. Thanks for helping me out of a mean situation, Mason. If you'd wanted to be tough about being searched, it would have put me in an awful spot. As an officer, I'd have hated to watch you walk out of that room *without* being searched, but I'd hate like hell to have had to make a search without a warrant, you being a lawyer and all that."

Mason said, "Don't mention it, Perkins. You know your business, but I really think the place for you is keeping an eye on Manning."

6

■

MASON LOOKED over the crowd which milled around the gambling tables. He made certain Sylvia Oxman was not at any of those tables, nor did he see the detective Paul Drake had delegated to shadow her.

He left the gambling salon for the fog-swept moisture of the decks. A little knot of people were grouped about the raised boat landing. A man standing out near the end was pounding on a rivet which held the grated landing stage. One of the group asked irritably, "How much longer is it going to be?"

Jimmy, the bartender, his white apron removed, a gold braided cap pulled low on his forehead, said in the soothing voice of a man who has learned his diplomacy dealing with drunks across a mahogany bar, "It won't be long now. We've got to get these rivets tightened up so they'll be safe. After all, you know, safety first. When we once get it fixed, it'll only take a minute to lower it and get you people started ashore. There are four speed boats working tonight, and they'll all be hanging around ready to unload, fill up and get going. . . . Why don't you folks go back inside where it's warm? We'll call you just as soon as the landing's fixed."

The man with the irritable voice said, "How do we know this isn't a stall to keep us from leaving the ship with our winnings? I'm almost a hundred dollars ahead and I don't like the way this thing's being handled."

"Aw, go on back in the bar and buy yourself a drink with some of your winnings. It'll make you feel better."

There was a chorus of laughter.

Mason mingled with the crowd. Sylvia Oxman was nowhere in sight. He stood at the rail and stared into the foggy darkness. He could see the dim outlines of red and green lights where two of the speed boats were standing by. The sounds of laughter and joking comments which drifted up from these speed boats showed that the passengers were inclined to take the whole thing as a lark, taking advantage of the informality of the occasion to get acquainted with the unescorted women who had journeyed out to try their luck aboard the craft.

Mason re-entered the lighted interior and went to the bar. A feminine voice said, "How do you do, Mr. Mason."

He turned to meet the whimsical challenge of Matilda Benson's gray eyes.

She seemed hardly more than in her late fifties, the low-cut evening gown showing the firm-fleshed, rounded contours of her throat, bosom and shoulders. Her snow-white hair was swept back from her head in a boyish bob. Her gown sparkled with silver, which glittered in the light as she moved, matching the sheen of her hair.

"Well," she asked, "are you going to buy me a drink? I presume you've already attended to your business."

Mason glanced swiftly about him. A young man had taken Jimmy's place behind the bar and was toiling frantically, trying to keep up with the suddenly increased demands for drinks. His hands were flying from the bottles behind the bar to the keys of the cash register. Several of the persons seated at the bar were attired in hats and coats, waiting for the landing-stage to be fixed. They seemed to be entirely engrossed with their own affairs. There was none of that hushed tension which would grip the people when they realized a murder had been committed.

"Come over here," he invited, "and sit down. I want to talk with you."

"Why so grim?" she asked, laughing. "Don't tell me they've got your goat. I saw a man in a gray suit running around here looking as worried as a taxpayer making out his income tax return. Someone called him 'Mr. Duncan,' asked him some questions, and got a curse for an answer. Surely, if you've got the opposition as worried as that, it's a good sign for us."

Mason said, "Lower your voice. Here, sit down at this table."

"You'll have to go to the bar if you want to get anything," she said. "I never saw such poor service. The bartender's away, and the man who was waiting on tables has had to take his place behind the bar, and . . ."

"We don't want service," Mason said, "we want to talk. This is a good place. All the others are crowding around the bar. Now, how long have you been here?"

"Quite a little while," she said chuckling. "I was here before you came aboard. I knew this was a pretty tough place and I thought I'd be on hand in case you needed reinforcements."

"Did you see Sam Grieb?"

"No."

Mason stared steadily at her and said, "Did you see *anyone* whom you knew?"

"Why?"

"Never mind why," Mason said, "go ahead and answer the question. Did you see anyone whom you knew?"

She said slowly, "Frank Oxman came out, but he didn't see me, and he didn't stay."

"How do you know he didn't see you?"

"Because I saw him first and took good care to keep out of his way."

"How long after you came here did he arrive?"

"About an hour and a half. I had dinner aboard, and it wasn't much of a dinner. However, I suppose . . ."

"Who else did you see?" Mason asked.

"What do you mean?"

"Go on," Mason told her.

"Why are you asking me these questions?"

"Because it's important."

"No one," she said, staring steadily at him.

"Did you know when I came aboard?"

She nodded and said, "I was out on deck, getting some fresh air. It was foggy, so I didn't stay long. I was there by the rail near the bow when you came aboard."

"Did you see anyone else whom you knew aboard the ship?"

"No."

"You'd swear to that?"

"Why, yes, if I had to." She settled back in her chair and said, "Now if you've quite finished, you might go to the bar and get me a Tom Collins. I can't satisfy my craving for tobacco by puffing at these insipid cigarettes. I'm dying for a *real* smoke. To tell you the truth, I went up on deck to find a place where I could puff on a cigar, but there was an amorous couple huddled against the rail and I was afraid the young man would go into a monastery and shave his head if I shattered his romantic ideals by letting him see what age and freedom will do for a woman."

Mason leaned across the table, studied the twinkling humor of the alert gray eyes and said abruptly, "Sam Grieb's been murdered."

Her face was an expressionless mask. "How do you know?" she asked.

Mason said slowly, *"You* knew he'd been murdered."

"I didn't know any such thing."

"Then why did you lie to me?"

The gray eyes glinted dangerously. "I'm not accustomed," she said, "to being talked to . . ."

"Why did you lie to me?" Mason asked.

"What do you mean?"

"You lied to me about Sylvia."

"What about her?"

"She was aboard, and you knew she was aboard. You saw her here."

The gray eyes faltered. She stretched a jeweled hand across the table and said, "Give me one of your cigarettes."

Mason opened his cigarette case. She took a cigarette, Mason scraped a match on the underside of the table, held the flame to her cigarette, took another cigarette for himself, lit it, and exhaled twin streams of white smoke through appreciative nostrils.

"I'm listening," he told her.

She avoided his eyes, puffed rapidly at the cigarette, took it from her lips, ground it into the ash tray and said, "Isn't there some place where we can *smoke?*"

"It may not be a good idea for us to be together at all," Mason said. "Right now this is the best place for us to talk. The gang's up at the bar with their backs turned to us . . . and I'm still listening."

She toyed with the rim of the ash tray with nervous fingers, then looked up at him and said, "Yes, Sylvia was out here."

"I know she was out here. Why didn't you tell me she was here?"

"Because . . . Well, because of lots of things."

"What, for instance?"

"The way Sylvia acted."

"For God's sake," Mason told her impatiently, "quit beating around the bush. I'm a lawyer retained by you to protect Sylvia's interests. How the devil can I do it if you keep playing button-button-who's-got-the-button? Inside of a few minutes the officers are going to show up, and the party may get rough. I want to know what happened, what I've got to guard against, and what I've got to meet."

She said slowly, "Sylvia went to the offices. I was afraid she was going to play right into Grieb's hand, and I didn't know what to do. I didn't want her to see me. That was why I went out on deck. I kept hoping you'd turn up. Sure enough, you came pretty soon after that.

I heaved a big sigh of relief. I thought you'd probably run into Sylvia in the office."

"Now wait a minute," Mason said, "let's get this straight. Sylvia came aboard before I did?"

"Yes."

"How many boats before?"

"I don't know. I didn't see her when she first came aboard. Naturally, I hadn't expected she would come here at all. Otherwise I'd have stayed away. I didn't want her to know I was taking an interest in her affairs. If she'd seen me, she'd have known at once . . ."

"Never mind that," Mason said. "Let's get down to brass tacks and stay there. Where was she when you first saw her?"

"She was just coming into the casino."

"What did you do?"

"I kept out of sight. She went to a table, said something to the croupier, and then headed straight for that corridor which goes into Grieb's office. . . . I slipped up the stairs and went out on deck."

"Was she betting?"

"No, she was asking something of the man at the wheel. I thought perhaps she was asking whether Grieb was in."

"So what?" Mason asked.

"Well, that's all. I went up on deck and stayed there. It was foggy and I got chilled, but I didn't dare go back for fear I'd run into her."

"Now, where was her husband?"

"Frank Oxman," she said, "must have come aboard earlier, perhaps while I was in the casino. The first I knew that he was aboard was when I saw him leave. He came out of the salon wearing a cap and overcoat, walked within a very few feet of me, and I was afraid he'd see me. Then he went to the place where passengers wait, and went down the stairs and took the boat which pulled out just a few minutes after you'd come aboard."

"Was anyone following him?" Mason asked.

She shook her head and said, "I don't think so," then said, "Wait a minute. There was a man who had been wandering around as though he was looking for someone. He kept hanging around but didn't gamble. He went back on the same speed boat Frank took. *He* may have been a detective."

"And I had arrived on board before that?"

"Yes. But not very long before. He left perhaps ten minutes after you arrived. You may have met him."

Mason frowned thoughtfully, then said, "I wouldn't have known him if I *had* met him. What about Sylvia?"

"I stayed out on deck. I didn't want Sylvia to see me. I must have been there ten or fifteen minutes when Sylvia came out. A man followed her. He said, 'Frank's aboard. Beat it,' and then he stepped back into the casino. Sylvia went . . ." She abruptly stopped in mid-sentence.

"Go on," Mason said, "went where?"

She kept her jeweled fingers busy with the edge of the cigarette tray and said, "Went back."

"Back where?"

"Back on the speed boat, of course."

Mason studied her face. "That wasn't what you were going to say."

"Yes, it was."

Mason said, "Don't be a fool. I *know* you started to say something else."

"Why?"

"Because the way you bit off that sentence showed that you'd almost betrayed yourself into saying something you didn't want to say. Then when I asked you where she went and you said that she went back to the shore, there was relief in your voice to think you hadn't gone far enough with your other sentence to keep from patching it up. Now I want to know where Sylvia went when she came out of the casino."

Matilda Benson lit another cigarette and puffed on it.

"Tell me where she went," Mason demanded insistently.

"She went to the rail."

"And what did she do at the rail?"

Matilda Benson said slowly, "She fumbled with her handbag, and a second or so later I heard something splash in the water."

"Something heavy?"

"It made a splash."

"Was it a gun?"

"I'm sure I couldn't tell you *what* it was."

"Did anyone else see her?"

Matilda Benson delayed the shake of her head for almost a second.

Mason said, "In other words, someone *did* see her."

"The young couple who were doing the necking *may* have seen her. I don't know. It depends upon how engrossed they were in what they were doing. You see, when Sylvia came out of the lighted interior her eyes were unaccustomed to the darkness and she stood quite close to the young couple, apparently without knowing it. Just before the sound of the splash, the neckers acted as though they'd seen something, and I heard them whisper excitedly. Then Sylvia ran down to the speed boat."

"Sylvia was standing close to you?"

"Quite close, yes."

"Now wait a minute," Mason went on. "There was a speed boat waiting at the landing?"

"Yes."

"Couldn't the people in that launch have seen her toss something overboard?"

"I don't know. I don't think so."

"Now, Sylvia came out of the casino and went right to the rail?"

"That's right. . . . This man told her Frank was aboard and to beat it. Then she went right to the rail."

"And from the rail she went right down to the speed boat?"

79

"Yes."

"Now, who was this man?"

"I don't know. It was someone who'd followed Sylvia up from the casino. He stuck his head out of the door, told her Frank was aboard and for her to beat it. Then he ducked back into the door and Sylvia crossed to the rail."

"You didn't *see* this man?"

"Only as a dim figure popping his head out of the door from the casino."

"Light was streaming through that door?"

"No, it opens from stairs and a curtained corridor. There was very little light."

"How was Sylvia dressed?"

"She had on a dark suit with a three-quarter length jacket."

"And a hat?"

"Yes."

"That was the same way she was dressed when you first saw her in the casino?"

"Yes."

"Now look here," Mason said, "she must have worn a coat over here."

"She has a very nice fur coat that . . ."

"I know she has," Mason said. "Now here's what I'm getting at: she must have checked that coat. Pretty soon the officers are going to come aboard. They'll get the names and addresses of everyone on the ship. After a while they'll let people go home. Then the check girl will report that someone has left a very valuable fur coat. The police will put two and two together. If Sylvia claims that fur coat, she'll be walking into a trap. If she doesn't claim it, it will be equivalent to a declaration of guilt. The police will trace that coat, and Sylvia will be in a sweet mess. Now do you suppose . . ."

She interrupted him and said, "Yes, I could go down

to the girl at the checking counter, tell her I'd lost my coat check, give her a dollar tip and . . ."

"Could you describe the fur coat well enough to get it?" Mason asked.

"Yes. I bought the coat for Sylvia. There's a tag on the inside of the pocket with Sylvia's name printed on it and the number of an insurance policy. I could tell the girl I was Sylvia, and get the coat."

Mason surveyed the full-fleshed arms in rather critical appraisal. She nodded and said, "Yes, I can wear the coat. I wouldn't try to button it."

"That," Mason told her, "will leave *your* coat unaccounted for. You checked it?"

"Well, yes, but I can go down and present my check, get my coat, park it somewhere, then go back and make the stall about Sylvia's coat and go ashore with both coats. I'll go . . ."

"No," Mason interrupted, "you can't do that. The girl in the check room might remember you, and you haven't enough time to wait more than a minute or two in between trips. It's too dangerous."

"There's no other way out," she said.

"Give me your check," Mason told her, "and wait here."

She opened her handbag, handed the lawyer a printed oblong pasteboard, and remarked, "I like the way you're handling things. I'm going to show my gratitude in a substantial way."

"Yes," the lawyer told her, "you can send me pies and cakes while I'm in jail."

She stared at him with speculative eyes and said, "Apparently you don't mean that as a wise-crack."

"I don't," he told her. "When they check up on me, I'm going to be in a spot. Sylvia left me holding the sack. You wait here."

He walked down the passageway to the checking room, pushed the numbered pasteboard across the counter to the girl on duty and dropped a fifty-cent piece into her outstretched hand. "My wife's seasick," he explained. "Get me that coat in a rush."

"Seasick! Why there's hardly any motion . . ."

Mason made a grimace and said, *"She* thinks she's seasick. Suppose you go argue with *her?"*

The girl's laughter rang out merrily as she handed Mason the coat. Her brown eyes swept the lawyer's broad shoulders and clean-cut features in swift appraisal. "We hope *you* won't stop coming out," she said, "just because your wife gets seasick."

"I won't," Mason assured her, and took the coat to Matilda Benson. "Here you are," he said. "I'll leave it to you to get the other coat. You may have to . . ." He broke off as from the outer darkness came the sound of a speed boat roaring through the fog. "That," he said, "sounds like the officers. We'll have to hurry."

"Shall I give them my right name?"

"Not unless you have to," he told her, "but be careful. They'll probably want to see some identification, driver's license or something of that sort. You can tell what you're up against by getting a place near the last of the line-up. There are probably quite a few men and women on board who'd just as soon not give their right names. It'll be a tedious process weeding them out. Along toward the last, the officers may get tired and let down the bars a bit. Be careful you don't get caught in a lie."

She tilted her head back, squared her jaw and said with calm confidence, "I've told some whoppers in my time and made them stick. You'd better go out that door to the left, because I'm going out through the door to the right."

Mason said, "Happy landing," and walked out through the door to the left, into the casino. He was half way to the roulette tables when a man in a rubber raincoat which still glistened with fog and spray, called out, "Attention, everybody! A murder's been committed aboard this ship. No one's going to be allowed to leave. You will all kindly remain inside and not try to leave this room. If you'll co-operate with us, it won't be long. If you don't co-operate, you'll be here all night."

7

PERRY MASON stood near the end of the long line which serpentined its way toward a table where two officers sat taking names, addresses, and checking credentials.

The deserted gambling tables were an incongruous reminder of the gaiety which had been stilled by death. Laughter, the rattle of chips, and the whirring roulette balls no longer assailed the ears. The only sounds which broke the silence were the gruff voices of the officers, the frightened replies of the patrons, and the slow, rhythmic creaking of the old ship as it swayed on the lazy swells of the fog-covered ocean.

Mason surveyed the line in frowning anxiety. He could find no trace of Matilda Benson, yet every person aboard the ship had been mustered into that line. It was certain that no one could have gone down the companionway without presenting a written pass signed by the officers who were conducting the examination.

In the executive offices, men were busy with the details incident to murder cases. Photographs had been taken showing the location and position of the body. The furniture was being dusted with special powders, designed to bring out latent fingerprints. Men came and went from the entrance to the offices, and the frightened line of shuffling spectators turned anxious faces to regard these hurrying officers with morbid curiosity.

A man emerged from the L-shaped hallway, approached the line and called out, "Where's Perry Mason, the lawyer?"

Mason held up his hand.

"This way," the officer said, turned on his heel, and strode back through the door. Mason followed him. He could hear the sound of voices as he walked down the corridor, voices which held the deep rumble of ominous interrogation. Then he heard the sound of Charlie Duncan's voice, raised in high-pitched, vehement denial.

Mason followed the officer through the door into the outer office. Grim-faced officers were interrogating Duncan. As Mason entered the room, Duncan was saying, ". . . of *course* I had difficulties with him. I didn't like the way he was running things. I filed suit against him this afternoon, but I didn't do it to take advantage of him. I did it because I wasn't going to be ruined by the goofy ideas of a man who doesn't know the business . . ."

He stopped talking as he saw Mason.

One of the officers said, "Are you Perry Mason, the lawyer?"

Mason nodded.

"You were in this room when the body was discovered?"

"Yes."

"What were you doing here?"

"Sitting here, waiting."

"Waiting for what?"

"For someone to come in."

"Had you knocked at the door of the inner office?"

"Yes."

"You didn't get any answer?"

"No."

"Did you try the knob of the door?"

Mason frowned thoughtfully and said, "It's hard to

tell, looking back on it, just what I *did* do. When I came in here, I regarded my visit as just a routine call, and, naturally, didn't pay any great attention to a lot of details which didn't impress me as being important or significant."

One of the officers said, "Well, they aren't unimportant and they aren't insignificant."

Mason smiled affably. "It's *so* difficult to tell in advance—which is probably why our hindsight is better than our foresight."

There was a moment of silence, during which Mason studied the faces of the officers. They had evidently been recruited from various channels, and rushed out to make an investigation. One of the men was apparently a city police officer, with the rank of sergeant. Another was undoubtedly a motorcycle traffic officer. The third was a plainclothesman, apparently a detective. The other was probably a deputy sheriff or marshal, or both.

While Mason was watching them, one of the officers entered the room with Arthur Manning. Accompanying Manning were two people, a young man in his middle twenties, and a girl, who was wearing a beige sport suit. A dark brown scarf, knotted loosely about her throat, matched her brown shoes and bag. She carried a coat with a fur collar over her arm.

Manning said, "I've just found . . ."

The sergeant checked him by holding up a warning hand and said, "Let's finish with this phase of the inquiry first. Now you, Mr. Mason, were waiting here in the outer office?"

"Yes."

"How long had you been here?"

"Perhaps five minutes, perhaps not that long. I can't tell exactly."

"You were waiting to see Mr. Grieb?"

"Yes."

"Why?"

"I had business with him."

"What was the nature of the business?"

Mason shook his head smilingly. "As an attorney I can't be interrogated about the affairs of my clients."

"You refuse to answer?"

"Yes."

"That's not the law," the sergeant protested angrily. "The only thing you can hold out is a confidential communication made to you by your client. I happen to know, because I heard the point argued in court once."

Mason said deprecatingly, "You can hear *so* much argued in court, Sergeant, that it's quite discouraging. I, myself, have heard many court arguments."

The plainclothesman grinned. The sergeant flushed, turned to Duncan and said, "When you came in the office, where was Mr. Mason sitting?"

"In that chair."

"What was he doing?"

"Looking at a magazine."

"You don't know what he was reading?"

"No, I don't. He made some remark about the magazine being an old one. I can't remember just what it was."

"The door to the inner office was locked?"

"Yes."

"You had a key for it?"

"Yes."

"Were there any other keys?"

"Only the one Grieb had."

"The one we found on his key ring?"

"Yes."

"It was customary to keep this door locked?"

"Absolutely. That was one rule we never violated. This door was kept closed, locked and barred at all times."

"So that Mr. Grieb, himself, must have opened this door?"

"Yes."

"And then returned to his desk, after admitting some visitor?"

"That's right."

"Now, there's no way of reaching that inner office, except through this door; is that right?"

"That's right."

"How about the porthole?" Mason asked. "There's a porthole directly over the desk, and another on either side. Wouldn't it have been possible for someone to have lowered himself down the side of the ship and fired a shot . . ."

"No," the sergeant interrupted, "it would have been impossible. Excluding a theory of suicide, which the evidence won't support, the person who fired the fatal shot must have stood near the corner of Grieb's desk, and shot him with a .38 caliber automatic. Moreover, the empty shell was ejected and was found on the floor." He turned back to Duncan. "You opened the door to the inner office," he said, "and found Grieb's body in the chair. Then what did you do?"

"I was pretty excited," Duncan said. "Naturally, it knocked me for a loop. I remember going over to make certain he was dead, and then I said something to Mason and . . . Oh, yes, we looked around for a gun. There was some question about whether it was suicide."

"Do you remember anything else?"

Duncan shook his head and said, "No. We came on out. Mason was making a few wise-cracks. I wanted him searched . . ."

"*Why* did you want him searched?"

"Because he'd been sitting here in the office. Naturally I was suspicious. . . . That is, I thought it would be a good idea to search him and see if perhaps he had a key to that door, or a gun, or . . . Well, he might have had a lot of things in his pockets."

"Did Mason object to being searched?"

"On the contrary," Mason interpolated, smiling, "I

demanded it. Mr. Perkins, an officer who came aboard with Mr. Duncan, handcuffed me, so I couldn't take anything from my pockets, took me into another room, had me undress, and searched me from the skin out. But Mr. Duncan was alone with the body for several minutes."

"No, I wasn't," Duncan retorted angrily. "And that reminds me of something else I did. I pushed the alarm button which called Manning. That button sounds buzzers in various places and turns on a red light in all four corners of the gambling room. Manning came in here within a matter of seconds."

"That's right," the blue-coated special officer corroborated. "I was over at the far corner of the casino, watching a man who looked like a crook. He was rolling dice on the crap table, and he was pretty lucky. Most of the time I hang around by the entrance to these offices, but when I see something that looks suspicious, I go give it the once-over. As a matter of fact, Grieb had given me the tip-off on this guy, himself. That was about fifteen or twenty minutes before Duncan put on the lights for me. I saw the light come on and started for the office. It couldn't have been fifteen seconds until I got there."

"During that fifteen seconds did you see anyone leave the offices?" the sergeant asked.

"Sure. I saw Perry Mason, and this officer who came aboard with Mr. Duncan—Perkins, I think his name was. They tell me that he put handcuffs on Mr. Mason, but I couldn't see the handcuffs. The way they strolled out, arm in arm, I thought they were just buddies, going into the bar to get a drink."

"You saw us leave?"

"I wasn't over six feet from you. You'd have seen me if you'd turned around. I was moving pretty fast. I thought there might be some sort of an emergency."

"Where was Duncan when you entered the room?"

Duncan started to say something, but the sergeant silenced him with a gesture and said, "Just at present, Mr. Duncan, we're questioning Manning. Where was he, Manning?"

"He was right over at that chair where you're sitting," Manning said. "He'd pulled up the cushion and was looking around." Duncan looked sheepish.

"What were you doing there?" the sergeant asked Duncan.

"That was the chair Mason had been sitting in," Duncan said. "He looked just a little too smug and smooth when I came in. I don't know. I can't put my finger on just *what* it was, but I didn't like the way he looked. And I thought maybe he'd known he was going to be searched, and had ditched something. You see, he must have heard Perkins and me coming four or five seconds before we came in through the door."

"What did you think he might have concealed?"

Duncan said lamely, "I don't know. It might have been a gun."

"Perhaps," Mason suggested, "Duncan picked up something in the inner office and wanted to plant it in the chair where I'd been sitting, but was interrupted by Manning's prompt arrival."

"That's a lie," Duncan yelled, "and you know it's a lie. You were still in the room when I pressed the buzzer for Manning. If I'd wanted time to stall around, I'd never have pressed that button . . ."

The sergeant interrupted, "That'll do. Now, just how long was it, Manning, from the time you saw Mason leave until you saw Duncan bending over this chair?"

"I don't think it was over four seconds, at the outside," Manning said. "I came down that corridor on the double-quick."

Mason said, "It took us six or eight seconds to walk down that corridor. That gave Duncan ten or twelve seconds."

The sergeant ignored Mason's comment, but kept his

eyes on Manning. "Then what did you do, Manning?" he asked.

"Duncan asked me to help him look around. He told me what had happened. I looked through the door into the other room, but Duncan kept on looking around through chairs in this room, and I came over and helped him."

"Did he say what he wanted you to search for?"

"No, he didn't say."

"Did you enter the inner office at all?"

"Just stood in the doorway," Manning said, "and looked in. I asked Mr. Duncan if it was suicide or murder, and he said it was murder if we couldn't find any gun, and that I was to lock up the place and stand guard . . ."

"One other thing," Duncan interrupted, "speaking about locking up the place reminds me:—are you going to want the vault opened?"

The sergeant said, "Of course we're going to want the vault opened."

"Well," Duncan said, "when you do that, I've got something to say about the way things are handled."

"Just what do you mean?" the sergeant asked.

"I came out here with a deputy marshal and an order to show cause why a receiver shouldn't be appointed, and I was going to make Grieb take a physical inventory in the presence of the deputy. Now, I'm sorry Sammy's dead; but that doesn't alter the fact that he tried to play me for a sucker. He's short in his accounts, and I know he's short, and that's why he . . ."

"Why he what?" Mason asked coldly, as Duncan paused.

"Why he didn't want to face me," Duncan finished lamely.

"What makes you think he didn't want to face you?" Mason asked.

Duncan turned pleadingly to the sergeant and said,

"For God's sake, make this guy keep his trap shut while I'm trying to explain things."

The sergeant said tonelessly, "Shut up, Mason. What were you trying to say, Duncan?"

"Grieb left heirs somewhere," Duncan said. "I don't know just who they are, but they'll be snooping around and making trouble, claiming half of the business. With Sam alive, I could have had a show-down in court and put a receiver in charge. Now that Sam's dead, I've got to go through a lot of red tape with administrators and stuff, and if there's any shortage, in place of my being able to show that Sam lifted the stuff, they'll claim *I* got away with it *after* Sam died. So I want you fellows to make a complete inventory of every single thing in that vault and in the coin safe."

The sergeant frowned. "You mean you think something's missing?"

"I know damn well something's missing."

"Making an inventory is out of *our* line," the sergeant pointed out. "It'll take more time than I can spare right now."

"Well then, how about sealing the vault up?"

"We'll want to look inside of it."

"The minute that vault's opened," Duncan said obstinately, "there's going to be an inventory made."

The sergeant hesitated a moment, then said, "All right, Duncan, we'll make an inventory. Perhaps, after all, we might find something that'll throw light on the motive for the murder."

"Before you open that vault," Manning ventured, "you'd better talk with these two people. They saw a woman throw a gun overboard."

The sergeant stiffened to attention. "Throw a gun overboard!" he exclaimed.

Manning nodded.

"Well, why the devil didn't you say so?"

"I tried to," Manning said, "but . . ."

"That'll do," the sergeant interrupted, and said to the young man who was staring with apprehensive eyes, "what's your name?"

The man swallowed twice and said, "Bert Custer."

"Where do you work?"

"In a service station at Seventy-ninth and Main."

"What were you doing out here?"

"I took my girl . . . I mean Marilyn Smith here, out to the ship."

"You were going to do some gambling?"

Custer lowered his eyes, grinned sheepishly and said, "No."

"Then what *did* you come out here for?"

"For dinner and the trip. You see, they serve a cheap dinner here, with a little floor show, because they want to get folks to come out to the ship. And the speed boats make a low fare for the same reason. I don't have an awful lot of money to spend and I like to get the most I can for my money. Marilyn and I . . . Well, we had some things we wanted to talk over, and so we came out here . . . Well, you know how it is. It doesn't cost much to come out in the speed boats, have dinner and then go out on deck and talk. I was showing her a good time without getting stuck for it. Of course, it was pretty cold out there because of the fog, but it had been hot all day and I thought it would be nice to sit out on deck and . . ."

"And do a little necking?" the sergeant interrupted, grinning.

Custer stiffened and said indignantly, "We were talking."

It was the girl who answered the question. "Sure we were necking," she said. "What'd you *think* we came out here for?"

"No offense," the sergeant said, laughing. "Now, you were out on deck?"

"Yes," Custer said.

"Where?"

"Amidships . . . Come to think of it we must have been right above this office."

"And what did you see?"

"A woman with a silver dress and white hair came out of the cabin where they have the gambling, and she acted awfully funny. Both Marilyn and I thought there was something wrong, the way she acted. She seemed to be trying to hide."

"Go on," the sergeant said.

"Well, she stood there for a minute and then another woman came out, and this woman in the silver dress ducked back in the shadows and then Marilyn grabbed my arm and whispered, 'Look!' and I looked just in time to see a gun that this woman in the silver dress had thrown overboard."

"What sort of a gun?" the sergeant asked.

"Well, it was an automatic, but I couldn't tell what make it was nor what caliber. It was a gun. That's about all I can tell."

"You know the difference between an automatic and a revolver?"

"Yes, sure. An automatic is more at right angles, and a revolver has sort of a curve. They're built different. I can't describe them exactly, but I know all about 'em. I sold guns once."

"And this woman in the silver dress threw it overboard?"

"Yes."

"Then what did she do?"

"She stuck around on the deck for quite a while until after the other woman had gone away. And then she walked back down the deck. She was about fifty, I should judge."

"About fifty-five," the girl interrupted. "She had a silver lamé dress, as nearly as I could tell, silver slippers, and a string of pearls."

"Just a moment," Mason said; "it sounds strange to

me that the woman would have thrown away the gun under those circumstances. As I understand it, you two saw the gun go over the side. Now, isn't it possible that it was thrown by the *other* woman who had just come out of the casino?"

"That'll do," the sergeant said. "You're not here to pull any cross-examination of witnesses, Mr. Mason. *I'll* ask the questions."

"But we owe it to all concerned to get this thing straight," Mason asserted.

The girl said, in a low voice, *"I* wasn't certain who threw the gun. I can't swear which one of the women did it."

"Sure the white-haired dame threw it," Custer said positively, "otherwise what did she want to duck back in the shadows for? She was hiding something, and . . ."

"But *you* didn't see the gun until after Miss Smith grabbed your arm and said, 'Look,'" Mason said. "You . . ."

The sergeant got to his feet and roared, "Now, that's enough! Don't you go trying to mix up these witnesses. I don't know what your interest in this thing is—not yet."

Mason bowed and said, "Of course, Sergeant, you're in charge. I thought you were investigating the facts and would like to have them clarified as you went along. I felt perhaps that such experience as I may have had might be of some assistance."

"Well," the sergeant told him, "I'm fully capable of handling this matter. I don't like the way you're trying to confuse the witnesses."

"I'm not trying to confuse the witnesses. I'm trying to establish the facts."

"Trying to establish them the way you want 'em established. How about this woman in the silver dress? What's your interest in her?"

"Why not ask *her?*" Mason suggested.

There was a moment of silence, during which the officers exchanged glances. The sergeant said to the man in the traffic officer's uniform, "Go and round up that woman in the silver dress, Jerry. Bring her in. She should be a cinch with the description we've got."

Steps sounded in the outer corridor. The door opened, Perkins entered and said to the sergeant, "I'm all finished out there, Sergeant. Anything else I can do?"

"Yes. We're going to open the vault. Duncan wants you to take inventory."

"Can't we postpone that?"

"No, I want to take a look through the vault. It'll have to be opened, and we should have a complete inventory. We can take a quick look first to make certain that robbery wasn't the motive, and then start taking a detailed inventory. I also want to go through the desk and . . ."

"I'd like to have the vault and coin safe opened right now," Duncan interrupted. "You see, Sergeant, in addition to the cash used in operating the business, there's nine thousand five hundred that was to have been paid in on some notes early this evening. Sammy may have received this money and put it in the coin safe. It's important that I know . . ."

"So," Mason interrupted, "you sold them for a two-thousand-dollar bonus, did you?"

Duncan said, "You keep out of this."

"And stay out!" the sergeant snapped.

Mason shrugged his shoulders.

"It makes a lot of difference," Duncan pleaded, "and I think I'm entitled to know."

The sergeant said, "Okay, Duncan. We'll open the vault and the coin safe. I'll have the boys list everything."

"Particularly the stuff in the coin safe," Duncan said.

"Everything," the sergeant snapped. "Come on, Perkins, you come along with Duncan and me. And you come too, Walter. The rest of you stay here. Now, remember, men, I don't want you touching things in the inner office.

And particularly, don't go near the desk. I want that glass top for evidence."

Duncan spun the dials of the vault door, opened it and switched on an electric light. The men vanished inside the vault. From the interior came the low hum of voices.

Mason moved casually to Marilyn Smith's side and said, "How about the woman who came to the rail? Could you describe her?"

"Not very well. She had on a dark suit of some kind. It didn't show up in the dark at all; but this woman with the white hair certainly acted suspicious. Bert and I talked about it even before this other woman showed up. But the minute this other woman came out, you could see from the way she acted—the white-haired woman, I mean—that she was afraid, and . . ."

Bert Custer crowded protectingly forward and said, "I don't want Marilyn to make any statements until the officers are here. This man's a lawyer, Marilyn, and . . ."

"Bosh and nonsense!" she said. "All this business about lawyers, and getting rattled, and all that stuff makes me sick. We know what we saw, and we'll tell what we saw just the way we saw it. When you come right down to it, Bert, you know as well as I do the reason I thought the white-haired woman threw the gun was because of the way she'd been acting. If you were under oath, you'd have to swear that the first time you saw the gun it was in the air."

"I saw the white-headed woman make some sort of a throwing motion. She did something with her hand, as though she was tossing something," Custer insisted doggedly.

"Bert, you never saw any such thing! You weren't even looking at her. You were looking at me. You had your arms wrapped around me, and you were . . ." She broke off with a giggle.

"Well," Custer said sullenly, "I could see her out of the corner of my eye, couldn't I?"

Marilyn Smith smiled at Perry Mason and said, "*I* saw the gun first. I saw it after it had been thrown over the rail. I grabbed Bert's arm, and said, 'Look, Bert.' That was the first he saw of it. You see, there was light streaming out of a porthole and the gun fell across the path of light."

"You were standing almost amidships and on this side of the ship?" Mason asked.

"Yes."

"Then it's possible you saw the gun as it fell across the path of light which was thrown from *this* porthole, isn't it?"

"Well . . . perhaps. This probably is the porthole. There's a bright light here, and the illumination sort of fans out into a cone. You could see the path of light in the fog."

"What sort of gun was it?" Mason asked. "Could you see?"

Custer beat her to the answer. "It was an automatic. I guess I should know. I worked in a hardware store and I've sold lots of guns. It was a blued-steel automatic with a wooden handle. Just judging from the size of it, I'd say it was a .38, but you can't tell. Some companies make a pretty heavy .32. And then there's one .45 that's not so much different in size from a .38. You know, just looking at it for a second or two that way, it's hard to tell."

"So," Mason said gravely, "you think it was a .38, if it wasn't a .45 or a .32. Is that right?"

"Yes."

"But it may have been a .45?"

"It might have been."

"Or it might have been a .32?"

"Yes."

"Don't they make a .22 caliber automatic with a heavy frame and a long barrel?"

"Well, yes, they do."

"Could it have been a .22?"

Custer frowned thoughtfully. Marilyn Smith laughed and said, "Just because you sold guns, Bert, you try to know too much about them. You couldn't tell what caliber that gun was. Why, we just saw it for a fraction of a second, as it went down through that shaft of light that was coming from the porthole."

Mason said, "Thank you, Miss Smith."

He stepped to the door of the inner office, and the plain-clothesman said, "Don't go in there."

"I'm just looking through the door," Mason said.

The body had been removed. The glass top which had been on the desk was standing on edge, propped against the wall. Powder had been dusted on it to bring out hundreds of latent fingerprints, and near the center of the glass was the print of a whole hand, where apparently someone had leaned over on the glass. The imprint seemed to have been made by a woman's hand.

Mason casually moved over toward Arthur Manning. "Is this going to make quite a change for you?" he asked.

The uniformed special watchman nodded and said gloomily, "I'll say it is."

"Won't you get along okay with Duncan?"

"Well, you know how it is," Manning said. "They were both of them fighting. Duncan gave me my job, but Grieb handled most of the inside business and all the cash, and I naturally saw more of Sam Grieb than I did of Duncan. Grieb gave me orders and I tried to please him. So, the first thing I knew, I was in the position of sort of taking sides with Grieb. Not that I did, at all, but I know Duncan felt that way about me. Now that he's in charge, he'll let me out. He didn't like what I told the officers about the chairs."

Mason said, "I might be able to get you a job. At least a temporary job, with a detective agency."

Manning's eyes brightened.

"Think you'd like that?" Mason asked.

"I'd like any job that pays wages," Manning said, "and I've always wanted to get in a detective agency. I think I could make good in that business and perhaps work up."

"Well," the lawyer went on in a low voice, "suppose you drop into my office first thing tomorrow. Don't tell anyone about it, though. Just drop in on your own. Do you think you could do that?"

"Sure, unless they tie me up here so I can't get ashore. I don't know how long this investigation's going to last."

"Well, just drop in any time," Mason said. "Ask for Miss Street. She's my secretary. I'll speak to her, so you won't be delayed. It'll only take a few minutes. Just run in and I'll introduce you to the head of the detective agency that handles my business."

"Okay, Mr. Mason. Thanks a lot," Manning said.

The men who had been in the vault came back into the room. Duncan pulled the door shut, slammed the bolts into place, and spun the combination savagely. There was no trace of a smile on his face. The sergeant took a roll of gummed paper from his pocket, tore off two pieces, wrote his name across them, moistened them on his tongue, and stuck them across the edges of the vault door.

"Now, I don't want anyone opening that vault until after the Marshal gets here," he said. "You understand that, Duncan?"

"I understand it," Duncan blazed, "but it's a hell of a note when you seal up a man's place of business and say he can't get into it! Now, there's something wrong here. We're ninety-five hundred dollars short that I know of. You said you were going to take a complete inventory. Why don't you go ahead with it?"

"Because there's too much junk in there. It'd keep us

busy until morning if we did that. I've sealed the vault door. That will hold things intact until . . ."

"Intact, hell!" Duncan blazed. "A man could steam off that paper, and . . ."

"Well, I'll put a guard on duty. How will that be?"

Duncan was mollified. "That might be okay," he conceded.

"Now, how about this ninety-five hundred? You said that was to have been paid in tonight. That might have been a motive for the killing."

Duncan stared at Perry Mason in somber appraisal and said, "I'm not making any statements just yet. Let's take a look through the desk."

"Now, I'll be the one who does that," the sergeant said. "You fellows keep away."

He opened the top left-hand drawer in the desk and exclaimed, "Here's your nine thousand five hundred, Duncan."

Duncan pushed eagerly forward. The sergeant's right hand pressed against the gambler's chest. "Keep away, Duncan, I don't want you touching things here."

He scooped the money from the drawer, slowly counting it. As the bills fell to the desk and the count mounted up, Duncan's lips twisted back in a smile so that his gold teeth were once more visible. Then, after the six-thousand-dollar mark was reached, Duncan's smile slowly vanished as his appraising eyes took stock of the bills remaining in the sergeant's hand. By the time the count was completed, Duncan's lips were once more pressed tightly together.

"Seventy-five hundred," the sergeant announced. "Now, that's two thousand dollars short of the amount you mentioned, Duncan."

Duncan said, "You haven't gone through the desk yet. There may be some more in one of the other drawers."

"That's not the point," the officer remarked. "Grieb was sitting at this desk when he was killed. Now, someone paid him a big sum of money. He evidently hadn't had time to put the money in the coin safe. He certainly wouldn't have planned on letting it stay here in his desk. Therefore, the man who paid this money *may* have been the last man to see Grieb alive. I want to know who he was."

"I don't know who paid it," Duncan said, his eyes carefully avoiding Mason's.

"You have an idea who *might* have paid it, haven't you?"

"I haven't any ideas that I'm spilling right now," Duncan said obstinately. "After all, this is our business, and it's confidential."

"I order you to tell me."

"Order and be damned!" Duncan blazed. "I don't know who you think you are. We're still out on the high seas. I'm in charge of this ship."

Perkins coughed, hesitated, then blurted, "There was some talk between Mason and Duncan about some I O U's. It was when we first came aboard, before Mason knew about the murder. I think they said something about seventy-five hundred dollars. Those I O U's may have been what . . ."

The sergeant whirled to Perry Mason. "Did *you* pay that money?" he asked.

Mason said casually, "I don't think I have anything to add to Mr. Duncan's statement. It seems to cover the point admirably, Sergeant. I might add that there's quite a difference between seventy-five hundred dollars in obligations and a ninety-five hundred dollar shortage."

"Oh, you're going to get technical, are you?"

"You can express it that way if you wish."

"You were here when the body was discovered," the sergeant pointed out.

Mason quite casually took a cigarette case from his pocket, inserted a cigarette between his lips, struck a match, and not until after he had held the flame to the tip of the cigarette did he say, "Oh, no, I wasn't, Sergeant. I was in the *outer* office. The door between me and the dead man was locked. I didn't have a key to it. Furthermore, if I *had* come here to pay seventy-five hundred dollars, and the seventy-five hundred dollars had actually been paid, it's reasonable to suppose that my business would have been completed and that I would, therefore, have left the offices. And if *I'd* murdered Sam Grieb in order to get possession of something, it's hardly reasonable to suppose I'd have dropped seventy-five hundred dollars in his desk drawer, and then sat around waiting for the corpse to come to life."

The sergeant regarded Mason in frowning appraisal. "I still don't like the looks of the whole business," he said.

Mason nodded and said soothingly, "*I* never like murder cases either, Sergeant."

Marilyn Smith tittered. The sergeant said savagely, "You're under orders not to leave this ship until I tell you you can."

"You mean," Mason said, "that you're taking the responsibility of placing me under arrest on a ship which is at present beyond the twelve-mile limit?"

"I mean just what I said," the sergeant snapped. "You're not to leave this ship until I tell you you can. And I don't intend to indulge in a lot of argument about the legal effect of my order."

The man in the traffic officer's uniform burst excitedly into the outer office and said, "Sergeant, that woman's hiding somewhere aboard the ship."

"Hiding!" the sergeant exclaimed. "What are you talking about?"

"Just what I said. She isn't in the line-up and the officer at the desk swears she hasn't gone through. But quite a few people remember having seen her aboard the ship. I've got half a dozen people who can give detailed descriptions of her. She was seen *after* we came aboard, so she hasn't gone ashore. And there are two people who saw her sitting at a table back of the bar talking with this lawyer."

And the officer pointed a dramatic forefinger at Perry Mason.

8

■

MASON WAS the first to break the silence which followed the officer's dramatic accusation. "Come to think of it," he drawled, "I believe I *was* talking with a woman who answered that description."

"What was her name?" the sergeant demanded, frowning.

"I'm sure I couldn't give you her name, Sergeant."

"You mean you don't know who she was?"

"I mean," Mason said, "that I couldn't give you her name."

"But you won't say you don't know who she is."

Mason merely smiled.

"Look here, Mason, your conduct in this thing is open to a good deal of criticism," the sergeant said.

"So I gather from your remarks," Mason told him.

"You can't pull this stuff and get away with it."

"Pull what stuff?" Mason asked innocently.

"The stuff you're pulling."

"Well," Mason said, judicially inspecting the end of his cigarette with critical eyes, "since I've already pulled it, the only question between us is whether I can, as you term it, get away with it. That, I suppose, is a matter of opinion."

The sergeant said to the traffic officer, "Take this guy and lock him up. Don't let him talk to anyone, and don't let him see anyone. You stay in the room with him, and if he tries to talk with you or asks you questions, don't answer them."

"Of course," Mason said, "I'll want it understood that I'm protesting vigorously against such unwarranted and high-handed action."

"Protest and be damned," the sergeant told him. "I've had enough of your lip. Jerry, go ahead and take him out of here, and then I'll search this damned boat from one end to the other until I find that white-headed woman in the silver gown, and don't let anyone else go ashore, no matter whether they have passes or not. I'm going to sew this ship up until I find that woman. She might try to ditch that silver dress and put on men's clothes, or something. The way it looks right now, she's the one who committed the murder, and Perry Mason's her lawyer."

The sergeant turned to Bert Custer and said, "Now *you're* willing to swear that she came out on deck and threw an automatic out over the rail, aren't you?"

"Yes," Custer said.

Marilyn Smith interposed firmly to say, "No, he isn't. He can only swear that she and another woman were standing out on the deck at the time he saw a gun thrown overboard."

The sergeant said angrily, "That's what comes of letting this damned lawyer stay in here and raise hell with our witnesses! Take him out and lock him up, Jerry."

The traffic officer, his holstered gun ominously in evidence, clapped his left hand on Perry Mason's shoulder. "On your way, buddy," he said.

"But," Mason objected, "I protest . . ."

The traffic officer spun him around facing the door and said, "You've done too damn much protesting already. Do you want to go sensibly, or do you want to be taken?"

"Oh, sensibly, by all means," Mason said, smiling, and

accompanied the officer down a corridor and into a room, where he was held for more than three hours.

It was still foggy when Mason was released from the room. A tall, raw-boned individual with a lazy drawl in his speech, a black sombrero on his head, and a manner of calm unhurried efficiency greeted Mason and said, "I'm the United States Marshal. What were you doing aboard the ship?"

"Visiting."

"Did you have business with Sam Grieb?"

"Yes."

"What was that business?"

"It was business I was handling for a client. I came aboard the ship to see Mr. Grieb. For all I know, he was dead when I got here. I didn't see him alive. I don't know who murdered him, and I'm not making any statement."

The marshal nodded and said, "You know I can take you before the grand jury and make you talk, don't you?"

Mason smiled and said, "You can take me before a grand jury. Whether you can make me talk is a matter of opinion. My personal idea is that you can't."

A slow smile of whimsical humor twisted the lips of the marshal. The sergeant who had been conducting the investigation said belligerently, "Well, we can hold you on suspicion of murder and stick you in a cell and . . ."

"I'm running this, Sergeant," the marshal interrupted. "That's all, Mr. Mason."

"When can I go ashore?" Mason asked.

"Any time," the marshal said.

"Did you find out anything?" Mason inquired.

The marshal merely smiled.

"Locate the woman in the silver gown?" Mason asked.

The marshal's smile became a grin. "Try reading the papers, Mr. Mason. You'll find a speed boat at the bottom of the landing-stage. Your coat and hat are over there on the table."

Mason struggled into the overcoat, turned up the collar, and silently walked along the hallway, through the deserted bar and casino to the deck.

There was virtually no motion to the ship. The fog had settled like a thick blanket. Moisture slimed the deck, the stairway, and the rope which served as a handhold. A speed boat was waiting at the foot of the landing-stage. Mason was the only passenger, and, so far as he could observe, save for the crew and the officers, no one remained aboard the gambling ship.

He took his seat near the stern of the speed boat, which immediately roared into motion. A moment later the hulk of the gambling ship was swallowed by the gray pall through which the speed boat roared on a compass course toward the shore.

The amusement pier was deserted when Mason landed. Contrary to his expectations, there were no newspaper reporters awaiting him. He found his car, climbed in it, and drove to his office building. He slid the car to a stop at the curb, entered the lobby and rang for the elevator. The night janitor brought up the cage, grinned at Mason, and said, "Pretty late for you to be working so hard, Mr. Mason. Your secretary's up in your office waiting for you."

Mason's face showed surprise. "Been there ever since around eleven o'clock," the janitor said.

Mason thanked him and signed the register while the elevator was shooting upward. His steps echoed down the deserted corridor. He turned a corner and saw lights in his office, transforming the frosted glass of the entrance doorway into a golden oblong, against which appeared in black letters:

PERRY MASON
ATTORNEY AT LAW
Entrance

Mason passed by the door to the entrance room and went to his private office. He opened the plain mahogany door with his key and saw Della Street tilted back in his big swivel chair, her feet propped upon the desk, ankles crossed. She was sound asleep.

She looked up as the latch clicked into place when the door closed. Her eyes, swollen with sleep, blinked in the bright light. " 'Lo, Chief," she said sleepily. She lowered her feet from the desk, rubbed her eyes with her knuckles, grinned and said, "I fell asleep after the midnight news broadcast. That's the last one."

She indicated the portable radio which she had placed on the corner of Mason's desk, stretched her arms, yawned, made a little grimace, stamped her feet, and said, "Gosh, my legs have gone to sleep. What time is it?"

"Half past two," he told her. She tried to walk, but swayed on her numb feet. The lawyer caught her in his arms as she staggered. "Steady," he told her, holding her close to him.

She smiled sleepily and said, "I'm all pins and needles from my knees down. Gosh, I've been asleep a long time. That's one of the best sleeping chairs I ever sat in."

He slid an arm around her shoulders while she pillowed her cheek against his coat and closed her eyes.

"Why did you come up here?" he asked.

"There was a news flash on the ten o'clock broadcast that Sam Grieb had been murdered on his gambling ship and that everyone aboard was being held pending a complete investigation, so I thought you might want something, or try to get some message to me, and I figured I could work things better from here than from the apartment house where I hang out."

"Did anything else come in?" Mason asked.

She puckered her forehead into a frown and said, "Gee, Chief, those legs are driving me nuts. Let me walk around."

He circled her waist with his arm. Together, they started walking around the office, Della Street stamping her feet, making little grimaces of pain. "Let me see," she said. . . . "There was some hot stuff in the midnight broadcast. It seems that Perry Mason, the noted attorney, was aboard the ship at the time of the murder, and was detained by authorities for questioning. The police are looking for a mysterious white-haired woman somewhere around fifty or fifty-five years of age, who wore a silver gown, silver slippers, a string of pearls about her neck and had snow-white hair cut in a boyish bob. Everyone described her appearance as striking. . . . Tell me, Chief, why did Mrs. Benson go aboard? Were you to meet her out there?"

"No," he said, "she claims she went out to back me up in case I got into any trouble."

"Then she must have been carrying a gun," Della said.

"How are your legs?" the lawyer inquired.

"Better. I can feel the floor now, but we were talking about a gun. Look here, Chief, are you keeping something from me?"

"Lots of things," he told her.

She looked down at her legs and said, "Regretfully, Chief, I must inform you that my circulation is now restored."

He released her. She danced a swift jig step, perched herself on the corner of the office desk, and said, "Let's get this straight while we have a chance. The landlady out at my apartment house is absolutely okay. She's a friend of mine and perfectly swell. I told her I had some friends coming to see me and I didn't have room to put them up in my apartment, so I wanted to rent the adjoining apartment for a few days. You see, my apartment was once part of a double, but they made it into two singles, and the other single is vacant. I paid her a week's rent and then went out to your place and picked up a suitcase. Gee, Chief, I hope I got everything you need. I didn't have room to put in an extra suit of clothes, but I got socks, shirts, underwear, ties, shaving things, tooth-brushes and pajamas. I also put in the pair of bedroom slippers that were under the edge of your bed. . . . I thought you might want to hide out."

"What did you do with the suitcase?" he asked.

"Planted it in this apartment I was telling you about. I figured that after they let you go they'd be watching you, and if they saw you leave *your* apartment with a suitcase they might . . ."

"Good girl," he interrupted. "Switch out those lights. We're on our way."

"You see," she said, turning out the lights, "in this way you can keep in touch with me and no one will be the wiser. There's a connecting door between the apartments, and I could have you in for meals and . . ."

He slipped an arm around her waist and said, "Della, you're a life saver. As a matter of fact, I have an idea they'll be trying to serve a subpœna on me within the next two hours."

"And you don't want to be subpœnaed?" she asked.

"Absolutely not. Where's your car, Della?"

"In the parking lot."

"Okay," he told her, "I'll get in my car and drive around the block. In case I'm shadowed, I'll ditch the shadows before I come out. If I'm not, I'll follow you out. After you get out to your apartment, put in a call for Paul Drake. Get him out of bed. Now, they may have tapped your line. So just ask him if he's seen me or heard anything from me. He'll tell you that he hasn't. Then you tell him it's important as the devil that you see him right away, and ask him if he can come out to your apartment. Tell him you're worried about me. Don't let him stall you along, but make him get in his car and come out at once. Do you follow me?"

"I," she proclaimed, "am two paragraphs ahead of you."

9

PAUL DRAKE tapped at the door of Della Street's apartment. She flung open the door and said, "Come in, Paul."

He regarded her with a droll smile and said, "You're as bad as your boss. I was hoping I *might* get a couple of hours of sleep."

"I'm worried about Perry," Della said, "awfully worried about him. The news flash came through that he was out on that gambling ship when . . ."

Drake interrupted her to say, *"He* was out there, Sylvia Oxman was out there, Frank Oxman was out there, and some woman in a silver evening gown who tossed a gun overboard after the murder, was out there. Perry had lots of company. They can't pin anything on him just because he was there—but they're sure going to try!"

"Well," she said, "I don't know too much about it, but the chief's gone into hiding."

"Gone into hiding," Drake echoed. "Well, *that's* food for thought. Where did he go? Where is he?"

"I don't know. He telephoned in some instructions from a pay station. He says he may be classed as a fugitive from justice, and he doesn't want to get me implicated. He's worked out a method of communicating with me, though."

Della Street picked up a shorthand notebook and said, "Here are his instructions: You're to find out everything you can about the murder, and particularly, he wants you to get a photograph from the newspaper men of the fingerprints that were developed on the glass top of Grieb's desk. It seems the fingerprint men got a lot of latent prints from it. There was one print of a hand, and the chief thinks it's a woman's hand. He couldn't see it clearly. He wants to get a copy of that latent print, if he can."

"Okay, what else?"

"The chief wants to find out exactly what Duncan's doing. Now there's a man on the ship by the name of Arthur Manning, who works as guard and bouncer. He figures he's due to lose his job as soon as Duncan takes over, because he'd sided with Grieb. The chief made a play to get Manning lined up with us, and thinks it's going to work. Manning's coming in to see me sometime after nine this morning. I'll get in touch with you when he comes in.

"Now, the chief figures that by sticking up for his rights, Manning can demand two weeks' notice and perhaps make it stick. Duncan will probably fire him, and the chief wants you to promise him a two months' job at a fair salary, with a chance to stay on regularly if he makes good. He's not to let anyone know that he's working for you, and he's to keep on out at the gambling ship just as long as he can. He'll make secret reports to you. The chief figures he can find out things.

"As soon as you've hired him, so the man's sympathies will be with you, the chief wants you to turn him inside out about just what he saw, and particularly just what Duncan was doing when Manning came into the office in response to the buzzer signal. Duncan may have been trying to plant some evidence in the chair where the chief had been sitting. Perry figures Manning might not have told all he knows about that—you know, figuring on trying to hold his job."

Drake nodded and said, "Okay, I'll put Manning to work. What else?"

"You're to report to me from time to time everything you've found out about the case, but you're to come into the office and do it personally. You're not to use the telephone. The chief thinks they may be looking for him and may try tapping telephone lines and . . ."

"For God's sake, is he going to stay hidden if they put out a dragnet for him?" Drake asked.

"That's what he said."

"He can't do it," Drake said positively. "They'll find him. He's mixed in this thing the way it is. He was waiting in the outer office when Duncan came in and discovered the murder. You can't let him . . ."

"Paul," Della Street interrupted in a tone of finality, "when the chief tells me to do something, I do it. I've learned by experience that it doesn't do any good to argue with him."

"Well, *I* want to talk with him," Drake said. "He's going to be in bad on this thing. He may even be accused of murder."

Della Street nodded lugubriously. "I'll tell him you want to talk with him the next time he gets in touch with me. And, in the meantime, he wanted you to give me a detailed report about what you know."

Drake said, "There isn't much to report. Sylvia Oxman went out aboard the ship about half or three-quarters of an hour before Mason went out, and Frank Oxman went out a short time later. Now, that's where the breaks went against my man. He tailed Oxman right down to the wharf and up to the point where Oxman bought a ticket for the speed boat. Then he ran into some tough luck. Oxman was the last passenger aboard the boat, which was loaded to capacity. As soon as he got aboard, the speed boat shoved off, and my man couldn't possibly get aboard. He had to wait quite a while before another launch was ready to shove off. Then, when he did get out to the gambling ship, he couldn't find a trace of Oxman anywhere. He searched all over the place for fifteen or twenty minutes. Finally he spotted Oxman just boarding one of the shore launches. So he got aboard that launch and tailed Oxman to the Breeden Hotel, where he's staying. I'd already stationed a plant—an operative staked out in the lobby—so if Oxman spotted his shadow, the operative in the lobby could carry on. Oxman was suspicious, and waited around in the lobby for a little while to make certain he wasn't being followed. So the tail turned him over to the plant. After a while Oxman went up to the desk and said he had some money he wanted to deposit in the hotel safe. He said it was money that belonged to someone else and he was particularly anxious to be relieved of the responsibility, so he made the clerk count it with him and check the amount, put it in an envelope, and deposit it in the safe.

"The money amounted to nine thousand five hundred bucks. You tell Perry about that and see if that means anything to him. I think it will. I've put a shadow on Oxman and we'll follow every move he makes.

"My men couldn't pick up Sylvia Oxman right away. She'd been out all day, but along late in the afternoon her maid came out carrying a fur coat, so one of the boys followed her and picked up Sylvia. Perry knows all about that. The shadow's name was Belgrade and I sent a relief for him down to the pier, but Sylvia had got aboard the ship before the relief arrived. Tell Perry that Belgrade shadowed her aboard and his report shows that she parked her coat with the hat check girl, stuck around for a while, and finally went into Sam Grieb's office. Now she'd been in there for maybe two or three minutes when a man who answered the description of Frank Oxman went down the corridor and was gone just a minute or two. Then he came out. Then, later on, Perry went in. Then Sylvia went out. Belgrade's instructions were to tag Sylvia, but Belgrade knew Perry was in there, and figured Perry might be having some trouble, so he stuck around, trying to keep Sylvia lined up and also watch the office entrance. Sylvia was nervous, did a little gambling and kept looking back at the offices.

"Then Duncan and a tall chap in a tweed suit went in,

and a few minutes later the tall chap brought Mason out, and Mason's wrists were handcuffed. Sylvia went white as a sheet when she saw that, and dropped into a chair as though her legs had gone weak. She stayed there for three or four minutes. Then Duncan came out of the office, and Sylvia got up and started for the deck. Belgrade followed her up to the deck, then down to one of the speed launches.

"Now, there were a couple of neckers out on deck who saw some woman toss a gun overboard. Apparently Perry got to talk with them, and by the time he got through, about all they dare swear to is that they saw a gun somewhere in the air, just before it struck the water.

"Well, Sylvia went ashore, and when she landed Staples relieved Belgrade. Belgrade phoned in his report, and I told him to go pound his ear for a while. Staples made a good job of following Sylvia. He says she acted as if she was scared to death over something. She parked her car in the Central Garage at Fifth and Adams, then took a taxicab to the Pacific Greyhound Depot and bought a ticket on a bus that was leaving for San Francisco. Her ticket read as far as Ventura, but when the bus pulled into the depot at Hollywood, she got out and didn't get back aboard. My man followed her and she went to the Christy Hotel and registered under the name of Nell Yardley, and gave her address as 1260 Polk Street, San Francisco. She was given Room 318 and hasn't gone out since."

"You have men watching the place?" Della asked.

"Sewed up tighter than a drum," Drake told her.

"Okay, the chief wants you to keep her and Frank Oxman shadowed and he wants you to locate a Matilda Benson who lives at 1090 Wedgewood Drive, and shadow her. The chief says she's pretty cagey and you'll have some trouble with her. She's the white-haired woman in the silver dress who figures in the case, and the chief wants to find out if the officers have learned who she is.

If they have, they'll be watching the house and your men can spot them. Let us know just as soon as any other men get on the job. And locate her if you can. She'll be under cover somewhere."

Drake said, "All right, I've got that. How about Duncan? He worked all day getting papers issued. He's filed a suit alleging the dissolution of the partnership and asking for an accounting in the federal court. Post, Wiker, Jones & Grayson are his lawyers and they're a reputable firm. After Duncan got the papers filed and an order issued to show cause why a receiver shouldn't be appointed, he and Dick Perkins, a deputy who specializes in serving papers, started down to the gambling ship.

"Mason only wanted a tail on Duncan long enough to find out when Duncan was starting out to serve the paper, so my man checked out when Duncan and the deputy reached the pier. Belgrade, the operative who was tailing Sylvia, knows Duncan personally. He identifies Duncan as one of the men who went into the offices, and the chap who was with him answers the description of the deputy marshal, Perkins. Perry will know because he was there."

"Then Frank Oxman went down the corridor to those offices while Sylvia was still there?" Della Street asked.

"That's right. The description checks."

"And that was after his wife had gone in, and *before* Perry arrived?"

"Yes."

"And Frank Oxman came right out?"

"That's right. He was only in there a minute or so."

"Then he went ashore and went to the Breeden Hotel and left nine thousand five hundred dollars with the clerk. Is that right?"

"Check."

"And his wife had been staying there at the same hotel?"

"No, they've separated. The wife has an apartment

at the Huxley Arms, but now she's staying at the Christy Hotel as Nell Yardley."

"Anything else?" Della Street asked.

Drake shook his head.

"All right, Paul, keep on the job. I'll let you know as soon as I have any more instructions."

Drake frowned and said, "Now listen, Della, it's up to you to snap Perry out of this. He's going to get himself in an awful mess if he isn't careful. Somebody murdered Sam Grieb at just about the time he was out there. Now, my man, Belgrade, knows that Sylvia Oxman was there when Mason went in. I think I can trust Belgrade to keep his mouth shut, but that information's simply dynamite, and if it should get out to the officers or to the newspapers it would put Perry in an awful spot. Then there's that couple on the ship who saw the gun tossed overboard. That business isn't going to help any. By the time they get on the witness stand they'll have Sylvia taking that gun out of her handbag. That'll pin an accessory-after-the-fact charge right on Mr. Perry Mason. Now, you tell Perry I want to talk with him. He's sitting on a volcano."

"Okay," Della said wearily, "I'll *tell* him, but it probably won't do any good. He's the champion volcano-sitter."

"Going to buy me a drink?" Drake asked.

"What do you want?"

"Scotch and soda, if you've got it. And, just to show you I'm a good scout, I'll buy a bottle of Scotch and bring it up the next time I come. It'll be on the expense account as entertainment, and neither Perry nor his client will know who got it."

"Swell," she told him, and went to the ice box, brought out ice cubes, Scotch and soda, poured two drinks and clicked glasses with the detective.

"Confusion to our enemies," she toasted.

Drake gulped down three big swallows of the light amber drink. "You don't need to wish any confusion on them. The whole case is worse than a jigsaw puzzle." He slipped his arm around her waist and said, "Gee, Della, you're a good kid! I wish I could get someone who had just one percent as much loyalty for me as you have for Perry. How does he work it?"

Della laughed. "Take your arm away, Paul. Experience has taught me that when a man sticks around my apartment about daylight, drinking Scotch and soda and talking about my wonderful loyalty, he's getting ready to go out of control."

Drake sighed. "I see you're a good judge of character as well as a darned efficient secretary. Going to kiss me good-by when I leave, Della?"

"No. If I did you wouldn't leave."

"Well," Drake said, "there's no harm in asking. I'll drop in at the office later on and give you all the dirt I can dig up. So long, Della, and thanks for the drink."

"Don't forget that bottle of Scotch," she told him as she closed the door behind him.

Perry Mason stepped out from behind the screen where he had been sitting. "The big palooka, trying to kiss my secretary! Where the hell does he get that noise?"

Della Street laughed at him. "If you're going to spy on my unguarded moments you'll hear a lot worse than that. He was positively platonic."

"And padding his expense account," Mason grinned. "So *that's* why his expenses are so big. Hand over that bottle of Scotch. If you're going to get another one on the expense account I might as well make a hole in this one."

10

PERRY MASON was sleeping soundly when Della Street pulled up the shades and let sunshine filter into the apartment. She was trimly dressed in a neat-fitting gray tailored suit, as freshly radiant as though she had been in bed by nine o'clock.

"Hi, Chief," she said, "I hate to do this, but it's necessary."

Mason muttered a mumbling protest in a voice which was thick with sleep.

"Hurry up," she said, "I have to get to the office, because I'm working for a slave driver who insists on my being there by nine-thirty every morning and *prefers* to have me there to open the mail at nine o'clock."

Mason opened his eyes, blinked in protest against the sunlight and said, "Fire the boss, Della, and get a new one. Why not work for me? I'll let you stay in bed until noon every day."

"Well," she said slowly, as though deliberating his proposal, "I *should* give the other boss notice, shouldn't I?"

"To hell with the notice," Mason said sleepily, "give him two weeks' salary. And how about my breakfast?"

"All laid out on the table for you," she said. "Coffee in the percolator, orange juice in the ice box, eggs all ready to drop in the boiling water that's on the stove, and a plate of bread by the electric toaster, plenty of butter, strawberry jam and broiled bacon being kept warm in the oven. I let you sleep just as long as I dared, Chief."

Mason sat up in bed, rumpled his hair with his fingers and said, "Young woman, you're begging the question.

How about quitting your other boss and going to work for me?"

"I'd have to get in touch with him first," she said, "and no one knows where he is."

He grinned. "You're trying to make me get witty, think up come-backs to your wise-cracks, so I won't go back to sleep after you leave. I'm on to you! Why all the early morning calls?"

"The newspaper," she said, "with an account of the crime, a diagram, a cross marking the spot, a statement from Perry Mason, the attorney, seems to have disappeared, and an awful wallop right between the eyes: one of Drake's men sold out."

"Give me that paper," Mason commanded.

"Not yet, Chief. You shower, breakfast, and think it over. Don't do anything until you've gone over it carefully. I'm going to open up the office. If I don't do that, some smart detective may figure I'm with you and start frisking my apartment."

"Who sold out?"

"George Belgrade."

"Whom did he sell us out to?"

"The newspapers. They paid a top price for his story."

"Let's see, Belgrade was the one who knew Duncan, wasn't he?"

"Yes, he was the man who was shadowing Sylvia Oxman. He sure put both of you in a sweet spot. She was in those offices when you went in, and she came out *before* you did. Therefore, she must have been in there either when the murder was committed, after it was committed, or before it was committed."

He grinned and said, "That's logical. And she must have either been sitting down, standing up or walking around."

"No," Della Street said, "I'm serious, Chief. This is the way the newspaper has doped it out: If she went in there *after* the murder was committed, there would have been

119

no reason for you to have protected her. If she was in there *while* the murder was being committed, she must have done the killing. If she left *before* the murder was committed, you must have done it.

"Belgrade admits he was hired as a detective by Paul Drake, that he knows Paul Drake does your work, and thinks he was working for you on this case; that you apparently were representing Sylvia Oxman because you're trying to cover up for her. The newspaper's dishing out a lot of dirt, and it's putting you in an awful spot.

"Now, here's something else: the eight-thirty Newspaper-of-the-Air announces that the woman in the silver gown was Matilda Benson, the grandmother of Sylvia Oxman. Both women were evidently aboard the gambling ship at the time the murder was committed. Both women have vanished. Matilda Benson apparently committed suicide by jumping overboard."

Mason flung his legs out of bed and made a grab for the newspaper.

She tossed him the paper and said, "That isn't in the newspaper. It came over the radio as a news flash."

"How do they know she committed suicide?"

"They found her fur coat wrapped around the anchor chain of the gambling ship when it came daylight. Her name was in the coat, and it's been identified by some of her friends."

Mason laughed. "I know the answer to that. It isn't suicide."

"Okay, Chief, have breakfast and read the paper. I'm going up to the office and go through the motions of frantically wondering where you are. Now I won't dare to come back here before five o'clock tonight. You may want to get in touch with me in the meantime. If you want to give me any instructions, you can telephone Paul Drake and leave the message with him. He'll see that I get it. I've brought in my portable radio. There's a card with station numbers and the hours of news broadcasts beside it."

"What time is it?" Mason asked.

"Twenty minutes to nine. I want to be up at the office early so I can answer questions about you."

He nodded and said, "Where's the breakfast, Della, in your apartment or here?"

"Here," she told him. "I brought supplies over from my place. You lock the connecting door after I leave and keep it locked, because some smart dick may start prowling around my apartment."

"Okay, Della," he told her, drawing up his feet to sit cross-legged on the bed while he spread the newspaper open.

"Go on and get your breakfast," she told him. "You'll probably want to explode into some action, and you'll need food in your stomach. You can read while you're eating. I'm on my way. Toodle-oo." She blew him a saucy kiss and gently closed the connecting door to her apartment.

Mason found his bedroom slippers placed under the edge of his bed.

"The perfect secretary," he muttered, grinning, thrusting his feet into his slippers and straightening his pajamas. He went into the kitchenette where a coffee pot was sending forth steaming aromas. Water was briskly boiling on the stove. Three eggs were in a saucer near the water. Mason glanced across at the table, with its white cloth, glittering silver, coffee cup, cream, sugar, jam, butter, bread and electric toaster. He dropped the three eggs into the water, poured himself a cup of coffee, noted the time, and stood over the eggs to wait for the three-minute interval to elapse. He spread the paper flat against the wall, holding it with his left hand pressed against the upper left-hand corner, while his right held the cup of coffee. As he read the paper, he sipped the coffee. The three minutes passed unnoticed, lengthened into five. Mason set down his empty coffee cup. The eggs danced about in the briskly boiling water.

Mason opened the paper to the inside page and studied the diagram of the gambling ship, the photographs of the hull, waded through a lot of extraneous detail concerning the previous history of the ship and its transition from a proud, square-rigged vessel which sailed the seven seas, to a fishing barge and then a gambling ship.

Suddenly he thought of the eggs, and glanced at his watch. The eggs had been in exactly fifteen minutes.

He turned out the fire, dumped eggs and water into the sink with a frown of disgust, poured himself another cup of coffee, took it over to the table, placed two slices of bread in the electric toaster and switched on the current. He buried his nose once more in the paper and studied the statement of George Belgrade with a frowning concentration which prevented him from noticing the wisping streamers which began to drift upward from the bread in the electric toaster. The streamers grew into a cloud. The apartment was filled with the odor of burning toast. Mason groped with his free hand for the handle of his coffee cup, raised the rim of the cup to his lips and then caught sight of the smoke billowing up from the toaster. With an exclamation, he switched off the toaster. He gulped down the rest of his coffee, forgot about the bacon, dropped the newspaper on the floor, divested himself of his pajamas on the way to the bathroom, showered and shaved. While he was shaving, he was staring with unseeing eyes at his reflection in the mirror. The motions of his shaving were purely mechanical.

Mason foraged around in the cupboard and the icebox and found no food. He tentatively opened one of the hard-boiled eggs in the sink, but it presented too substantial a problem for a breakfast dish. He took the charred toast from the toaster, dropped in two more slices of bread and switched on the radio. He kept a watchful eye on the toast, turned it when one side was a golden brown. The voice of the announcer on the radio finished droning through routine news and announced a flash. Officers who had been searching for Perry Mason, the noted criminal attorney, seeking to serve a subpœna on him to appear for questioning before the grand jury, were now seeking him on a much more serious charge. While they would not divulge the exact nature of the charge, informed sources stated that he was to be arrested upon suspicion of murder, criminal conspiracy, and compounding a felony. Following the spectacular statement of George Belgrade, which had been exclusively released through a local newspaper, the Federal Grand Jury had issued a subpœna for Belgrade. There had followed a battle of wits between the newspaper which had paid Belgrade for his exclusive statement, and the United States Marshal's office, which had been seeking to serve the subpœna and bring Belgrade before the grand jury forthwith. The marshal had won out. Belgrade had been found where he had been concealed by representatives of the newspaper which had hoped to print an exclusive follow-up story. A subpœna had also been issued for Paul Drake, head of the Drake Detective Bureau.

The radio announcer promised to report latest developments in the murder case at the next news broadcasting period. In the meantime, a search of Perry Mason's usual haunts had been fruitless. Perry Mason, Sylvia Oxman and Matilda Benson were all three missing.

By the time the broadcaster had concluded his statement, Perry Mason ruefully inspected the charred remains of his second attempt at toast making and switched off the current.

For more than half an hour, Mason paced the floor in frowning concentration, then, having reached a decision, he dressed, put on his hat, locked the door of the apartment, descended to the street and walked to the boulevard. He called Paul Drake's office from a pay station, asked to be connected with Drake, and a moment later heard the detective's voice on the line.

"Hello, Paul," Mason said. "You know who this is?"

"Yes. Where are you telephoning from?"

"A pay station."

"Where?"

"In a drug store. Is it safe to talk, Paul?"

"I think so. Listen, Perry, I'm sorry as hell about this Belgrade business. You know how it is. I pick my men the best way I can and I never put men on your work unless I've first tested them for honesty and ability and . . ."

"Forget it," Mason interrupted. "There's no use crying over spilled milk. Hell, Paul, we can't waste time swapping words over what . . ."

"I know," Drake interrupted. "But I want you to know how I feel."

"I know how you feel. You can't help what happened."

"Well, now I've got that off my chest," Drake said, "I want to see you. Manning's here in the office with some important information. I've been subpœnaed to appear this afternoon at two o'clock before the grand jury. I'm afraid Manning may be subpœnaed, and I think you'd better talk with him. Then you *may* want to let him stick around and get a subpœna. You know, of course, they're looking for you."

"Yes."

"I want to talk with you about that. You can't . . ."

"Think you can get away from your office without being followed, Paul?" Mason interrupted.

"I think so. I'll have a couple of the boys tail me, and if anyone's tagging along they can tip me off."

"Okay. You tell Della to leave any messages at your office. You bring Manning with you. Make sure you're not being followed, and go to the corner of Adams and Figueroa. Wait there on the corner. I'll pick up a taxicab, and if no one's on *my* trail I'll drive by to pick you up. If the coast is clear, take off your hat and stand on the corner with your hat in your hand. If you're at all suspicious, leave your hat on your head and I'll whiz

124

right on by and call your office to pick another meeting place."

"Okay," Drake said. "I think I've got an out for you, Perry."

"That," Mason proclaimed, "will help."

"It's a swell break for you," Drake said. "It's spectacular, dramatic and logical. It clears you and your clients."

Mason said slowly, "Perhaps you think *that* won't be welcome. How soon can you make it, Paul?"

"If we're not followed, I can be there in ten or fifteen minutes. I'm bringing Manning with me. If we're followed, it'll take a while to ditch the shadows."

"Okay," Mason told him, ". . . be seeing you," and hung up the telephone. He stopped at the lunch counter in the drug store, ate two soft-boiled eggs, toast and bacon, then waited on the corner for a cruising cab. When one came along, he had it drive to a side street address. He paused there uncertainly, as though debating with himself, then said to the cab driver, "Turn around, go out Figueroa to Adams, turn west on Adams, and then I'll tell you where to go."

The cab driver nodded, turned the car and sent it into speed. Mason leaned forward in the seat, said, "Not too fast as you round the corner into Adams. I want to look at some property there."

"Okay," the driver told him.

Mason saw Paul Drake and Arthur Manning standing on the corner. Drake was holding his hat in his hand.

Mason said, "I think I'll stop and take a good look at this property. Here's enough to cover the meter and leave you a couple of cigars."

The cab driver pulled in to the curb, rang down the meter, opened the door of the cab and said, "I can wait if you ain't going to be long."

"No," Mason told him, "it may be some little time. Don't wait."

The cab driver thanked him and drove on. Drake continued to stand with his hat in his hand, taking no notice whatever of Mason. Not until the cab had rounded the corner, did Drake touch Manning's arm and move on toward the lawyer. He said, "My car's parked around the corner, Perry. We can talk there."

Mason nodded. Manning said, "I sure want to thank you, Mr. Mason, for what you've done for me. Mr. Drake's given me a job. He's going to try me out for a couple of months, and I think I can make good."

"How about Duncan?" Mason asked. "Has he said anything about firing you?"

Manning shook his head and said, "In some ways I feel like a rat with Duncan. He certainly has been square and aboveboard as far as I'm concerned. I took sides against him with Grieb, but Duncan called me in and said he wasn't holding any hard feelings, that he understood just how I'd been situated, and that I couldn't have done anything different. It was damn white of him. He said I could stay on in my regular job."

"Then perhaps you'd prefer to do that instead of working for Drake," Mason said, flashing Drake a warning look.

"No," Manning said slowly, "I think this job has a future, and I'm afraid of Duncan. I can't trust him."

"How do you mean?" Mason asked. "You think he's just kidding you along?"

"That's right. Duncan's clever as hell. Right now he needs me. *I'm the only one who can back his story.*"

Drake said, "Here's the car, Perry. Wait until you hear his story. I've heard it, so you'd better let me ask the questions."

"Okay," Mason said, climbing in the back of the car. Drake slid behind the driver's wheel, and Manning sat next to him.

Drake said, "I want you to talk with Manning, Perry, and hear his story. Before we start on that, I've got something to tell you about Frank Oxman."

126

"What is it?"

"Something's in the wind there, Perry, sure as hell. Early this morning Oxman dashed out of the Breeden Hotel and went to the offices of Worsham & Weaver. They're lawyers, you know. P. C. Worsham, the senior partner, was there, and after a while a stenographer showed up. My men covered the corridor. They couldn't hear what was going on in the office, but they did hear the clack of a typewriter; and a little later a couple of detectives from the homicide squad came in. There was quite a bit of talking. When the dicks left, they took Oxman with them."

"Under arrest?" Mason asked.

"It looked like it."

"Where is he now?"

"At the D.A.'s office, apparently being turned inside out. Something's happening in a big way and one of the newspapers has a tip-off. A reporter is hanging around the Breeden Hotel waiting for Oxman to come back to his room."

Mason said slowly, "Then it isn't a pinch, Paul. If the newspaper has a tip-off and is waiting for Oxman to come *back,* that means the newspaper knows Oxman's going to be released."

"That's right," Drake agreed. "I hadn't thought of it in just that way."

Mason narrowed his eyes and said, "That *could* complicate matters, Paul."

For a moment they sat in silence. Then Drake said, "Perry, I want to explain to you about this man Belgrade, who sold us out. You see . . ."

"Forget it," Mason interrupted. "He sold us out, and that's that. You can't apologize it away, and you can't explain it away. It's happened, and that's all there is to it. It's one of those things that are bound to happen when you have to work through operatives. You can't expect a man who draws eight dollars a day and expenses to pass up a juicy chunk of coin when a newspaper offers it to him."

Drake fidgeted uneasily and said, "I should never have hired the fellow in the first place. His record isn't any too good. And I certainly shouldn't have let him get aboard that ship, in view of the fact that he knew Duncan and Grieb. I sent Staples down to the pier to relieve him. Sylvia Oxman had gone aboard before Staples got there, so he didn't pick her up until after she'd left the ship. Then he relieved Belgrade and took up the shadowing job. Staples was the man I wanted for the job all along. He'd been covering her apartment."

Mason said slowly, "Then Belgrade was relieved *before* Sylvia went into hiding, is that right?"

"Yes."

"Therefore," Mason went on, "Belgrade can't tip the newspaper off to where Sylvia is now?"

"That's right. Staples picked her up at the wharf and shadowed her into the Christy Hotel, and bribed a bellboy to give him her room number—318. I reported to Della."

"Yes, I know," Mason interrupted, "Della told me."

Drake said, "Well, I wanted to get that off my mind, Perry. You've been damned white about it, but it was a blunder on my part. I shouldn't have let Belgrade have anything to do with the case. So much for the bad part. Now for the good part: I think we've got something that's going to put us in the clear."

Drake turned to Manning, said, "Turn around, Arthur, so Mr. Mason can see your face. I'm going to ask you some questions and I want you to . . ."

"I can tell my story," Manning said eagerly, "and then you can . . ."

"No," Drake interrupted, "I want to ask you questions. That's the way your story would come out in court or in front of a grand jury, and I want Mason to see how you handle yourself on answering questions."

"Okay," Manning said with a grin, "fire away."

"How long have you been out there on the gambling ship?"

"Ever since it started."

"And you were friendly to Grieb and unfriendly to Duncan?"

"Not exactly. My *original* contact was with Duncan. He got me the job. But Duncan was the outside man. Grieb was the inside man. Duncan was in the city most of the time buying supplies, handling publicity, making arrangements with the speed boat men, looking after political fences to keep the beach cities from passing ordinances putting the speed boat men out of business, and all that sort of stuff. So naturally I was thrown more and more in contact with Sam Grieb. Then they commenced to start fighting over little things, and I tried to keep neutral. Gradually I found Duncan was steering clear of me, and Grieb was taking me into his confidence. I tried to keep things from drifting too far that way, but I didn't want to put myself in a position where I had *both* Grieb and Duncan sore at me; and I figured Grieb was going to come out on top because he was the one who had the money."

"Now then," Drake said, glancing meaningly at Mason, "who murdered Grieb?"

"Nobody."

"How do you figure that?" Drake asked.

"Well, Grieb and Duncan had some I O U's signed by Sylvia Oxman. Grieb was trying to peddle them at a premium, if he could. He had an idea Frank Oxman would pay a bonus to get hold of them.

"Duncan was anxious to get them in the form of cash, because Duncan knew there was going to be a bust-up of the partnership and he figured it would be easier to divide cash than to hold the sack of notes. So Duncan and Grieb had a big fight yesterday afternoon and Duncan made Grieb promise that he'd get those I O U's reduced to cash by seven o'clock that night. Grieb was going to get a pre-

129

mium for them if he could, and, if he couldn't, he was going to let them go for their face value. It seems Mr. Mason had thrown an awful scare into them when he started handling Sylvia's case.

"Now, I was sticking around the offices until about fifteen or twenty minutes before Duncan came in and discovered the murder, and I know Grieb was alive when I left. He sent for me and said the crap table had a slicker working the game, and sent me over there to take a look. Now, no one had come in who could have paid off those I O U's *before* I went over to the crap table. Three people went in afterward—Sylvia, Frank Oxman, and Mr. Mason. *After* Duncan found the body, the I O U's were gone, and there was seventy-five hundred bucks in the desk drawer. That was just the amount of those I O U's, so I figured Oxman must have paid them off. Sam held out for a premium and Oxman wouldn't give it to him, so finally Sam took just the face value of the I O U's."

"Then Oxman must have been in there long enough to have talked with Grieb. Is that right?" Drake asked.

"Yes, that's right. I saw him go in. I didn't see him come out. I thought I was keeping my eye peeled all the time, but you know how it is when you're watching a dice slicker, and Oxman must have gone out without my seeing him. It's a cinch *someone* paid off those I O U's. I don't think the dame did it. She didn't have the dough for one thing."

"Well, then," Mason said, "what you're getting at is that Oxman must have killed him."

"No," Manning said, vigorously shaking his head, "it all builds up to the fact that Oxman *didn't* kill him."

Drake said, "Wait a minute, Perry, and let me handle this. I know the whole story. . . . Now, Arthur, why do you think Oxman didn't kill him?"

"Because if Oxman had paid off those I O U's and then killed him, he certainly wouldn't have left the seventy-five hundred dollars in the desk drawer, and if he'd killed him *before* he'd paid the I O U's, he'd never have left the money there."

Mason's face showed disappointment. He said, "I'm sorry, Paul, but this isn't getting us anywhere. This guy's deductions are just deductions. Anyone can guess what happened from . . ."

"Wait a minute," Drake interrupted significantly.

Mason caught the look in the detective's eye and became silent.

"Now then," Drake said, "having figured that Oxman didn't kill him, who did?

"Well, like I said," Manning remarked, "*I* don't think anyone killed him."

"How did he die, then?"

"He committed suicide."

"What makes you think he committed suicide?"

"I think Duncan had the goods on him. I think Sam had been dipping into the partnership funds. Duncan suspected it. Grieb put most of his money in the business and then had some losses in the stock market. Grieb handled all the money. I think he knew Duncan was calling for a showdown and knew that, as soon as a receiver stepped in, Duncan could send him to jail, and he knew Duncan wouldn't want anything better than that.

"The only chance Grieb had to make a killing was to get Oxman to pay a fancy sum for those I O U's. I think at first Grieb thought he could get maybe ten thousand bucks premium and make Oxman promise never to say anything about it. Then Grieb could have told Duncan that Oxman wouldn't pay any premium for the notes and he'd had to let them go for their face value. That would have suited Duncan all right for he'd never have checked up on it, and Grieb could have used the extra cash to square off his shortage."

Mason said impatiently, "Damn it, Paul, this isn't *getting* us anywhere. I can think up a dozen different theories that . . ."

He once more stopped in mid-sentence as he caught the look in Drake's eyes.

"Now, what makes you think Grieb could have committed suicide?" Drake asked. "The police experts all say it was murder."

"I know they do, but the reason they say that is because they can't find the gun. Now, Grieb was killed with a .38 caliber automatic that he ordinarily kept in the upper left-hand drawer of his desk."

"How do you know?" the detective asked.

"Why, we went over all that in your office," Manning said.

"Never mind what we went over in my office," Drake told him. "You just begin from scratch and tell Mr. Mason the whole story. I want him to hear it the way you tell it and not the way I'd try to tell it."

"Well," Manning said, "it's this way. First, you've got to consider the type of man you're dealing with. Charlie Duncan is a smart hombre. He keeps his face buttoned up until he's ready to say something, and when he says something it's a mouthful. But most of the time he's just sitting on the side lines sizing things up; but he doesn't give you that impression, because of those gold teeth of his. He keeps his mouth open in a grin and the gold teeth sort of draw attention to the fact that he's grinning. People don't look at his eyes, they look at his teeth. Now, I know this, because I know Charlie Duncan. I've known Charlie Duncan for ten years, and I know the way he works. He thinks fast and he doesn't say much. Most people figured Sam Grieb was the big-shot of the business, because Sam was always acting like the big executive. Sam liked to sit behind his desk and impress people, while Duncan liked to get out on the firing line and slip things over. Left to himself, Grieb could never have kept that business going because he didn't have brains enough to handle the political end."

"All right," Drake said, glancing again at Mason,

"that gives us a pretty good sketch of Duncan's character. What's that got to do with the suicide?"

"Well, when they started business," Manning said, "they took out one of these policies of business insurance by which each man insured his life in favor of the other for twenty thousand dollars. If one of them died, the twenty thousand dollars was to go to the other partner, who would use that twenty thousand to pay the heirs of the dead partner for the dead man's share in the business. That's usual in lots of partnerships, I understand. Anyway, that's what the insurance salesman told them. I was there when he talked with Sam. You see, when a partner dies, the surviving partner has to wind up the business and then he has to turn over half of the net assets to an administrator or something. That means that the business is wrecked, because the living partner isn't supposed to buy it in; but when the partners all agree on having an insurance provision of this kind, it's legal, and the other partner simply takes the twenty thousand, pays it over to the heirs in the form of cash, and that represents the value of the dead partner's share in the business. Anyway, that's the way the insurance man put it up to them, and . . ."

"Mason's a lawyer. He knows all about business and partnership insurance," Drake interrupted. "Go ahead and tell us the rest of it."

"Well, those policies had a provision that if a partner committed suicide within the first year, the insurance company only had to pay the amount of the premiums which had been paid in. On the other hand, if the death took place by violence or by accident, the surviving partner got double the face of the policy. Now then, you see where that leaves Charlie Duncan. If Sammy committed suicide, Duncan can't collect a cent under the policy except a few hundred dollars which were paid as premiums. He has to wind up the partnership business and he has to give one-half of all the assets to Sammy's heirs.

But if he could prove Sammy was murdered, then he'd get *forty* thousand dollars instead of twenty. He could keep the whole partnership business, and he'd only have to pay over *twenty* thousand to the heirs.

"You see what I mean. When they took out the partnership insurance, the insurance had this clause about death by violence, but in the agreement they overlooked that and agreed on a payment of a flat amount of twenty thousand dollars, which one partner would pay to the other."

Perry Mason pursed his lips in thought, met Drake's significant glance and nodded his head.

"Go ahead, Arthur," Drake said.

"Well, Charlie's a quick thinker. Now, I'm just betting that as soon as he walked into that room and saw Grieb dead, he realized the position that he'd be in. I think he knew Sammy had been dipping into the till, and that was one of the reasons he was so anxious to have a receiver appointed.

"Now then. Charlie busted into that room and saw Sammy sitting at his desk, dead. He knew damn well it was a suicide, but Perry Mason, the lawyer, was right there in the office, and Charlie had a deputy United States marshal with him who had been called in to serve the papers on Sammy. Now, I think that Charlie knew there was evidence there which would prove Sammy had killed himself, and what he wanted was to ditch that evidence. In order to do it, he had to get rid of *both* this man Perkins and Perry Mason, and the best way he could think of was to pretend Perry Mason had bumped Sammy off, and, of course, to protect his own interests, he kept yelling murder right from the start. Charlie's an awfully smooth guy when he has to be. He's a fast worker and a quick thinker, and . . ."

"Yes, you've told us all that before," Drake interrupted.

"Well, the logical thing for Charlie to do was to make

a build-up so he could accuse Perry Mason of murder and order Perkins to take Mason and lock him up somewhere. Now, Charlie knew just as well as I do—in fact a damned sight better—that it wasn't murder, that it was a case of suicide, but he wanted to get Mason and Perkins out of there, so he accused Mr. Mason of the murder and got Perkins and Mason to go out.

"Now, I was watching that runway which led to the offices, and I saw Perkins and Mason go out. I went in just a second after they went out. I told the officers that Charlie was looking around in the chair in the entrance room when I went in there, and that's the truth, but *before* I went in that room, Duncan had been in the room where Sammy's body was slumped over the desk. I *know* that because when I opened the door to the outer office I could hear the sound of someone moving fast on the other side of the door, just as though Charlie had come running out of that inside office.

"Now, I'd gone in there on an emergency signal. I didn't know what was up and when I heard all the noise of running feet I stopped long enough to get my gun out of my holster and into my fist. I wasn't going to walk in and have someone stick a gun in *my* ribs.

"My gun didn't come out easy, and maybe I was a little yellow. I hated like hell to push that door open the rest of the way, but I did it—and there was Charlie fumbling around in the chair, just like I told the officers.

"Now, I think that Sammy killed himself, that the gun had slipped down from his hand and was lying on the floor by the desk, that Charlie saw it there. He got rid of Mason and Perkins long enough to run in and pick up that gun. At first he intended to frame the killing on Mr. Mason. So he figured he'd slip the gun down in the cushions of the chair in which Mason had been sitting. But I came in there and found him fussing around that chair, and he didn't dare to do it then, because he was afraid I'd squeal. So he kept the gun in his pocket and ditched it later."

"How do you know what gun Grieb was killed with?" Mason asked.

Drake nodded and said, "That's the part that's important, Arthur. Just *how* do you know that?"

"Well," Manning said, "I know something about guns. I fooled around quite a bit with ballistics when I was in the army. The marks on a gun barrel fingerprint a bullet which goes through it just the same as a man's fingerprints on a piece of glass . . ."

"Yes, we know all about that," Drake said. "Go on."

"Something else that isn't so generally known," Manning said, "is that the firing pin leaves a distinctive mark on the exploded shell. Firing pins aren't centered dead to rights. They're always a little bit to one side or the other.

"Well, one day Charlie Duncan and Sammy Grieb got in an argument about who was the best shot. They were both army men. Charlie bet Grieb fifty bucks he could come closer to a mark than Sammy could. Sammy got sore and put up the fifty. I was in the room at the time and they used me as stake holder. We went below the casino into a long storeroom where there were some heavy timbers and put up a target."

"Who won?" Mason asked.

"Grieb did. That was where he outsmarted Charlie. Charlie's a crack shot, but Grieb was familiar with the gun and Grieb stipulated that they were only to shoot one shot apiece.

"Now, after I got to thinking about what might have happened, I went down there below decks and started prowling around. Sure enough, I found one of the exploded shells that had been ejected by the gun and dug one of the bullets out of this heavy beam. Now I can swear those bullets came from Sam's gun and that's the same gun that Sam was killed with."

Mason raised his head and said to Paul Drake, "Have you checked up on this, Paul?"

Drake nodded. "I've got a photograph of the exploded shell which they found on the floor in the room where Grieb was killed and checked the mark made by the firing pin with that on the shell Manning found down there in the passageway beneath the casino. There's no question but that they were both fired from the same gun."

"And how about the bullet he dug out of the beam?" Mason asked.

Drake took a little glass tube from his pocket. The tube had been sealed up with a strip of gummed paper, on which appeared words written in pen and ink and a scrawled signature.

"I put the bullet Arthur gave me in this tube and sealed it up in his presence," Drake said. "That tube can't be opened without breaking the seal. You see, I've put the wax over the paper at the top."

"Good work," Mason said. "They'd probably accuse us of switching bullets if they could. Have you made a microscopic examination, Paul?"

"No, because I'll have to pull a few wires to get enlarged microscopic photographs of the fatal bullet, but it's a cinch the indentations made by the firing pin on both shells are the same."

Mason said slowly, "You know, Paul, this is important as hell."

"Of course it is," Drake said. "That's why I wanted you to hear Manning's story yourself."

"It's important to a lot of people," Mason went on slowly. "It means the insurance company can save forty thousand bucks in hard cash. It means Charlie Duncan will be out forty thousand bucks, hard cash. It means that, no matter what else happened aboard that ship, a murder charge can't be pinned on anyone for Grieb's death. Now that's going to make quite a commotion in a lot of places."

Drake nodded.

Manning said, "I hope it's going to help you, Mr. Mason. You and Mr. Drake have been on the square with me."

"It'll help us, all right," Mason said, "but I don't know yet just *how* I'm going to spring it, or *when* I'm going to spring it. I want you to forget all about this for the time being, Arthur, and don't tell anyone anything about it."

Manning said, "Whatever you two say."

"Well," Mason pointed out, "they *may* subpœna you before the grand jury that's making the investigation. If they do, you answer questions, don't tell any lies; but, answer the questions in such a way you don't volunteer any information—that is, unless Paul instructs you to play it differently."

"Yes, sir," Manning said, "I can play the game, all right."

"Who else knows about this shooting match?" Mason asked.

"No one except Charlie Duncan, and of course he isn't going to talk."

"Where did you say it took place?"

"Right under the casino; there's a long passageway running the length of the storeroom. They keep a lot of canned goods down there."

"Which way did they shoot, toward the bow or toward the stern?"

"Toward the bow."

"What was the distance?"

"Oh, I'd say about thirty or forty feet."

"And Grieb beat Duncan shooting?"

"Yes."

"But Duncan's a good shot?"

"Yes, but you see, it was Grieb's gun and Grieb knew just how to handle it."

"Is Duncan left-handed?"

"No, he's right-handed. Sam was left-handed. That's

why he kept the gun in the upper left-hand drawer of his desk."

"They shot into a beam at the end of the passageway?"

"That's right."

"What was the target they were shooting at?"

"A round piece of tin they'd cut from a can with a can opener."

"How did they hold it in place?"

"Drove a nail through it and stuck it into the beam."

"That piece of tin would have been about two or three inches in diameter?" Mason asked.

"Yes, you know, just the top of a tin can, an average-sized tin can."

"But neither one of them hit it, did they?"

"Sure they did. Grieb hit it almost dead center. Duncan missed the center by about half an inch."

Mason regarded Paul Drake with speculative eyes and said, "How about Duncan, Paul? Is he telling the truth about having been ashore filing papers and all that stuff?"

Drake said, "Yes, Perkins was with him, and then you'll remember that I had men shadowing him. Why, Perry? You don't think . . ."

"How about those fingerprints on the glass top of the desk? Did you find out anything about them?" Mason interrupted.

"A leak from the D.A.'s office," Drake said, "is that the print of the hand and fingers on the desk was made by Sylvia Oxman. I don't know how they found out, perhaps by getting her fingerprints from the articles in her house. It's a cinch they haven't been able to take any fingerprints from *her*. She's crawled into a hole and pulled the hole in after her."

Mason said thoughtfully, "And you don't think the police know where she is?"

"No. . . . What do you think about this Benson suicide, Perry?"

Mason said, "I don't think, Paul," and closed one eye in a warning wink. "You'd better go back to the office and tip Della off to play 'em close to her chest. And it'd be a good plan to put Manning some place where the dicks can't find him."

"You're not going to release this story now?" Drake asked.

"No. I want to wait until Duncan has sewed himself up good and tight on the incidental details. I want to let the police build up a swell case against Sylvia. Then I want to smash down the house of cards with one big grandstand. I want to do it in a way that'll stampede the witnesses and hit the grand jury with such a smash the whole case will blow up. There are some things about what Sylvia did that would be better hushed up. And I'm not in such a sweet spot myself if the going gets rough. To make Manning's story hold water it's got to be played up just right. . . . You, Manning, keep absolutely quiet about this. Paul will hide you somewhere . . ."

"You won't need me out on the ship?" Manning asked. "Getting stuff on Duncan?"

"Hell, no," Mason said. "Not now. We've got enough on him now to raise merry hell with a murder case. That's all I want. *I'm* not representing the insurance company."

"How about you, Perry?" Drake asked. "Can I take you some place?"

Mason shook his head and opened the car door. "I'm on my way," he said, reaching through the open window on the driver's side to give the detective's shoulder a reassuring squeeze. "Damn good work, Paul," he said. "It's probably saved my bacon."

■

11

MASON, DRIVING a rented car, slid into a parking space
opposite the Christy Hotel, looked up and down the street,
then crossed Hollywood Boulevard. A newsboy waved a
paper in his face and Mason caught a glimpse of headlines reading:

LAWYER WANTED
IN CONNECTION WITH
GAMBLING SHIP MURDER

He bought a paper, walked through the lobby of the
hotel, toward the elevator. He paused abruptly as he saw
the trim figure of Sylvia Oxman emerge from one of the
cages and stand for a moment searching the lobby with
her eyes.

Mason abruptly whipped open the newspaper, held it
up so it concealed his chest, shoulders, and the lower part
of his face, only his eyes being visible over the upper
edge.

Sylvia Oxman, her survey of the lobby completed,
walked directly to the telephone booths. Mason followed. Still holding the newspaper in front of his face, he
stood where he could observe her through the glass door
of the telephone booth. She dropped a dime into the
slot and dialed a number. Mason was at some pains to
watch her gloved forefinger as it spun the dial. He men-
tally checked each number as she dialed it.

She was, he realized, calling his office.

He stepped into an adjoining booth, and pulled the door

shut behind him. Through the partition he could hear Sylvia Oxman's voice. "I want to speak to Mr. Mason, please. . . . This is a client. . . . He'll want to speak with me, I'm sure. . . . Well, when *do* you expect him? . . . Will you *please* tell him that he was called by Miss I O U. I'd better spell that for you. It's I, for Irma, O, for Olga, Y-e-w, but please see that he gets the name as just Miss I. O. Yew. Tell him that I'll call later."

She hung up the receiver. Mason cupped his hands about his mouth, leaned against the thin partition, and called, "Hello, Sylvia, this is Mr. Mason talking."

He could hear her grab at the receiver in the other booth, heard her frantic "Hello! Hello!"—then silence. He stood leaning against the partition, grinning and listening.

Abruptly the door behind him opened, and he turned to confront Sylvia Oxman's smile. "Do you know," she asked, "that you scared me to death for a minute? I recognized your voice and couldn't imagine where in the world it was coming from. . . . Why don't you stay in your office during office hours?"

"Can't," Mason told her.

"Why not?"

By way of answer, he unfolded the newspaper and let her read the headlines.

"Oh!" she exclaimed, her eyes dark with consternation, "I didn't know it would be anything like *that*."

"It is," Mason told her. "Why did you run out on me?"

"I had to. Frank was aboard."

"How did you know?"

"A man told me."

"Who was the man?"

"I don't know."

Mason said, "Look here. We'd better get where we can talk. How about your room?"

"How did you know I was registered here?"

"A little bird told me."

"The maid's making the room up," she said. "That's

142

why I came downstairs to use the telephone. Let's go over in a corner of the lobby."

"All right," Mason said, and followed her to a comfortable nook. He seated himself beside her, stretched out his long legs, and gravely offered her a cigarette. They lit from the same match, and Mason said, "All right. Let's talk."

She motioned toward the newspaper. "How much of this," she asked, "is because of what you did for me?"

"All of it."

"I'm frightfully sorry. Would it . . . Would it have helped any if I hadn't run out on you?"

"Not a bit," he told her. "The breaks went against me. But, first, suppose you tell me *your* story."

"I'm in a mess," she said.

"How much of a mess?"

"The worst possible."

"Go ahead and tell me."

"I lied to you last night," she said. "I haven't been able to sleep thinking about it. Tell me, how can I square myself?"

"By telling me the truth now," the lawyer told her.

"All right, I will. I gave Grieb and Duncan my I O U's for a gambling debt. Yesterday afternoon someone rang me up and told me that Sam Grieb was going to sell those I O U's to my husband. He said Frank was going to use them to keep me from getting my trust fund, and as evidence that I wasn't a proper person to have custody of our child, and couldn't be trusted to handle the monies she'd receive under her trust."

"What did you do?" Mason asked.

"I went right out to the ship, of course. I wanted to see if I couldn't do something about it."

"Did you have any money?"

"About two thousand dollars. That was all I'd been able to raise. I thought perhaps I could pay that as a cash bonus and get them to wait for the rest of it."

"Go ahead," Mason told her.

"I went aboard the ship," she said, "and went down to Grieb's office. There was no one in the reception room. The door to the private office wasn't closed. Before, whenever I called on Grieb, he'd hear the electric buzzer and push back the peephole in the door to see who it was."

"Had you ever found the door unlocked or open on any of your prior visits?" Mason asked.

"No. It was always locked and barred."

"What did you do this time?"

"I stood in front of the door for several seconds, waiting for Grieb to come. When he didn't come, I tapped on the door and called, 'Yoo-hoo. Anyone home?' or something like that. Then, after a moment, I said, 'This is Sylvia Oxman. May I come in?'"

"What happened?" Mason asked, studying her intently over the tip of his cigarette.

"Nothing. No one came to the door so I pushed it open and . . . There he was."

"You mean he was dead then?"

"Yes. Just like you found him."

"What did you do?"

"At first," she said, "I started to run. Then I realized that the papers on the desk might be my I O U's. I'd just caught a glimpse of them as I pushed the door open. But you know how something like that impresses itself on your mind. It was just as though the whole scene had been etched on my consciousness."

"Go ahead," Mason told her.

"I tiptoed over to the desk," she said. "I didn't want to touch the papers unless they were my I O U's, so I leaned across the desk to look down at them. I found they were my notes, and was just reaching for them when you came down the corridor. That rang the electric signal and threw me into a panic. At first I started to grab the I O U's, hide them and claim I'd paid cash for them be-

144

fore Grieb was murdered, but I realized there *might* not be seventy-five hundred dollars in the safe. So I decided to dash out in the other room, leave the door partially open, as I'd found it, and wait to see who was coming. Then, later on, I might be able to get rid of whoever it was and get the notes. So I ran back to the office, carefully pulled the door so it lacked about an inch of being closed, went over and sat down. I picked up a movie magazine and pretended to read."

"Then what?" Mason asked.

"Then after a while you came in," she said.

Mason scowled at her and said, "Are you telling me the truth, Sylvia?"

She nodded.

"Why didn't you want me to search your handbag?" he asked abruptly.

She met his eyes steadily and frankly, "Because I had a gun in that bag."

"What did you do with it?"

"I went up on deck and tossed it overboard. I didn't dare to let anyone know I had that gun."

"What sort of gun was it?" the lawyer asked.

"A .32 Smith and Wesson Special."

Mason studied her through half-closed eyes and said abruptly, "Sylvia, you're lying."

She straightened in her chair. Her face flushed under the make-up, then grew white. "Don't you *dare* accuse me of lying, Perry Mason," she said.

The lawyer made a casual gesture with the hand which held his cigarette, "All right, then," he said, "I'll point out to you the places where your story doesn't hang together."

"Go ahead," she challenged.

"In the first place, I was walking rather rapidly when I came down the corridor which leads to the office. That section of flooring which is wired to the office is within thirty feet of the door. I covered that thirty feet within six seconds. The things you've *said* that you did would have taken a lot more time than that."

"But it *was* a long time," she insisted. "You didn't open that office door for two or three minutes after the signal sounded. You must have been standing by the door or something."

Mason shook his head. "It wasn't more than six seconds at the most."

"I know better," she told him. "I heard the sound of the buzzer. That frightened me. At first I was so scared I couldn't do anything. I just stood there, leaning over the desk. Then I straightened, faced the door and waited. When nothing happened, I decided I might be able to sneak out into the other office. I didn't waste any time doing it, but I took pains to adjust the door rather carefully. Then I went over, sat down, picked up a magazine and pretended I was reading. It was quite a while after that when you opened the door. It might have been two or three minutes."

"You were excited," he told her, watching her closely. "Your judgment of time . . ."

"Forget my judgment of time," she interrupted. "The fact remains you didn't come right down that corridor as you claim. You paused for a minute or two outside the door."

Mason shook his head.

Her mouth was obstinate. "I *heard* the signal," she insisted.

"Wait a minute," Mason said, "is there any chance someone could have been hiding somewhere in that outer office? Then he could have slipped out when you went into the private office, and the signal you heard . . ."

"Not a chance," she interrupted.

"You're sure?"

"Yes."

"All right, we'll pass that up for the moment. You say you had a gun in your bag?"

"Yes, that's why I didn't dare to let you touch it."

"And you went on deck and threw the gun overboard?"

"Yes."

"But you didn't kill Grieb?"

"*I* kill Grieb? Of course not."

"Then *why* did you throw the gun overboard?"

"Because I'd been in that room, and Grieb had been shot. I didn't want to have people think I'd done it."

"Don't you know," he said, "that a gun leaves distinctive marks on every bullet which goes through the barrel? Don't you know that the experts can tell absolutely what gun fired a fatal bullet?"

"I've heard something like that," she admitted. "But I'd been in a room where a man had been murdered. I thought the safest thing to do was to get rid of my gun. So I got rid of it."

"And in doing that, put it forever out of my power to show that your gun did *not* kill Grieb," Mason said.

"No one needs to know I had a gun."

"How long had you been carrying it?"

"Some little time. I'd been doing quite a bit of gambling. Sometimes I won and sometimes I lost. I carried considerable cash with me on occasion and I didn't want to be held up."

Mason smoked for a few moments in thoughtful silence, then said, "That story doesn't hang together. It doesn't fit in with the other facts. No jury on earth would ever believe it. But years of practicing law have taught me to put more reliance in my judgment of character than in my ability to correlate events. Looking at you when you talk, I feel you're telling the truth. I'm going to stick with you, Sylvia; but God help you if you ever have to tell *that* story to a jury."

"But I won't have to," she said. "No one knows I was in there . . . except you."

He shook his head, watched the smoke eddy upward

from the tip of his cigarette, and said, "In addition to Belgrade's sell-out, there's another hurdle. You left fingerprints, Sylvia."

"Where?"

"On the desk. When you put your left hand on the glass top and leaned over to look at the I O U's, you left a perfect print of your palm and fingers."

She frowned. "Couldn't you claim that had been done earlier in the day?"

"No. They know better, Sylvia. There were no other prints on top of that hand print. It wasn't even smudged."

"All right," she said, "I'll take my medicine if I have to. But don't think you'll ever get me to go on the witness stand and tell a story which isn't the truth. I'll tell the truth if it kills me."

"It probably will," Mason said grimly. . . . "Why did you run out on me, Sylvia?"

"I told you why. Because I'd learned my husband was aboard."

"How did you learn it?"

"A man told me."

"Who was this man?"

"I don't know."

"Had you ever seen him before?"

"Not before that night, but I'd seen him two or three times during the evening. I . . ."

"Go on," he urged, as her voice trailed away into silence.

"I have an idea he may have been following me."

"What did he say to you?"

"He said, 'Beat it, Sylvia, your husband's aboard,' or something like that. I remember he used the words, 'Beat it.' "

"When did he tell you that?"

"Just as I stepped out on deck."

"Could you describe him?"

"Yes. He wore a blue serge suit, black shoes with thick soles, a blue-and-black striped tie with an opal tie pin. He was about fifty years old, with thick, black hair, and a stubby black mustache. He wasn't particularly tall, but he was quite heavy."

"Had you spoken to him during the evening?"

"No."

"And you thought he might be following you?"

"Well, you understand how it is with an unattached woman on a gambling ship. People look her over. Some of the more persistent hang around."

"In other words, you thought this man was a masher?"

"Yes."

"Do you still think so?"

"I don't know."

"He evidently knew your husband."

She nodded.

"And for some reason warned you that your husband was aboard."

Again she nodded.

"Did *you* see your husband?"

"No."

Mason ground out the stub of his cigarette in the ash tray, doubled up his knees, leaned forward, placed his elbows on them, interlaced his fingers, and stared thoughtfully at the carpet. "This didn't look so hot when I started in, Sylvia," he said, "and it keeps getting worse as we go along."

"Well, I can't help it. I've told you the truth, and . . ."

She broke off as a newsboy delivered an armload of papers to the bellboy. As the bellboy stacked the papers on the glass top of the cigar stand, Mason, glancing at Sylvia Oxman's face, saw her eyes widen.

"What is it?" he asked, without taking his eyes from her face.

"Those newspapers."

"What newspapers?"

"The ones the boy just brought in."

"What about them?"

"Look at the headlines. . . . No, he's turned the papers down now so you can't see the headlines. . . . Here, boy . . ."

"Wait a minute," Mason interrupted. "You sit tight. *I'll* stroll by and pick up a couple of papers."

He sauntered over to the cigar stand, bought a package of cigarettes, and then, as an afterthought, bought two of the noon editions. Huge headlines across the front page read:

OXMAN ACCUSES WIFE IN GAMBLING SHIP MURDER

Down below appeared in smaller headlines:

PROMINENT ATTORNEY SHIELDING WIFE, BROKER CLAIMS.

Mason tucked the papers under his arm, crossed over to where Sylvia Oxman was waiting, sat down beside her and said, "This looks bad, Sylvia. I think it's a jolt you're going to have to take right on the chin. Don't show any emotion. Someone *may* be watching us. Read it as though you were only casually interested."

The cold tips of her fingers brushed across the back of his hand as she took one of the papers, nodded, and settled back in the chair. Mason hitched his chair around so the light came over his shoulder, and read:

"In a surprise statement made to police today, Frank Oxman, well-known broker and popular clubman, disclosed evidence which police claim completely solves the mysterious murder of Sam Grieb, proprietor of the gambling ship, *The Horn of Plenty*.

"Prior to Oxman's statement, the case had presented some of the most spectacular and mystifying angles ever encountered by local police. While there is a technical question of legal jurisdiction, because, at the time of the murder, the gambling ship was anchored beyond the twelve-mile limit, both local police and the sheriff's office are co-operating with the federal authorities in an attempt to solve the murder. The federal authorities, following their usual procedure, refused to comment, other than to state they were making progress. It was, however, learned from a source high in police circles that the case is now completely solved. It only remains to dispose of incidental matters, including among others, the part played by a well-known criminal attorney whose recent spectacular successes have made his name a family byword.

"The authorities were frantically running down numerous clues in the most mystifying murder of the year, when Frank Oxman's surprise statement, released through Worsham & Weaver, his attorneys, came with the force of a bombshell. Its repercussions will undoubtedly involve at least one well-known lawyer, and may drag a wealthy, white-haired great-grandmother into the toils of the law. This woman was at one time supposed to have committed suicide. In the light of Oxman's statement, police are now inclined to scout the suicide theory.

"While the broker's statement was given secretly by his attorneys to the authorities, it is understood the police may shortly make the statement public. In the meantime, while Worsham & Weaver refused to discuss any matters contained in the statement, they did admit such a statement had been prepared in their offices and submitted to the federal investigators. The attorneys refused to divulge the location of their client, but Oxman was run to earth by an Associated Press reporter, and admitted he had disclosed facts involving his wife in the murder.

"Evidently in the grip of strong emotion, he admitted

that he and his wife had been estranged for some weeks. A mutual love for their child had, according to the broker, been instrumental in delaying the institution of legal action seeking to dissolve the marriage.

"In short broken sentences, Oxman, pacing the floor of a downtown-hotel bedroom, told a story so filled with drama, so startling in its implications, as to rival any situation ever created in the field of mystery fiction.

" 'My wife and I had been separated for several weeks,' he said. 'I didn't know whether she intended to file a divorce complaint, but presumed she did. I was waiting for her to take the initiative. Then, by chance, I learned that not only had she lost all of her available cash, but had given demand I O U's to a firm of gamblers.

" 'I had, of course, known she made trips to Ensenada and Reno. I knew that she liked to gamble, but had supposed she did it only as an amusement. I had no idea she was jeopardizing her future as well as that of our child, by plunging wildly at the tables.

" 'Immediately upon learning the true situation, I tried, without success, to get in touch with my wife. Twice during the day the gamblers advised me that, unless these I O U's were taken up before midnight, they were going to collect by legal proceedings. I saw no reason why I should take up my wife's gambling debts; but I wanted to spare our daughter the publicity which I knew would result if suit were filed.

" 'So I raised the amount of the I O U's in cash and took the money out to the gambling ship. It was exactly seventy-five hundred dollars. I don't know at just what time I reached the vessel, but it was during the early evening. I asked an attendant to direct me to the offices, and was sent down an L-shaped passageway to an entrance room, and told to knock upon a heavy wooden door. I did so, and a wicket shot back. A man asked me what I wanted. At the time, I didn't know this was Mr. Grieb as I had never seen him before.

" 'I told him who I was. He said he was Grieb. He opened the door, let me come into the private office, and closed the door behind me. He explained he had to keep this door locked because the ship was on the high seas and beyond police protection and they kept a lot of money aboard.

" 'I found Grieb affable but businesslike. He was, he explained, not in the banking business. He claimed my wife had given the I O U's with the positive assurance they would be taken up within forty-eight hours. Grieb said he didn't intend to be left, as he expressed it, "holding the sack." He said unless the I O U's were taken up immediately, he was going to commence proceedings to subordinate the trust fund to the lien of his notes.

" 'I pointed out to him that he couldn't do that. The I O U's were given for a gambling debt. No court would subject a trust fund to any such lien. Grieb knew that I was prepared to take up the I O U's rather than have any publicity. While he didn't say so in so many words, he intimated that publicity was his chief weapon. I had to pay, and he knew it. I paid him seventy-five hundred dollars in cash and received in return three I O U's signed by my wife. I naturally expected eventually to collect these from her. I have a good brokerage business, but I'm not wealthy, and my entire assets are small as compared with the large amount of money which will be coming to my wife within a few months. I wanted to spare our child the publicity incident to a suit such as Grieb might have filed; but I certainly didn't intend to stretch my credit to pay for my wife's gambling.

" 'I put the I O U's in my wallet and left the gambling ship, refusing an invitation from Mr. Grieb to be shown around the ship. Mr. Grieb was obdurate insofar as the business transaction was concerned, but was very affable once it had been concluded.

" 'I left his offices, went into the bar, and had a couple of drinks. I went to the dining room and had a steak sandwich. I started to leave the ship, and then remembered that Grieb had given me no receipt and had made no written assignment of the I O U's. Under ordinary circumstances this wouldn't have been necessary, but my relationship to Sylvia, coupled with the fact that these I O U's were demand notes upon printed forms, convinced me I should have a written assignment. I'd had to borrow some money to get the necessary cash and I wanted to have everything done properly. I walked down the L-shaped passageway which led to Grieb's offices, paused while I took the I O U's from my wallet. Then I pushed open the door to the reception office. As I did so, I noticed that the door of the inner office was standing wide open.

" 'I was surprised at this, because Grieb had explained to me this door was always kept closed and locked.

" 'I tiptoed across the outer office, being afraid that I might perhaps be interrupting a business conference. What I saw left me utterly speechless.

" 'My wife was standing in the inner office, an automatic in her right hand. I saw Grieb slumped over the desk, his head and shoulder resting on the corner of the desk. There was a gaping wound in the left-hand side of his head, and blood was trickling from this wound.

" 'For a moment I was at a complete loss. I wasn't certain but what my wife might turn the gun on me. So I stepped back into the outer office, then walked rapidly down the corridor, intending to wait for Sylvia to come out, then ask her what she had done, and demand that she surrender to the police. I was badly shaken by what I had seen.

" 'I was standing near the entrance to the offices when I saw a tall, athletic-looking man with broad shoulders start for the offices. I couldn't place this man at first, but within a second or two I identified him as Perry Mason,

154

the noted attorney. Mr. Mason had been pointed out to me once at a banquet, and he is not one to be readily forgotten.

" 'I knew then that he must inevitably stumble upon a scene such as I had encountered. I was, therefore, content to leave the responsibility on the lawyer's shoulders. So I went at once to the deck, where I waited for a few minutes, trying to compose myself, and wondering what I should do. I remembered reading somewhere that a husband couldn't testify against his wife in court, but I wasn't certain whether my failure to report what I'd seen would make me a legal accessory to the murder.

" 'I decided to go ashore and see a lawyer.

" 'The only lawyer I trusted was Mr. P. C. Worsham, of Worsham & Weaver. Mr. Worsham has handled all my legal business, and knows Sylvia and knows me. I tried to reach him by telephone, but didn't actually talk with him until nearly daylight this morning. He went to his office at once and I told him exactly what I had seen. He insisted I should prepare a written statement. He said I owed it to myself and to the authorities to report what I had seen. Under his direction I prepared such a statement.

" 'I don't know what happened after Perry Mason went into those offices. But I do know he walked down that corridor leading to the offices, while my wife was there. I didn't see either my wife or Perry Mason come out. I didn't wait for that. I went to the deck of the ship, and remained there for several minutes, trying to clarify my thoughts. I don't know exactly how long I was on deck. Unfortunately, I didn't think to look at my watch. I was completely unnerved.'

"Oxman refused to state whether he retained a copy of the written statement he had prepared at the suggestion of his attorneys and which has, it is understood, been submitted to the federal authorities. He was in a highly nervous condition when interviewed. The three I O U's which he had redeemed were in his possession and he produced these readily enough.

"It was learned that police have accepted Oxman's statement at its face value, as it is supported by an array of corroborating facts. Oxman was questioned, and released upon his assurance that he would appear before the Federal Grand Jury late this afternoon."

(Continued on page three.)

Mason turned the newspaper to page three, and saw facsimiles of three I O U's bearing the signature of Sylvia Oxman. There were also photographs of the gambling ship, a picture of Sylvia Oxman, and one of Frank Oxman. Various articles rehashed the front-page story from different angles: . . . sob-sister had written about the plight of a husband who must testify against the woman who has borne him a child; another article took up the Matilda Benson disappearance. Glancing hastily through it, Mason saw there was conjecture as to whether Sylvia Oxman's grandmother had learned of Sylvia's connection with the crime and committed suicide, or if, perhaps, she had been an accomplice whose disappearance was connected with that of Sylvia Oxman. Some prominence was given to the statement of an eye-witness who claimed to have seen Perry Mason and a woman who answered the description of Matilda Benson talking earnestly in the bar of the gambling ship shortly before the arrival of the officers. The witness was positive that this was after the murder had been discovered, because he had tried to leave the ship. The crew were making repairs to the landing-stage, repairs which were admittedly unnecessary, and which had been ordered following the discovery of the murder, as a subterfuge to keep patrons aboard the ship until the officers could arrive.

Mason looked across at Sylvia Oxman. "How much of that," he asked, "is the truth?"

"None of it," she said. "He *didn't* see me in that office. He's lying."

"And he didn't see you with the gun?"

"Of course not. That's Frank Oxman for you. You can't trust him for a minute. He'll stab you in the back whenever he has an opportunity. He wanted to divorce me. . . . Sending me to prison on a murder charge would suit his purpose just that much better."

Mason indicated the facsimiles of the I O U's. "Where did he get those, Sylvia?" he asked.

"Why," she said, "he must have picked them up from Sam Grieb's desk . . . unless . . . unless he got them through you in some way."

Mason pulled another cigarette from his cigarette case, tapped it on his thumb, and said, "Sylvia, I paid off those I O U's."

"You did what?"

"Paid them off."

"But you couldn't have. They were there when . . ."

"I know," he told her. "I burned them before Duncan came in."

"But isn't that illegal?" she asked. "Couldn't they . . . ?"

"No," Mason said. "I paid them off. Acting as an attorney who had been retained to represent your interests, I found those I O U's and paid them."

"But couldn't they make trouble for you over that?" she asked.

"They could make trouble for me," he admitted, "over lots of things I do. That doesn't keep me from doing what I think is right. And when I'm doing something which furthers the ultimate ends of justice, I think it's right. Take another look at those I O U's, Sylvia."

She studied the facsimiles carefully, then leaned forward to stare more intently at the paper. "Why," she said, "they're forgeries!"

"Good forgeries?" Mason asked.

"Yes, they look exactly like my signature. I know that

they're forgeries, however, because I remember that I didn't have my own fountain pen with me when I signed the first of those I O U's. I had to use a pen Grieb gave me, and it wasn't suited to my style of writing. The pen point ran through the paper at one place and made a blot. I thought perhaps I'd better make a new note, but Grieb said that one would be all right. I remember it particularly, because I noticed that blot on the signature last night when I saw the notes on Grieb's desk."

Mason said, "Come to think of it, I noticed it myself. Well, that's that." He smoked in thoughtful silence for several minutes while Sylvia finished reading the newspaper account of Oxman's accusation and the current developments in the case.

Sylvia Oxman folded the paper and said indignantly, "It makes me sick! Of all the lies . . ."

Mason interrupted her to say, "Wait a minute, Sylvia. I think I can tell you what happened."

"What?" she asked.

"There's some chance," he told her, "that Frank actually did see you in that office."

"I tell you it's a lie! He's just . . ."

"Hold everything," Mason warned. "Don't jump at conclusions. The evidence of the man who was shadowing you is that Frank Oxman went down the corridor to the offices while you were still in the offices. He was only gone a minute or so, then turned around and came out. Now then, let's suppose, just for the sake of the argument, that while you were sitting in the outer office, you couldn't have heard the electric buzzer in the inner office. Now, let's suppose that Frank Oxman came down the passageway while you were *still in the outer office,* but just as you were about to push open the door to the inner office. You, therefore, wouldn't have heard the buzzer which announced his *coming* down the corridor. His statement says he hesitated for some little time in front of the door to the outer office. Let's suppose, for the sake of the argument, that he did.

"Then he opened the door, walked in, saw you leaning over the desk, and saw Grieb's body. He was at first frightened, then recognized the wonderful opportunity he'd have to pin a murder charge on you. He felt, of course, that you'd take and destroy the I O U's which were lying in plain sight on Sam Grieb's desk. Having done that, he felt that you were completely in his power. So he retraced his steps back down the corridor. As he went over that wired section of floor, you heard the signal, because you were then in the *inner* office. You thought it was someone *coming,* so you went back to the outer office, picked up the magazine and sat reading. A few minutes later, I came down the corridor, but you couldn't hear the electric signal then, because you were in the *outer* office. That would tie everything together. What you heard when you were in the inner office wasn't the signal of my *approach,* but the signal made by Frank Oxman as he *left.*"

There was dismay in her eyes. "You make it sound so d-d-damn logical," she said. "I could almost hate you for it."

"Keep cool," Mason told her, "and don't cry."

"I'm not crying," she said in a harsh, strained voice.

Mason flipped ashes from his cigarette and said, "Okay, Sylvia, I think I know what to do."

"What?"

"I had to destroy those I O U's," he said, "because I didn't want them found on the scene of the crime, and I certainly didn't want them found on *me.* But you're the only one who knows I destroyed them. Now then, I'm going to step into a stationery store and get a book of blank notes. I can find exactly the same form which Grieb and Duncan kept aboard the ship. Then, using these facsimiles to go by, we'll make duplicate I O U's, duly signed and dated."

"But won't that put my head right back in the noose?" she asked.

"It will if we make them public," he said, "but think of the spot it's going to put Frank Oxman in if he thinks the *original* I O U's are in the hands of the district attorney. That will brand *his* I O U's as forgeries and his whole statement as a lie, fabricated out of whole cloth."

She nodded and said, "I see your point. Go get the blanks."

12

MASON CALLED Paul Drake from a pay station in an isolated side-street restaurant. "Hello, Paul," he said cautiously when he heard the detective's voice on the line. "What's new?"

Drake said, "Seen the papers?"

"Yes."

"How do you figure it?"

"I don't figure it yet. Where's Oxman?"

"He signed that written statement and was released. He went to his hotel. A couple of reporters nailed him there for an interview. Then he sneaked out the back way and went out to Hollywood. He's registered in the Christy Hotel in five-nineteen, under the name of Sydney French."

Mason gave a low whistle. "Think he knows his wife is there?"

"I don't see how he can."

"Then what's his idea?"

"I think he's trying to dodge reporters."

Mason said slowly, "I don't like it, Paul."

"Well, after all," the detective said, "it's a reasonably

prominent hotel. It may be just a coincidence they both picked it."

Mason thought for a moment, then said, "Hardly a coincidence, Paul, but it may be that the hotel has associations for them or they may have used it before when they wanted to hide out. . . . Tell me, Paul, what's the latest on Belgrade?"

Drake's voice was bitter. "If I told you what I think of that snake it'd melt the telephone wire."

"Never mind what you *think* of him, what's he *doing*, Paul?"

"Hell, I don't know, Perry. I haven't kept tabs on *him*. They served him with a subpœna to appear before the Federal Grand Jury this afternoon. They also served one on me and they're trying their damnedest to serve one on you. One of the newspapers was trying to keep Belgrade sewed up, but after the subpœna was served it was no dice."

"Where did he spend the night, Paul?"

"How the devil should I know? . . . Who cares where he spent the night?"

"I do."

"Why?"

"Because," Mason said, "he's going to be wanting some clean clothes, a bath, a shirt, socks, change of underwear, and, if he's going before the Federal Grand Jury and have his picture taken for the newspapers, he'll probably want to put on his best suit."

"So what?"

"So," Mason went on, "I thought perhaps we could drop around to his house and find him there."

"Now listen, Perry, if we go around there and start making a beef, it won't do us a damn bit of good and the first thing *he'll* do will be to get on the line and tell the detectives where they can find you. I feel the same way you do about him, but . . ."

"Forget it," Mason interrupted. "I'm working on an entirely different theory. What does he look like, Paul?"

"You mean a physical description?"

"Yes."

"He's around fifty, weighs about a hundred and ninety pounds, is five feet six-and-a-half inches, wears a short mustache, and has a little scar on the top of his right ear where a bullet nicked him, and . . ."

"What kind of a suit was he wearing?"

"He wears a blue serge suit when he's on duty," Drake said. "Figures it's less conspicuous and blends well in the dark. Most of the men who do shadow work wear dark clothes."

"What's his residence address, Paul?"

"A little bungalow just off Washington Boulevard on Fifth Avenue. It's pretty well out."

"How far from Washington?"

"Only a couple of blocks, as I remember the place. I drove out to see him two or three days ago."

"Tell you what you do, Paul," Mason said. "Climb in your car and meet me out at the corner of Fifth Avenue and Washington. I'm in Hollywood, driving a rented car. We should get there just about the same time."

"Now wait a minute, Perry. You're in bad enough on this thing already. For God's sake, don't go messing around . . ."

"Better start right now," Mason said, and hung up the receiver.

The lawyer beat Paul Drake to the rendezvous by more than five minutes. Drake drove up, parked his car, and came across to the lawyer and renewed his protestations. "I don't think this is going to get us anywhere, Perry," he said.

"Well," Mason told him, "I want you to know more about Belgrade. He's the only one of your men who was on the ship when the murder was discovered. I'm particularly anxious to know whether his report of what happened out there is accurate."

"He's a double-crosser, or he'd never have betrayed you," Drake commented bitterly. "I'll see he never gets another detective-agency job as long as he lives."

"Forget it," the lawyer told him. "It was a chance for a clean-up and he fell for it. Aside from that one slip, he may be okay."

They walked in silence for a block, then Drake said, "There's the house over there, the one which sits back from the street."

"Does his wife know you?"

"Yes."

"But she doesn't know me?"

"I don't think so. Not unless she's seen your picture somewhere."

Mason said, "That'll be swell. Now, what I want to do is to get into that house, so don't make any explanations, don't perform any introductions. When his wife comes to the door, put on an act and we both go in, see?"

"Maybe we both go *out*," Drake said.

"What sort of woman is she?"

"A blonde. She does things with her eyes."

"Think she's on the up-and-up?"

"Not this baby. I've seen her only once, but I wouldn't trust her around the block. She has one of those baby stares veneered on a face that's hard as cement, if you know what I mean."

"I know what you mean," Mason told him. "The last time I saw an expression like that was on the face of a nineteen-year-old blackmailer." He chuckled and added, "While she was waiting in the outer office, I asked Della Street what she looked like, and Della said she looked like a synthetic virgin."

"That's the type," Drake said. "Only this dame is in the late thirties."

"Okay," Mason told him, "let's barge in."

They turned from the sidewalk, walked up the narrow strip of cement to the porch stairs. Mason hung behind while Drake climbed the stairs first and rang the bell.

A few moments later a woman wearing a printed house dress opened the door and said with over-effusive cordiality, "Why, it's Mr. Drake! Why, *good morning*, Mr. Drake! How do you do? Did you want to see George?"

Drake said, "Yes," and stepped forward.

For a moment the woman's eyes became hard as blue quartz, but her full red lips maintained a fixed smile. "He isn't here," she said.

"I'm to meet him here," Drake told her, very apparently waiting for her to move.

"Oh, all right," she said sullenly, and stepped to one side. As Mason was walking past her, she said, "Won't you gentlemen come in and sit down? When was George to meet you here?"

Mason selected a comfortable chair, caught Drake's questioning glance, and asked, "When did *you* see him last, Mrs. Belgrade?"

She turned to face Mason, her eyes cautious, her face expressionless. "You're Mr. Mason, aren't you?"

"Yes."

"I thought so."

"When did you last see your husband?"

"Why?"

"I just wanted to know."

"Not since last night. He couldn't get home. He was detained."

"How was he dressed when you last saw him?" Mason asked.

"Why do you want to know?"

The lawyer indicated Paul Drake and said, "After all, he's working for Mr. Drake. He's been out on a case. We want to talk with him."

"You mean," she asked Paul Drake, "that he's still working for you?"

"Of course."

"He thought perhaps you'd feel sore at what you read in the papers and . . ."

Her voice trailed away into silence, and Drake said, "Of course I'm sore; but, after all, he's still working for me."

Mason inquired again, "How was he dressed, Mrs. Belgrade?"

"Why, he wore his business suit, his blue serge suit."

Mason said casually, "Well, we're all subpœnaed to appear before the Federal Grand Jury this afternoon. I thought it might be a good plan for us to have an informal chat before they ask us questions."

A look of relief came over the woman's face. "Oh," she said, *"that's* it. Well, I'm glad you men feel that way. George had a chance to make some big money giving a story to the newspaper. He'd have been a chump *not* to have done it. I can understand how you gentlemen feel; but you must make allowances for a man who's working on wages. Both of *you* make big money. George doesn't. Lots of times we have to struggle along to make both ends meet."

Mason nodded. "Yes, I know how he must have felt. Too bad he got gypped."

She said bitterly. "That subpœna certainly put George on the skids. He was in a position to sell some follow-ups to the newspaper. Then this subpœna was served, and the newspaper wouldn't have anything more to do with him. They figure whatever he says now is going to become public property."

Mason nodded, said, "Uh-huh," looked at his watch, asked, "How soon were you expecting him?"

"He telephoned me about an hour ago and said he'd be home in an hour. I'm expecting him any minute. He wanted to change his clothes."

Drake looked at his wristwatch, then glanced across at Mason. Mrs. Belgrade said nervously, "I think he'll be here any minute now. . . . That sounds like his car." The worn rivets on brake linings squeaked against drums as a dilapidated car swung wide in the street and turned into the driveway.

"There he is," Mrs. Belgrade said. Mason nodded, walked to the door.

Steps sounded on the porch. Mason pulled the door open and said to the heavy-set individual who was pounding his way across the porch, "Welcome home, George. Come in and join the party."

Belgrade came to a dead stop. Paul Drake appeared in the doorway beside Mason and said, "Well, don't stand there gawking. Come on in."

Belgrade slowly walked toward the door, his eyes glancing about him apprehensively as though he were seeking some means of escape.

"I'd feel the same way myself if I'd sold out a client," Paul Drake said.

"Skip it, Paul," Mason cautioned.

Belgrade, avoiding their eyes, entered the house. His wife came running across, flung her arms about him, and clung to him for several seconds.

Drake coughed, and they separated.

Belgrade said, "I'm sorry about this whole business, Mr. Mason. I owe you an apology. I know how you fellows must feel. You think I'm a two-time, chiseling crook."

Mason said, "Suppose we sit down and talk things over for a while, George. I've practiced law long enough to know that people are only human, after all."

Belgrade glanced across at his wife. "You got my things all ready, Flo?" he asked.

She nodded.

"Sit down, George," Drake said.

Belgrade kept his eyes fixed on his wife. "How about mixing up some Scotch and soda, Flo? Perhaps the gentlemen would like . . ."

"Would like nothing better than to have Mrs. Belgrade stay right here in the room," Mason said, grinning.

Belgrade looked puzzled.

"She might want to telephone a friend," Drake explained.

"Oh," Belgrade said.

When they were all seated, Belgrade looked across at Drake. "So I'm all washed up in the detective business, am I?" he asked.

"That depends," Mason told him, before Drake could answer. "We want you to tell us just how you happened to sell out, George. Perhaps it won't look so bad after we hear your side of it."

Belgrade turned to him. *"You're* certainly taking this mighty fine, Mr. Mason. You make me feel like an awful heel. I don't know as I can explain it, but I'd like to have you gentlemen understand my position. I haven't been working steady, and I have a wife to support, a house to keep up, and all sorts of expenses.

"Well, I went out on that gambling ship and walked right into the middle of a murder case. It's the first time I've ever stacked up against anything quite like it in all the time I've been working as an operative. I was tailing Sylvia Oxman, you'll remember, and when I'd followed her back to the wharf, Staples stepped up and said he'd been instructed to relieve me. That left me standing there, all washed up for the evening. I telephoned in my report, and Drake said that'd be all. I knew Drake was working for you, Mr. Mason, and I knew you were still out aboard the ship, so I thought I might do you a good turn by going back to the ship and seeing if I could help you."

Drake said, "Wait a minute, Belgrade. Do I understand you went *back* to the ship?"

Belgrade nodded. "That's right."

"Why?"

"I told you why. I wanted to see if I could help Mr. Mason."

Drake said, "Why the devil didn't you go on home after I told you you were through for the night?"

"Well," Belgrade explained, shifting uncomfortably in his chair, ". . . well, to tell you the truth, Mr. Drake, I may as well come clean. I knew that Mr. Mason kept you busy most of the time. I didn't think I stood very high with you. There were too many men ahead of me who copped off all the important jobs. You remember, you'd given *me* the job of tailing Sylvia Oxman's maid. The only reason I got into the big-time stuff was because the maid went to Sylvia. And as soon as I contacted Sylvia, you yanked me off the case and put Staples on. Well, I figured that I might be able to make a good impression with Mr. Mason and then perhaps he'd speak to you about keeping me on his work regularly. Then I'd get the important jobs."

Drake said, "If that's the case, how did it happen you . . ."

"Wait a minute," Mason interrupted, without taking his eyes from Belgrade's face, "let me handle this, Paul."

Drake started to say something, then checked himself, and settled back in his chair.

"Then what happened?" Mason asked.

"Well," Belgrade said, "by the time the speed boat got back to the ship, the landing-stage had been pulled up and they told us they were making some repairs to it, that it would only be for a few minutes, and for us to stand by. We stuck around there for some little time, and then a launch came out with officers aboard, and we heard there'd been a murder. They told us to turn around and put back to the wharf, that no one could come aboard, and there'd be no more gambling.

"That started me thinking. I was doing a lot of thinking all the way back to the wharf. When we arrived, a bunch of newspaper men who'd been rushed down were questioning everyone who came off the speed boats. Now, one of the reporters knew me and knew what I did for a living. He started asking me questions, and found out from what I told him that I could give him a story if I wanted to, so he took me in and telephoned his city editor and the city editor sent another man down to cover the story on the boat and had my friend take me into Los Angeles.

"They made me a proposition and it just meant so much to me I couldn't afford to turn it down. I didn't figure it made any great amount of difference to you fellows. They told me that Mr. Mason was aboard and had been arrested; that the whole story was bound to come out within the next twenty-four hours, but they wanted an exclusive on it. They said I didn't have anything to gain by keeping quiet, and that I was going to lose a lot of money if I didn't tell them. It sounded reasonable to me, so I told them what I knew. Then the editor got the idea he could string it out for a couple of follow-ups and wanted to keep me sewed up where no one could get at me. But one of the other reporters had seen what happened, and somehow the Federal District Attorney got tipped off to where I was. The newspaper tried to keep me under cover, and the United States Marshal's office kept trying to serve a subpœna. The marshal's office won out, and just as soon as they served that subpœna on me, the newspaper dropped me like a hot potato. They figured I couldn't be any good to them any more. I got a piece of change for the first story and that's all."

"How about that report you telephoned me?" Drake asked.

"What do you mean, how about it?" Belgrade asked.

"I want to know whether it was accurate."

Belgrade flushed. "Of course it was accurate. I told you the absolute truth. Just because I saw an opportunity to make a piece of change on the side without hurting anyone, doesn't mean that I'm a crook."

"Have you," Mason asked, "reported *everything* which happened out on the gambling ship?"

"Why, yes, of course—that is, I reported it to Mr. Drake over the telephone."

"You followed Sylvia Oxman out to the ship?"

"Yes."

"Now, how long was she aboard before she went down to the offices?"

"Not very long. I didn't keep an accurate count of the minutes. She went in and had a drink, checked her coat, and then went down to the offices."

"How long after that before I showed up?"

"I'd say about eight or ten minutes, but remember, Mr. Mason, before *you* showed up, Frank Oxman was prowling around there."

"How did you know . . ." Drake began, but was silenced by a warning glance from the lawyer.

"Then, after Oxman had left, I entered. Is that right?" Mason asked.

"That's right. Then, after you'd been in there for a while, Sylvia Oxman came out. Then Duncan and this deputy marshal dashed in there. Then in about ten minutes the marshal brought you out and you were handcuffed."

"Now, let's get this straight," Mason interposed. "Sylvia had already left the offices?"

"That's right."

"And you were supposed to be shadowing her?"

"Yes, sir, I was."

"But after she went out, you still continued to keep an eye on the offices. Now which were you doing, watching the offices or shadowing Sylvia?"

"Both, Mr. Mason. Mrs. Oxman had taken a seat at one of the crap tables. I stood where I could watch her and the entrance to the offices at the same time."

"All right, go on—tell me what else you saw."

"Well, Duncan came out, and then Mrs. Oxman went up on deck. I followed her up there."

"How long after you saw me leaving the offices was it that Duncan came out?"

"Three or four minutes—not very long."

"How long after that did Sylvia go up on deck?"

"Almost immediately, Mr. Mason."

"Then what?"

"That's all. I followed Mrs. Oxman ashore, and then Staples told me to check out . . ."

"Now, wait a minute," Mason interrupted. "Have you told us absolutely *everything* that happened, Belgrade?"

"Why, yes, as nearly as I can remember it."

"Did you speak to Sylvia?"

Belgrade's face twisted with sudden expression. "Yes, that's right. I did tell Sylvia to beat it because her husband was aboard."

"Ah," Mason said. "Now we're getting somewhere. Just *why* did you tell Sylvia to beat it?"

Belgrade said, "I knew something was wrong. I didn't know what it was, but I could see that you were hand-cuffed when you came out of that office. Now, you're a big-time lawyer. No one's going to handcuff you unless something pretty serious has happened. I had an idea you were covering for Sylvia and that you'd want her off the ship, but I didn't know how to get her off. Then suddenly it occurred to me I could stick my head out the door and say, 'Your husband's aboard, beat it,' and then duck back out of sight, make a dash for the speed boat, and get myself aboard. I figured Sylvia would come rushing down from the deck and take that same speed boat. If she didn't, I could pretend I'd changed my mind and get off."

"And that's what you did?"

"Yes, sir. I ran down and got a seat in the speed boat and she followed within less than a minute."

"Now," Mason told him, "I'll ask a question Paul Drake was going to ask a minute ago. *How did you happen to know Sylvia Oxman's husband?*"

Belgrade twisted uneasily in his chair, glanced at his wife, then dropped his eyes to inspect the toes of his shoes.

"Go ahead," Mason told him. "You're in this thing pretty deep, George. Half-way measures won't get you out of it. You'll have to come clean."

Belgrade raised his eyes to Mason's. "I'd prefer not to answer that question, Mr. Mason."

"You'll have to."

"I'd be betraying a confidence someone had placed in me."

Drake's laugh was sarcastic. "You haven't shown any reticence about betraying confidences so far," he said.

"Shut up, Paul," Mason remarked, without taking his eyes from Belgrade's face. "What is it, George?"

"I worked for Frank Oxman," Belgrade blurted.

"When?"

"About a month ago."

"How long did you work for him?"

"A little over two weeks."

"How did you happen to work for him?"

"Oxman contacted an agency where I'd been doing some work," Belgrade said. "He was looking for an experienced operative. The agency took a cut and referred him to me.

"You understand how it is, Mr. Mason. Us detectives don't work steadily. We work by the job. For instance, you'll have a job for Drake's agency and Drake will hire ten or fifteen, or perhaps twenty of us boys who are registered with him. We're also registered with half a dozen other agencies. When we're not working for one agency we work for another. That enables us to work more or less steadily, but keeps the agencies from carrying a big pay-roll when they ain't busy."

"Then you register with various agencies in advance?" Mason asked.

"That's right."

"And you furnish references or something of that sort?"

"Oh, sure. We have to fill out a questionnaire, give references, tell all about our past employment, the amount of our experience, the type of work we're best adapted to, whether we can go out in evening clothes, whether we have a car of our own, and all that sort of stuff."

"Now, Frank Oxman wanted someone to shadow his wife?"

"Yes, sir."

"And you did the job?"

"Yes, sir."

"For how long?"

"Sixteen days, I think."

"What did you find out? Anything?" Mason asked.

Belgrade lowered his eyes. "I found out enough to sympathize with her," he said, "but sympathies don't put any butter on *my* bread. She's every inch a lady, but she's impulsive and she's out for a good time. A couple of times men picked her up on the gambling ship, and she played around a bit with them."

"What do you mean by playing around?"

"Nothing serious."

"You reported this to Frank Oxman?"

"Yes."

"Why didn't you tell *me* about this?" Drake asked.

"I never had a chance to," Belgrade said. "You told me you wanted me to do some work on a case Mr. Mason was interested in. You simply told me to go out to a certain address and shadow the maid who was working there. And you gave me a description. I recognized the address as that of Oxman's house, but I supposed you were working on the maid. *I* didn't know *you* were after Mrs. Oxman. Then, after a while, when I telephoned in a report that the maid was starting out with a fur coat, you told me to tail her and switch to Mrs. Oxman in case the maid contacted her. Even then, I supposed Mr. Mason was working for Frank Oxman and was getting ready to bring a divorce case or something. But, after we got on the ship, and I saw Mr. Mason apparently taking a rap for Mrs. Oxman, I knew he wasn't working for Oxman and figured there must be bigger game at stake."

"That's a hell of an explanation," Drake said skeptically.

"But it's the truth," Belgrade insisted.

"Did you know Oxman had gone ashore before his wife left the gambling ship?" Mason asked.

"No, sir, I didn't. I thought Oxman was still on the ship."

Drake said, "As far as I'm concerned, Belgrade, you're finished with detective work. You're altogether too damned loquacious for a detective."

"I'm sorry, Mr. Drake. I tried to give you a square deal."

Mrs. Belgrade's voice was bitter. "Don't give him anything, George. He pays you eight dollars a day and expenses, and expects you to give him your soul."

"Shut up, Flo," Belgrade said tonelessly.

"I won't either shut up. I think it's an outrage! You work day and night, take all sorts of chances, and are out in all kinds of weather, and what does it get you? The first time you . . ."

"You keep out of this, Flo," Belgrade said, raising his voice. "Don't you understand Mr. Drake can fix it so no other agency will ever employ me?"

"Well, what if he does? You got out of the detective business once, and you can get out of it again. There's lots of ways to make a living without working for a bunch of slave-drivers, who don't appreciate honesty when they see it."

"Did *you* see Sylvia Oxman toss a gun overboard?" Mason asked Belgrade, interrupting.

"No, sir, I didn't."

"Could she have done so without you seeing her?"

"I guess so. Yes. You see, I thought she'd taken a tumble to me. I wanted to get her off the gambling ship, and I wanted to be in the same speed boat she took; but I didn't want her to see me. I knew my only chance was to figure what speed boat she was going to take, and get aboard first. If I followed her down to the speed boat, I figured she might take a tumble. I just did the best I could, Mr. Mason."

Mason nodded to Drake and said, "I think that's all, Belgrade. Come on, Paul. Let's let Belgrade change his clothes."

"They've served you with a subpœna?" Belgrade asked Mason.

The lawyer avoided the question, saying easily as he started for the door: "You'll want to make a good impression with that Federal Grand Jury, George. I'm going to talk with Mr. Drake about you. The more I think things over, the more I realize you were placed in a very peculiar situation, one which wouldn't confront a detective once in ten years. I can understand just how you felt."

Drake's fingers closed about the lawyer's elbow. "Come on, Perry," he said.

"You're one swell guy, Mr. Mason," Belgrade said. "Do *you* forgive me, Mr. Drake?"

Mason said, "Don't press that question now, George. I'll have a chat with him and then we'll let you know the answer."

"Thanks a lot, Mr. Mason. I can't begin to tell you how much I appreciate the way you're taking this."

As the two men walked from the house, they could hear Florence Belgrade's voice rising in machine-gun rapidity. A door slammed shut, cutting off the sound. Drake remarked with feeling, "I wish you'd let me cut loose on that rat."

"No," Mason told him, "we can't afford to antagonize him now. He's important. He's going to be about the most important witness who'll appear before the Federal Grand

Jury. It might be a lot better to have him feeling friendly toward our side of the case, Paul. He's already received his money from the newspaper. Personally, I don't blame him too much. I know just how he felt. He'd been working on a salary, and suddenly had an opportunity to make a wad of dough by telling something to a newspaper that he thought wouldn't make any particular trouble for anyone."

Drake said, "I wish to hell I knew why you're so damned anxious to stick up for Belgrade."

"Because," Mason told him, "I make my living by dealing with people. Remember, Paul, if Belgrade was a man of outstanding ability, without *any* soft spots in his make-up, you couldn't hire him to work for you at eight dollars a day. You have to make allowances for people. Belgrade sold us out. That's admitted. He did it, not because he had anything against us, but because he needed the money. Now then, he's already received that money. He's facing the future. His ability to get work in the future depends a lot on placating you. If you let him feel, in advance, you're going to turn him down cold, he'll turn against you and be bitter. If you let him feel that you're holding his case under advisement, he'll do anything in the world to accommodate you. That means that when he gets in front of the Grand Jury he'll be trying to say what you want him to say—that is, as far as it's in accord with his recollection."

"Well," Drake admitted, "I see your point. But, as far as I'm concerned, he can go to hell. He sold us out."

The men walked to the corner in silence. Mason said, "Well, here are the cars, Paul. I guess I hadn't better stick around this neighborhood."

"Where are you going, Perry?"

"Oh, places," Mason said casually.

Drake stared steadily at him. "You're not going to the Christy Hotel, are you?"

"Why?"

"I have an idea you're figuring on calling on Frank Oxman."

"So what?"

"Don't do it," Drake said earnestly. "That man's dangerous, and you're already in one hell of a hot spot, Perry."

"It won't get any cooler if I stick around in that one spot," Mason told him.

"Well, lay off Frank Oxman. He's dangerous . . . Oh, by the way, Perry, I think we've found out who's backing him."

Mason, looking up and down the street to make certain there were no radio cars in sight, said, "All right, Paul. Give it to me fast."

"We're keeping a tail on Oxman, just as you instructed," Drake said, "and we find that he telephoned a man by the name of Carter C. Squires, at the Poindexter Hotel. Squires is the head of a gambling ring that dopes race horses, fixes prize fights, and bets on sure things. He spends most of his time in the lobby of the Poindexter and hanging around the bar. Incidentally, he has a police record somewhere, and he's crooked as a corkscrew, but he has money. He finances a lot of crooked schemes and takes a big cut. Oxman talked with Squires on the telephone. He seemed in an awful lather trying to get the call through."

"You couldn't get in on the conversation?" Mason asked.

"No, I couldn't. But Oxman was talking for almost ten minutes."

"That was after he went to the Christy Hotel?"

"Yes."

"Well," Mason said slowly, "I think I'll take a chance on Oxman, at that. . . . I have a little surprise for Oxman. . . . I want to see how he can take it. So far, he's only been dishing it out."

13

■

MASON ENTERED the lobby of the Christy Hotel, and paused to take mental inventory. Sylvia Oxman was nowhere in sight. Mason walked to the elevators, went to the fifth floor, walked rapidly down the corridor to Room 519, and tapped on the door. After a moment he heard motion, the sound of a bolt sliding back, and the door opened.

A thin, almost foppishly dressed man in a double-breasted gray suit stood on the threshold and surveyed Mason with hostile eyes.

Mason said simply, "I'm coming in, Oxman."

Oxman hesitated a moment, then stepped to one side, and held the door open. After Mason went in, he kicked the door shut and twisted the bolt.

"You left your hotel rather suddenly," Mason remarked affably.

Oxman indicated a chair with a well-manicured hand, on the third finger of which appeared a huge diamond. His hair, neatly waved back from his forehead, reflected glinting highlights from the window. His suit was spotless and freshly pressed, his shoes burnished to a resplendent shine. After Mason had seated himself, Oxman perched on the edge of the bed and propped pillows between his back and the wall. After a moment he said, "I wanted to dodge newspaper reporters."

"Any chance you wanted to dodge the police?" Mason asked.

A slight smile flirted about the corners of Oxman's mouth. "No," he said, "*I'm* not dodging the police."

Mason, staring steadily at him, said, "I'm Perry Mason, the lawyer."

"Yes, I knew who you were," Oxman said tonelessly. "*You* left *your* apartment rather suddenly, didn't you, Mason?"

Mason grinned. "Yes," he said, "I had business to attend to."

"Did you," Oxman inquired, "know the police were looking for you?"

Mason raised his eyebrows. "For me?"

"Yes."

"On what charge?"

"Murder," Oxman said. "Being an accessory after the fact is, I believe, the specific charge."

"Well," Mason told him, "it's fortunate I found you, then."

"Go on," Oxman told him, "spring it."

"I see by the paper," Mason said, "that you bought some I O U's from Grieb."

"What if I did?"

"And paid cash for them."

"Yes?"

"Cash which was found in the left-hand drawer of Grieb's desk."

"I believe so," Oxman agreed.

Mason slowly and impressively took from his pocket the three I O U's which Sylvia Oxman had signed that morning in the hotel. "Take a look at these, Oxman," he said.

Oxman moved forward on the bed. Mason, crossing his legs, held three I O U's pressed tightly against his leg so that Oxman could see the three signatures.

"So what?" Oxman asked.

"If these," Mason suggested, "are the *original* I O U's, where does that leave you, Oxman?"

Oxman yawned, patted his lips with four polite fingers,

and said, "Really, Mason, I'd have expected something far more clever from you."

"Has it ever occurred to you," Mason went on, "that if *I* hold those original I O U's, the ones you have are forgeries?"

"Oh, I don't think Sam Grieb would have sold me forged I O U's."

"We can prove in court that they're forgeries."

Oxman's tongue made clucking noises against the roof of his mouth. "Grieb shouldn't have sold me forgeries," he said. "That wasn't a nice thing for Grieb to have done. Of course, if they *are* forgeries, which remains to be proven, I can then recover the seventy-five hundred dollars from Grieb's estate. So you see, Mason, I personally have nothing to lose. Until you prove they're forgeries, I can collect on them as genuine. *If* you can prove they *are* forgeries, then, on the strength of the proof *you've* made, I can recover from Grieb's estate."

"So that's the way you figure it, is it?" Mason asked.

Oxman nodded.

"You've thought this all out in advance as an argument to use in case you were confronted with the original I O U's," the lawyer charged.

Oxman gestured contemptuously toward the three I O U's Mason was holding and said, "Keep your shirt on. Those notes don't prove a damn thing, Mason."

"Why not?"

"You're Sylvia's attorney. You've doubtless seen her since my signed statement was released to the papers. She can sign as many I O U's as she wants to. All she needs is a fountain pen. You can get the blanks in any stationery store. Probably you thought you could throw a scare into me by coming in here and flashing those I O U's on me. I'm not that simple. I'm surprised that you thought I was. You know, Mason, you're playing in big-time stuff now. You're not up against simple boobs you can twist around your fingers with a lot of cheap bluff. Those I O U's you have *may* have been signed by Sylvia. That doesn't mean the I O U's *I* have weren't signed by Sylvia. She can sign her name as many times as she wants to."

Mason said, "You can't get away with it, Oxman."

Oxman's laugh was sarcastic. "That's what *you* think. You're the one who can't get away with it. You're representing Sylvia. Sylvia murdered Grieb."

"Why?" Mason asked.

"To get possession of those I O U's."

"Why didn't she get them then?"

"Because I'd already bought them. Grieb didn't have them."

Mason stretched his legs out in front of him, crossed his ankles, exhaled cigarette smoke, and said, "That's the trouble with you, Oxman. You're not a logical thinker."

"All right," Oxman said, "go ahead and think some logic for me. I'll listen."

Mason said, "Grieb and Duncan were fighting. They wanted to reduce their assets to cash. They saw a chance to collect not only the face value of those I O U's, but a little bonus as well. They gave you to understand you could have them by paying a two-thousand-dollar bonus. You raised ninety-five hundred dollars, went out to the gambling ship to pick up the I O U's. You found your wife aboard and Grieb dead. At first it occurred to you you'd simply step out of the picture, then you figured it might be possible to involve Sylvia, have her convicted of murder, and put her out of the way.

"This morning you read the newspapers and learned that the police had discovered seven thousand five hundred dollars in cash in Grieb's desk. You suddenly saw an opportunity to do a little chiseling. You figured Sylvia had probably recovered and destroyed the original I O U's. You were planning to release a statement that you'd seen Sylvia in the room with Grieb's body. Why not claim that *you'd* paid the seventy-five hundred dollars for the I O U's? Forging Sylvia's signature wasn't so hard. You had letters and documents bearing her genuine signature. You secured notes and copied or traced her signature on them."

Oxman yawned ostentatiously and said, "You bore me, Mason. I'd really expected a man of your caliber would show more intelligence."

Mason went on doggedly, "When you first saw Sylvia, she was in the room with Grieb's body. Your first impulse was simply to get out, so you slipped back out of the way. Later on, when you realized Sylvia had failed to report the murder, and had also ducked out—but had left fingerprints on the top of Grieb's desk—you saw an opportunity to charge your wife with murder, claim you'd paid seventy-five hundred dollars for the I O U's, turn two thousand dollars back to your associates, together with the forged I O U's, and sit tight.

"If Sylvia had destroyed the original I O U's, she could never admit she'd done so. If someone else had paid cash for the notes, that person would never dare to come forward, because that would make him the last person to have seen Grieb alive. If . . ."

"All wrong, Mason," Oxman interrupted. "You must have been smoking marihuana."

"Or," Mason went on evenly, "you noticed the original I O U's on the desk when you saw Sylvia in the room, and figured she was going to destroy them. If anything happened, and the originals turned up in the hands of some individual who was willing to admit having paid seventy-five hundred dollars for them—about one chance in a thousand—you could still claim Grieb had blackmailed you by selling you forged promissory notes. There was no one to disprove your story."

Oxman said, "You know, Mason, this *is* boring me. Let's have a little more entertainment, or else let's call in the police, let them take you into custody, and have this rather tiresome visit over with."

Mason flicked ashes from the end of his cigarette and said, "You see, Oxman, I can *prove* what I'm saying."

Oxman raised politely incredulous eyebrows.

"A detective shadowed you all day yesterday," Mason said. "We know what time you went aboard the ship. And we know what you did after you boarded it. You went down the corridor once, and only once."

Oxman's face showed surprise. "My God, Mason, do you mean to say you have practiced law as long as you have, and still put confidence in private detectives? Your man, Drake, may be on the square, but the boys he hires are just like any other private dicks. About half of them are crooked as corkscrews."

"These reports check with the facts," Mason said with dogged patience.

Oxman laughed. "What a sap you are, Mason! And you're supposed to be a big-time lawyer! Good Lord, man, *I* know I was being shadowed. I got a kick out of it. But if my shadow claims he followed me aboard that gambling ship, he's a liar. I purposely stuck around the pier until there was room for only one more in the launch. Then I took that one seat. The man who was shadowing me tried to follow me but couldn't make it."

Mason said, "Another detective was on duty who saw you go down the passageway to the offices. He says you went down only once."

Oxman laughed scornfully. "The only detective you had out there was Belgrade. He wasn't shadowing *me*. He was covering Sylvia. He doesn't know where I was. What's more, he's sold you out to the newspapers. . . . Good Lord, Mason, what an easy mark you are! Come around some day when I have some time. I'd like to play a little poker with you. You're so damned simple and your bluffs are so obvious, you'd be duck soup for me."

Mason went on patiently, "Then, after you went ashore, my man shadowed you to your hotel."

"Good God, Mason, you surely didn't think *that* was any news to me, did you?" Oxman asked.

"You knew he was following you," Mason went on steadily, "and threw a scare into him by standing in the door of the hotel and looking ostentatiously behind you."

"Check on that," Oxman agreed easily. "This dick ducked into a doorway and then stuck around outside, watching the hotel. He was afraid to come in."

"But," Mason pointed out, "I'd anticipated all that, and had another man stationed in the lobby, an operative who was ready to pick you up as soon as you came in."

The easy, patronizing smile didn't leave Oxman's features, but, for a moment, the muscles tightened. Then he took a cigar from his pocket, cut off the tip and scraped a match on the sole of his shoe. He took a watch from his pocket and placed it on the bed beside him. "Mason," he said, "if you're just talking—killing time to keep me from calling the police—it isn't going to do you any good. In precisely three minutes I'm going to let the house detective know you're here."

"Now then," Mason said, ignoring the interruption, "we come to the really significant part of the entire transaction. You took particular pains to call the attention of the hotel night clerk to the fact that you were depositing ninety-five hundred dollars in the safe. The way I figure that, Oxman, is that you'd raised ninety-five hundred dollars with which to take up those I O U's. When you found out Grieb had been murdered, you were afraid you might be implicated in the murder, and were particularly anxious to build up an alibi which would show you hadn't accomplished your business with Grieb before he'd been killed.

"Later on, you thought it over, read the morning papers, and decided there was a chance to knock down seventy-five hundred dollars."

Oxman rotated the cigar in the flame of the match, in

184

order to get it burning evenly, shook the match out, and said, "You're a rotten bluffer, Mason."

"I'm not bluffing," the lawyer told him. "I can prove the ninety-five-hundred-dollar business by the night clerk in the hotel. I don't need to rely on my private detectives there."

"Yes," Oxman said, studying the tip of the cigar with thoughtful eyes, but still keeping the faintly scornful smile about the corners of his mouth, "you could do that all right. What you have overlooked is that you'd have to prove I had *only* ninety-five hundred dollars when I went aboard that gambling ship. As a matter of fact, I had seventeen thousand dollars. After I paid seventy-five hundred dollars for the I O U's, I had nine thousand five hundred left. I got the I O U's for about half what I expected I'd have to pay."

For a moment the two men smoked in silence. Gradually, the smile on Oxman's lips broadened into a grin. "You see, Mason," he said, "as a lawyer it should have occurred to you, but probably hasn't, that *you'd* have to prove I had only ninety-five hundred dollars when I went aboard the ship. There's no way on God's green earth you can prove it. As a matter of fact, it isn't so. I had seventeen thousand dollars."

Mason pinched out the end of his cigarette. "You don't understand what I'm getting at, Oxman. I'm not talking now about what I intend to prove in court. When I leave here, I'm going to Carter Squires. I'm going to tell him my story. Squires was financing you in this thing. *He* knows how much money you took aboard that ship. When he finds out you tried to double-cross him by knocking down seventy-five hundred dollars, leaving him holding the sack, he won't like it. From all I can hear, Squires is a poor man to cross. . . . Well, the three minutes are up, Oxman. Go ahead and telephone the house detective."

Oxman sat motionless on the bed, his eyes hard and glittering, staring at Mason with hatred and apprehension.

There was no trace of a smile about the corners of his mouth.

"All right, then," Mason said, "I'll be on my way." He started toward the door. Bed springs squeaked as Oxman jerked himself upright and started after the lawyer. "Now, wait a minute, Mason," he said. "Let's talk this thing over."

Mason turned toward him. "What do you want to talk over?" he asked.

Oxman said, "You're all wet, but I'd hate to have you go to Squires with a story like that."

"Well?" Mason inquired.

Oxman shrugged his shoulders and said, "Nothing. I'd just hate to have you do it. Squires can't make any trouble for me, you know, but I've been friendly with him for some time, and I'd hate to have you introduce an element of friction."

Mason stood facing Oxman, feet spread apart, shoulders squared, eyes studying the slender man with a cold scorn. Abruptly he pulled the I O U's from his pocket, tore them into pieces and stepped into the bathroom. A moment later he returned and said, "Okay, Oxman, we'll forget that about the forgeries and figure your I O U's are genuine."

Oxman's face showed sudden relief. "That's better," he said. "I thought you'd be sensible. Now, what do you want?"

"Nothing," Mason told him. "You *may* have walked down the corridor to those offices and seen Sylvia bending over the desk. You may have seen the original I O U's on the desk. I don't know. If you did, you'll never dare to admit it, because that would brand your story about paying seventy-five hundred dollars to Grieb as a lie."

"What are you getting at?" Oxman asked.

"Simply this," Mason said, grinning mirthlessly, "I thought I knew the answer, but I wanted to make sure. I wanted to find out definitely and positively that Carter

Squires could establish that you had only ninety-five hundred dollars with you when you went aboard that gambling ship. Nine thousand five hundred dollars which he'd given you with which to pick up those I O U's.

"Now then, you've admitted in writing that you saw Grieb after you went aboard the ship. You claim that you purchased the I O U's from him. You have those I O U's in your possession. You've allowed the newspapers to take photographs of them. And you returned from that gambling ship with the same amount of cash with which you boarded it—nine thousand five hundred dollars. Now then, according to your story, *you must have been the last person to see Grieb alive!* You received seven thousand five hundred dollars in I O U's from him and you didn't pay him any money.

"The question arises, how *did* you get them? The answer is you had a fight with Grieb, shot him through the head and took the I O U's. In case it's of any interest to you, Mr. Frank Oxman, your wife will go before the Federal Grand Jury, look at those I O U's and unhesitatingly and absolutely identify them as the original I O U's which she gave Sam Grieb. That'll cost her seventy-five hundred dollars in cash, but having you hung for murder will be worth it."

Mason strode to the door and threw back the bolt. He turned on the threshold to look at Frank Oxman.

Oxman's face showed startled consternation. "My God, Mason. You can't do that. Sylvia can't. You wouldn't . . ."

Mason stepped out into the hallway, pulled the door half shut behind him, grinned and said, "And I don't think I want to play poker with you, Oxman. It wouldn't do me any good to win your clothes. They're too small for a real man to wear. Good day!"

Mason slammed the door, walked down the corridor to the stairway, descended two floors, and tapped on the door of Sylvia Oxman's room. He heard the rustle of motion on the other side of the door, but no sound of the door being opened.

"Okay, Sylvia," Mason said in a low voice, "open up."

She opened the door and stared at him with anxious, apprehensive eyes.

"You can quit worrying about your husband," Mason announced.

"Why, what did you do?"

"Put him on the defensive," Mason told her grimly. "My best guess is he'll take a run-out powder."

"Tell me what you *did*."

"Made him the last man to see Grieb alive," the lawyer said. "That lying written statement really puts him in a jam. Now it's up to him to squirm out. By the way, Sylvia, he's here in the hotel."

She recoiled. "He's *where?*"

"Here in the hotel, upstairs, in five-nineteen. How did *you* happen to come here?"

"Why . . . why, we came here once when we were dodging some people we didn't want to see. We didn't want to be home, and . . . Oh, I should have *known* he'd come here, if I stopped to think of it. This hotel is his hide-out. . . . You didn't tell him I was here?"

"No, of course not."

"Do you think he knows?"

"I don't know. He may have seen you in the lobby. Do any of the bellboys know who you are?"

"No, I don't think so."

"Well," Mason told her, "you'd better sit tight. Keep your door locked and if anyone knocks, don't answer unless you know who it is."

She sat down on the edge of the bed as though her knees had lost their strength. "I don't want to stay here," she said. "I want to get out."

"No, Sylvia, that's the worst thing you could do. Remember, the officers are looking for you. You don't dare register now at any hotel. I think Frank will be leaving here within an hour."

She looked down at the carpet, then suddenly raised her eyes to his and said, "Mr. Mason, why are you doing this for me?"

"I want to see that you get a square deal," he told her.

"Why?"

"Oh, you're sort of a half-way client of mine," he said, making his voice casual.

"You said something like that once before. Now I want to know why." As he said nothing, but remained silent, she went on, "I saw you and another man aboard the gambling ship the other night when I went out to talk with Grieb about those notes. It impressed me at the time that there was something queer about the way everyone acted when I showed up. Now I realize what it must have been."

"What?" Mason asked her.

"You'd been out there trying to get those I O U's," she said. "And . . . and it must have been Grandmother Benson who retained you."

"What makes you think that?" Mason asked.

"You're just asking *me* questions," she charged, "so *you* won't have to answer *mine*. Now listen, Mr. Mason, I'm going to tell you something: if she went out there expecting trouble, she'd have carried a gun. I think you should know that. She's carried a gun for ten years, and lots of people know about that habit. They josh her about it. So don't be surprised if . . ."

"What kind of gun," he interrupted, "automatic or revolver?"

"I don't know. . . . It *may* have been an automatic."

"All right," the lawyer told her, "I'll watch out for that gun business. Now then, there's a thousand to one chance your husband came to this hotel because he knows you're here. You keep your door locked. No matter what happens, don't open that door unless I'm on the other side of it. In the meantime, if you want me, you can ring me at Vermont eight-seven-six-nine-two. That's my secret hideout. Don't call me unless it's some major emergency, and don't tell anyone that number under any circumstances. Do you understand?"

She nodded.

"Can you remember the number?"

She took a pencil from her purse and started to write. Mason said, "Don't write it down that way. Write it eighty-seven V six, nine, two. Then anyone who finds it will think it's an automobile license number."

She wrote down the number as he directed, then came to stand at his side, her hand on his arm. "I can never in the world thank you enough for what you're doing," she said.

He patted the back of her hand. "Don't try."

"Tell me, is there a chance they'll convict Frank of this murder?"

"Lots of chance," Mason told her, "—if there ever was any murder."

"What makes you say that?"

"I have a witness who thinks Grieb committed suicide."

She shook her head slowly and said, "Sam Grieb would never have done that. He was killed."

"Well, it might suit us to let the authorities think it was suicide."

She said slowly, "Don't let them bear down too heavy on Grandmother Benson. . . . She . . . keep their minds on Frank Oxman if you can."

"You don't care what happens to Frank?" he asked.

"No, I don't owe *him* anything. And anyway, you're Grandma Benson's lawyer. You mustn't let them pin anything on her."

"Now wait a minute," the lawyer told her significantly. "If I'm representing an innocent client, I'm going to prove that client's innocent. If I ever represent a guilty client *who lies to me,* and I find out the lies, it'll be just too bad—for the client. . . . That's the way I play the game, Sylvia."

He stepped quickly into the corridor and closed the door.

14

MASON CALLED Paul Drake from a pay station. "Still got your men on Oxman, Paul?" he said when Paul answered the phone.

"Yes. Why?"

"I have an idea he's going to take a run-out powder."

"He can't afford to do that," Drake said. "He . . ."

"He can't afford *not* to do it," Mason interrupted. "He's in a jam and he won't dare to show himself until he can make his peace with Squires. Now, when he leaves, I want to know where he goes. He's wise now that he's being tailed. He'll try to ditch the shadows. I want you to make things easy for him—not so easy he smells a rat, but easy enough so he feels certain he's on the loose."

"You mean you don't want him covered any longer?"

"No, I want him tailed, but if he *thinks* he's given his shadows the slip it'll make him easier to handle. So put a couple of men on the job who can be push-overs, and then plant some smooth operatives in the background who can carry on from there. Do you get me?"

"I get you," the detective said. . . . "Now, listen, I've got something for *you.* Della Street reports that the Benson woman has contacted her and wants to see you.

They're going out to Della's apartment. Can you meet them there? Della says she thinks it's important."

"All right," Mason said, "I'll go out there right away. What else is new?"

"I've managed to get micro-photographs of the fatal bullet," Drake said. "It checks with the bullet Manning dug out of the beam of the ship. That means Grieb was killed with his own gun. It commences to look more and more as though this would give you an out, Perry."

"Let's hope so," Mason told him, "but there are a few loose ends I'd like to tie up before the Federal Grand Jury starts an investigation. In the meantime, I'll go see Della Street, and you keep Frank Oxman under surveillance. He's put himself in a position where he's done some things he can't explain. We can make *him* the goat if we have to."

"That won't help for long," Drake said. "He really isn't guilty of anything, is he?"

"You never can tell," Mason told him. "In any event, he's put himself in a hot spot trying to chisel seventy-five hundred bucks. I'll get in touch with Della."

"Just in case it means anything to you, there's a whole army of plainclothesmen clamped around the office building here," Drake said. "They're waiting for you to come in."

"It doesn't mean a thing to me," Mason told him cheerfully. ". . . be seeing you, Paul."

"Yes," Drake said, "perhaps you'll have the adjoining cell."

Mason hung up, left the telephone booth, and drove to Della Street's apartment house. He went at once to his own apartment and started hurriedly packing a suitcase. He was awkwardly folding his pajamas when he heard a tap on the door which communicated with Della's apartment. He twisted back the bolt on his side of the door to encounter her anxious eyes and the keen gray eyes of Matilda Benson.

"Are things coming okay?" Della Street asked anxiously.

Mason grinned reassuringly. "We're making satisfactory progress. Come in and sit down."

Matilda Benson gave him her hand. "I want to thank you," she said. "No other man that I know of could have done what you've done."

"He's done too much," Della said. "He always does too much. He shouldn't jeopardize his career for some client who's in trouble, and no client has any right to ask him to take the chances he does."

Mrs. Benson settled herself comfortably in a chair. "No use trying to lock the stable door after the horse has been stolen," she observed. "What's been done has been done."

"How did you get off that ship?" Mason asked.

She grinned. "There wasn't anything to it. Some of the crew lowered a rope ladder over the stern and let people slip into a speed boat at twenty dollars a head. Twelve people went off that I know of."

"*Twelve* people went down that rope ladder?" Mason asked.

She nodded, opened her bag, took out her leather cigar case, clipped the end off a cigar, pulled out a card of matches bearing the imprint of the gambling ship, and said, "At *least* twelve. Apparently it's a great rendezvous for mixed couples."

"What do you mean by mixed couples?"

"Husbands who have their wives mixed, and vice versa," she said. "When a married man's stepping out with some blonde cutie and is afraid he may run into some of his wife's friends, he's apt to pick the gambling ship as a swell place for dinner, drinks, and a little action." She broke off to chuckle, scraped a match into flame, and lighted the cigar.

"How about the coat?" Mason asked.

"I tossed mine overboard. I thought it would sink, but,

as luck would have it, it caught on the anchor chain. That was a break against me. Otherwise they'd never have known I'd been on the ship. With that coat as a clue, they've made an investigation and are all ready to crack down on me as soon as they can find me.

"That was a great experience—giving the officers the slip. I never saw anything quite so funny as the bedraggled appearance of those frightened philanderers crawling down the side of that ship on a rope ladder. The crew were getting a great kick out of it. The people were frightened stiff."

"So you got away all right?" Mason asked.

"Sure. They pushed the speed boat loose and didn't start the motor until it had drifted away from the ship. I had planned to give a phoney name and address, but I found it wouldn't work. The officers were demanding evidence of identification and all that sort of stuff. So I just politely skipped out on them."

"Then what?" Mason asked.

"Then I kept under cover, of course. Now I want to see Sylvia. You know where she is. I want to talk with her."

"It would be dangerous for you to see her now," Mason said slowly. "You're wanted, and your appearance is sufficiently distinctive so you could be picked up from a description, where . . ." He broke off as the telephone burst into sound.

Della Street picked up the telephone, said, "Hello. . ." then after a moment, "Who shall I say wishes to speak with him? Very well, hold the phone, please."

She turned to Mason and nodded. The lawyer scooped the receiver to his ear and heard Sylvia Oxman's half-hysterical voice. "Something awful's happened!"

"What?" he asked. "Keep cool and tell me about it."

"I was lying on the bed, reading, when someone tossed something through the open transom. It fell on the floor. . . . It . . . it's a gun—a .38 automatic."

"Did you," Mason asked, "pick it up?"

"Yes. I was frightened."

"Where is it now?"

"Right here on my dresser. Shall I try to dispose of it, or . . ."

"Get ready," Mason said, "for the police. The officers will be there within a matter of seconds. Don't make any statement to anyone. And . . ."

"Someone's knocking at the door now," she said.

"Hang up your telephone!" Mason commanded.

He slammed the receiver back on its hook, turned to Della Street and said, "Sylvia's been framed. Someone tossed a gun into her room. The cops are pounding at the door. She got frightened and put through a call to this number. They'll trace that call as quickly as they can, then call the radio cars, and start sewing *this* place up. Let's go!"

He began to fling things helter-skelter into his suitcase. Matilda Benson pulled them out, folded them neatly and packed the suitcase with a swift efficiency.

"Don't wait, Chief," Della Street told him. "You get started. Never mind the suitcase."

"Don't you understand," he said, "if they find the suitcase here, they'll pinch you as an accessory after the fact, for aiding and abetting, compounding a felony, and a few other charges. We can't afford to let the officers ever suspect that you know I was here. This thing is getting too hot to handle, and . . ."

He broke off as a peremptory knock sounded on the door of Della Street's apartment. For a moment the lawyer and his secretary stared at each other in startled consternation. Matilda Benson calmly put the finishing touches to the packing. The knock was repeated, and a voice shouted, "Open up! This is the law. We have a search warrant for this apartment."

"It's all right," Della Street said in a quick whisper. "I'll go in there and let them search. You keep this door locked and . . ."

"Nothing doing," Mason said. "They'll search until they find me. There's only one way to keep you out of it. You leave it to me. Come on, Della."

Matilda Benson snapped the suitcase shut and said, "Do they need to know *I'm* here?"

"Not if you can get away," Mason told her, "but I don't think you can."

The knock was repeated for the third time, a thundering summons which made the door rattle.

"We've got to lock the connecting door from this side," Mason pointed out. "There's no *legitimate* explanation you can make for having that door unlocked, Della."

Matilda Benson pushed them toward the door. "Go on in," she said. "I'll lock the door of this apartment."

Mason picked up his suitcase, stepped into Della Street's apartment, flung his overcoat over the back of a chair, perched his hat on the back of his head, and called out, "Just a minute, boys. Don't make so much noise."

He heard the bolt click in the door of the connecting apartment, opened the door of Della Street's apartment, and bowed to the three men who were standing in the corridor.

"This," he said, "is an unexpected pleasure."

One of the men stepped forward and said, "You're Perry Mason?"

"Yes."

He handed Mason a folded oblong of paper. "A subpœna to appear forthwith before the Federal Grand Jury," he said, "and I might also tell you that you're under arrest."

"On what charge?"

"Compounding a felony, being an accessory after the fact, and on suspicion of murder."

The men pushed their way into the room. Della Street stood by the window, her eyes wide with alarm.

One of the men walked toward her and said, "All right, we'll hear from *you* now. Did you know your boss was a fugitive from justice while you were shielding him? You . . ."

Mason interrupted, "Don't be silly, she wasn't shielding me. I was on my way to take a plane. I dropped in to give her some last-minute instructions."

"Says you," the man sneered.

Mason gestured toward his overcoat on the back of the chair and the suitcase. "See for yourself," he said.

The men exchanged glances. The man in charge said, "Take a look through the suitcase, Bill."

They tossed the suitcase to an overstuffed chair, unfastened the buckles on the straps, flung back the lid. "Okay," one of the men said, "he's got his stuff in here."

"He did his packing after we started pounding on the door," the man in charge said, his voice showing his irritation.

Mason grinned at them. "Rather a neat job of packing to be done in five seconds, don't you think?"

"You were long enough about getting the door open."

"I was giving my secretary some last-minute instructions," Mason told him, casually lighting a cigarette.

"The stuff is sure packed, all right," Bill said. "All neatly folded and . . ."

"Never mind the comments, Bill," the leader interrupted. "How about the adjoining apartment? We hear you've rented that."

"Adjoining apartment?" Della Street asked, raising her eyebrows.

"Shut up, Della," Mason warned.

The leader glowered at him. "Like that, eh?" he asked.

"Like that," Mason said easily.

The leader nodded to his men. "If that door's locked smash it down."

"Got a search warrant?" Mason asked.

No one paid any attention to the question. Two of the men charged the door. The bolt-seat ripped out. The door banged open.

Matilda Benson, her clothes draped over the back of a chair, was sprawled out in bed, pillows under her head, a cigar in her mouth. She looked up and said, "Why the hell don't you knock?"

The officers fell back in surprise. The man who had assumed charge stepped forward. "I beg your pardon. We have a warrant to search this apartment. We had every reason to believe it had been rented for the purpose of concealing Perry Mason."

Matilda Benson exhaled a cloud of cigar smoke and said acidly, "You had no reason to believe anything of the sort. This is my apartment. Perry Mason is my lawyer. I wanted to be close to his secretary, so she got me this apartment. I'm quite comfortable here. And, while I have no false modesty, young man, I *do* object to having my morning smoke interrupted."

For a moment the leader paused uncertainly, then said, "Take a look around, boys."

"In case you don't know it," Mrs. Benson remarked, "this is a damned outrage." She pulled the sheet up around her neck, punched the pillows into a more comfortable position, and calmly resumed smoking her cigar.

The officers made a swift, hurried search of her apartment. "So," the leader said, "you've been up and had breakfast, eh?"

Matilda Benson raised her eyebrows. "What was the name?" she asked. "Dr. Watson . . . or is it Holmes himself?" Someone tittered.

"Where are your personal belongings?" the leader demanded.

"I haven't moved them in yet."

"And is it your custom to burn the toast, to leave bacon in the oven, and hard-boil your eggs?" the officer asked suspiciously.

Mrs. Benson sighed and said meekly, "None of my husbands cared much for my cooking." She meditatively inspected the end of her cigar, raised steady gray eyes to encounter those of the officer, and added with a smile, "But that's the *only* complaint they ever made, young man."

The officer stared at her in nonplused silence, then said with sudden determination, "Get up and dress. I'm going to see this thing through. You're going to the district attorney's office for questioning. You too, Miss Street. Bill, telephone the D.A. and tell him we're on our way up. Get him to round up the others."

15

■

BASIL WILSON, the Federal District Attorney, entered the room and nodded a perfunctory greeting. Two deputy United States marshals stood at the door.

Wilson, a man in his middle fifties, with a close-cropped, iron-gray mustache and deep pouches under tired-looking eyes, said in a deep-timbred voice which filled the room with musical resonance, "Let's see if we're all here: Sylvia Oxman, Paul Drake, Arthur Manning, Matilda Benson, Dick Perkins, George Belgrade, Della Street, Perry Mason, Charlie Duncan, Frank Oxman."

"Frank Oxman isn't here," one of the deputies at the door said. "He's not in his room at his hotel. He must have sneaked out the back door. The clerk swears he didn't go out past the desk."

The district attorney showed his irritation. "We want him," he said. "He's a material witness. We *can* make out a case without him, but his testimony corroborates the circumstantial evidence. Get him!"

"We're expecting to pick him up at any time," the deputy said, in a voice which somehow failed to carry assurance.

"Well, we have his signed statement and know what his story is," the district attorney remarked. "For the purpose of this inquiry, we'll take that statement as being true. He's under a subpœna and if he tries to skip out, it'll be that much the worse for him when we do catch him."

Mason stole a surreptitious glance at Paul Drake. The detective slowly closed his glassy eyes, almost imperceptibly nodded his head. Mason settled back in his chair.

Basil Wilson said, "I want you people to realize the position you're in. I'm not making any definite charges right now, but I think it's due to the influence of Mr. Mason that you've been playing fast and loose with the law. You can't do that and get away with it. You're all of you under subpœna to appear before the Federal Grand Jury, which is now in session. I'm not making any promises of immunity, and I'm not making any concessions, but I've called you together in this office to tell you that each and every one of you is going before the Federal Grand Jury and is going to be put under oath. I'm not particularly disposed to be harsh on those who have innocently followed the advice of an attorney.

"You can expedite matters in front of the Grand Jury if you'll state freely and frankly at this time exactly what you know about Grieb's murder."

Mason lit a cigarette and said cheerfully, "Well, if I'm going to be the goat in this thing, I should have an opportunity to say something in my own behalf."

The district attorney said, somewhat testily, "I don't care particularly about a statement from you, Mr. Mason. I *know* what you have done. You have made yourself an accessory after the fact and compounded a felony."

Mason said, "You'll agree with me that one can't be an

accessory after the fact unless the person he aids is actually guilty of a felony."

Wilson's mouth, under his frosty, gray mustache, became uncompromisingly hard. "If," he said, ominously, "you think you can find a legal loop-hole for Sylvia Oxman, your previous victories, which have been due largely to luck, have left you unduly optimistic."

Mason waved his hand in a gesture of dismissal, as though brushing the district attorney's comment aside. "The gun," he said, "which the officers found in Sylvia's room was planted there by someone who knew she was in the hotel and who tossed it over the transom of Sylvia's room. Find the one who did that, and you'll find the murderer."

"We've already heard that story," Wilson said, "and you are at liberty to raise the point in front of a jury if you wish. I think you will find that even the most impressionable masculine juror will consider that explanation too weird to be taken seriously."

Mason nodded to Arthur Manning.

"All right, Manning," he said, "do your stuff."

Manning raised his eyebrows and said, "You mean . . ."

"Yes," Mason said, "I mean tell them what you know."

Manning took a deep breath. "I know," he said, "that Sam Grieb committed suicide."

"Did *what!*" Basil Wilson exclaimed.

"Committed suicide."

"Impossible!" the district attorney said.

"Go ahead, Arthur," Mason said, "and tell the district attorney what you told me. Tell it as briefly as possible."

"Well," Manning said, "it's this way: Sam Grieb kept a .38 automatic in the upper left-hand drawer of his desk. He was left-handed. He'd been dipping into the partnership funds, I think. When he knew Charlie was going to have a receiver appointed, and the books audited, he pulled the gun out of the desk drawer and shot himself.

"I hate to say this, but . . ."

"That's all right," Mason said, "go right ahead, Arthur, and make your statement."

"Well," Manning went on, "you see, it was like this: Grieb and Duncan took out partnership insurance. The policies didn't pay anything if the man who was insured should commit suicide within a year. They paid twenty thousand if he died a natural death, and forty thousand if he died by violence. Charlie Duncan found Sammy Grieb had committed suicide, and he thought fast enough to know it'd make just forty thousand dollars difference to him if he could make it look like a murder. So he got Mason and the deputy marshal out of the office long enough to pick up Grieb's gun, where it had fallen under the desk, and pitch it overboard."

The Federal District Attorney frowned at Manning and said, "Do you understand what you're saying?"

"Of course I do," Manning said.

"Have you any proof, or is this just surmise?"

"Well," Manning said, "you can figure it out for yourself. Grieb was shot with his own gun. Charlie Duncan saw to it that he was left alone in the room with the body . . ."

"No, I didn't," Duncan blazed. "Mason, *you'll* have to admit that I pressed the button which gave the signal for Manning to come *before* you left the office. Didn't I?"

"Yes," Mason admitted, "you did."

"And how long was it after the signal lights went on before you got into the office, Arthur?" Duncan demanded.

"Well," Manning said, "it was a little while."

"Not over six or eight seconds, was it?"

"Well, I don't know exactly how long it was, but . . ."

"Where was Perry Mason when you started for the office?"

"He'd just left the office. Perkins had him hand-cuffed."

"And it didn't take you over four or five seconds to answer my call, did it?"

"Well, no. But you had plenty of time to throw a gun overboard, and I can prove that Sammy was killed with his own gun."

"How?" Duncan asked.

"You remember the time you and Sammy shot at that piece of tin can down below the casino?"

"Yes, what of it?"

"I dug out the bullets. They were fired from the same gun that killed Sammy. And you know you were using Sam's gun on that target practice."

"All right. What if we were?" Duncan asked. "That doesn't prove anything. And you're all wet about this insurance business. There wasn't any insurance."

"I was in the room when you signed the papers," Manning said. "Maybe you don't remember, but I was standing right by . . ."

Duncan interrupted him. "Sure you were, Arthur. We signed the applications, all right, but Sam couldn't pass the physical examination, so the policies were never is-sued."

Manning's face showed consternation. "You mean there wasn't any insurance?"

"Exactly!" Duncan said. "It didn't make a dime's worth of difference to me whether Sam was murdered or com-mitted suicide."

The Federal District Attorney glanced at Perry Mason and permitted himself a smile.

"So," he said, "that seems to dispose of that phase of the inquiry. And I'm willing to admit Grieb was killed with his own gun. Our ballistic experts have fired test shots from the weapon which was found in Sylvia Oxman's room when she was arrested, and there's no question but what it's the murder gun. Now, if you want to prove it was Grieb's gun, so much the better. That simply accounts for the fingerprints left by Sylvia Oxman when she leaned over the desk. She braced herself by leaning on her left hand when she jerked the gun from the drawer with her right hand."

Perry Mason asked easily, "Well then, how about Oxman?"

"What do you mean?" Wilson asked.

"Why did he skip out?"

"Probably because he feared publicity. Oxman's statement checks in every detail with the testimony of Mr. Belgrade."

Belgrade nodded, frowned, cleared his throat, and said, "Pardon me, Mr. Wilson."

The district attorney frowned. Mason said, "Go ahead, Belgrade."

Belgrade said importantly, "I was shadowing Sylvia Oxman. I saw her go into the offices. While she was in there, Frank Oxman went down the corridor, just as he says he did. Then he turned around and came out again. It couldn't have been more than seven or eight seconds. After he'd gone out, Mr. Mason went in. Then Sylvia Oxman came out and stuck around the casino. Then Charlie Duncan and Perkins went in. Then Mason and Perkins came out and, within a few seconds, Charlie Duncan came out, and Sylvia Oxman went up on deck. I followed her up on deck and saw her . . ."

"Wait a minute," Duncan interrupted. "You were where you could see the entrance to the offices, weren't you?"

"Yes."

"And you know how long it was after Mason and Perkins came out that I came out?"

"It couldn't have been over a few seconds."

"As much as a minute?" Duncan asked.

"No, Charlie, I don't think it was."

"You see," Duncan said to the Federal District Attorney, "this substantiates my statement that . . ."

"Fiddlesticks!" Mason interrupted. "If you were there alone for as much as three seconds, you had an opportunity to pitch a gun out of the porthole."

Basil Wilson said, "I think as far as *this* office is concerned, Duncan, you're out of it. The evidence points to Sylvia Oxman as being the guilty party. Do you wish to make any statement, Mrs. Oxman?"

"No," Mason said, "she doesn't."

Wilson frowned at Mason. "Do I understand that, as her attorney, you're advising her to make no statement?"

"That's right."

"The Federal Grand Jury," Wilson said coldly, "will hold that against her."

Mason nodded easily. "That's all right. You see, Wilson, *she* can't very well make a statement without implicating *me*."

The Federal District Attorney picked up a file of papers. "Well, we'll go into the Grand Jury room and . . . What was that last statement you made, Mason?"

"I said," Mason repeated, the corners of his mouth twisting into a smile, "that she couldn't very well make a statement without implicating me."

"I think I know what you mean," Wilson said, "but if you'd like to elaborate on your remark, I'd be willing to listen."

Mason said, "Sylvia Oxman went aboard the gambling ship to see Sam Grieb. She found the door of the office slightly ajar. She pushed it open and found Sam Grieb murdered. He was seated at his desk in exactly the position the officers subsequently found the body. The three I O U's she'd given him, in an amount of seventy-five hundred dollars, were on a corner of the desk. About that time, she was alarmed by the noise made by an electric signal, which indicated someone was coming down the corridor. She was rattled, and didn't know just what to do, so she turned around and ran into the outer office and sat down, pretending she was waiting for a chance to see

Grieb. A few moments later I entered that office and found her there. She was holding an open magazine. I said something to her, and then, noticing the door of the inner office was ajar, pushed it open and entered . . ."

"Wait a minute. . . . Wait a minute," the Federal District Attorney interrupted, jabbing frantically at the push-button on his desk, "I'm going to have this statement taken down in shorthand."

"Go ahead," Mason said easily.

Paul Drake looked across at Mason, an expression of startled incredulity on his face. Duncan glanced triumphantly about him and lit a cigar. A man with a shorthand notebook and fountain pen came hurrying in from an adjoining office. The Federal District Attorney said, jabbing his finger at Perry Mason, "This is Perry Mason, the lawyer. He's making a confession. Take it down."

"A confession?" Mason asked.

"Go right ahead," the Federal District Attorney said, "we won't quibble over words. You've already admitted pushing open the door. You've admitted Sylvia Oxman was in the outer office at the time, and *had* been in the private office. You gentlemen have heard that statement?"

Wilson's eyes swept the circle of faces, and received grave nods of acquiescence. "Let the record show," he said to the shorthand reporter, "that the people in this room all reply in the affirmative."

"Let the record show that I'm nodding too," Mason said, grinning, apparently enjoying himself hugely. . . . "Well, as I was remarking, I entered the inner office and found Grieb's body slumped over the desk. I grabbed Sylvia Oxman as she was leaving the office. She admitted then she'd been in there before. I told her to go on out. When she'd gone, I opened the drawer of Grieb's desk, deposited seventy-five hundred dollars, the face value of the three I O U's Sylvia Oxman had signed, touched a match to the I O U's and burned them up."

"You *what?*" the district attorney asked, his eyes wide.

"I burned them up."

"Didn't you know you were committing a crime when you did that, Mr. Mason?"

Mason raised his eyebrows and said, "Why, no. What crime?"

"Compounding a felony."

"In what way?"

"Those I O U's furnished a motive for the murder."

"*Did* they?" Mason said. "Well, of course, that's news to me."

"And when you destroyed them, you destroyed evidence. You were also guilty of a felony in wrongfully taking those I O U's."

"Personally," Mason said, "I don't think they're evidence of anything. Therefore, I wasn't guilty of anything when I destroyed them. Furthermore, I didn't *take* them, I paid for them."

"Wait a minute," Wilson said, frowning. "This doesn't agree with Oxman's statement."

"That's right," Mason said easily.

"I'm afraid," the Federal District Attorney went on, "that so far as the Federal Jury is concerned, Mr. Mason, they will be far more inclined to take Oxman's word than yours."

Mason shrugged his shoulders. "Well, that's all right. Let them. But I don't think they'll take Oxman's *written statement* against my *word*. Oxman had better show up and try to substantiate his story if he wants to make it stick."

The district attorney frowned. "I don't care to argue the point, Mr. Mason. Do you have any further statement to make?"

"Yes," Mason went on easily. "Shortly after I'd de-

207

stroyed the I O U's, an electric signal in the office announced someone was coming down the corridor. I slipped back into the outer office and pulled the door shut behind me just as Duncan and Perkins entered the office. I believe Mr. Duncan has correctly stated what happened after that. . . . Oh, yes, there's one point I wanted to make: you'll remember, Perkins, that Duncan crossed over to the vault, saying he wanted to open it. He grasped the door handle, and turned the knob of the combination. You advised him not to open it."

"That's right," Perkins said.

"That's true?" Mason asked Duncan.

Duncan mouthed his cigar for a second or two, and then slowly nodded and said, "Yes, that's true. I wanted to look in the vault and see what had happened to those I O U's."

Mason grinned at the district attorney and said, "Well, there's your murder case."

"What do you mean?" the district attorney asked.

"My God," Mason said, "do I have to draw you a diagram? Don't you see it yet?"

The district attorney flushed, and said with dignity, "I see, Mr. Mason, that, according to your own confession, you have involved yourself as an accessory after the fact. You have aided and abetted Sylvia Oxman in her escape. You have failed to do your duty as an attorney and an officer of the court."

Mason lit a cigarette, grinned across at the district attorney and said, "Where was Manning?"

Duncan said, *"You* know where Manning was. He was out in the casino. And as soon as I pressed the signal which summoned him, he entered the offices and took charge. Didn't you, Arthur?"

"Well," Manning said with slow deliberation, "there was a delay of a few seconds after you gave the signal, before I actually reached the offices."

Mason chuckled and the district attorney said acidly, "There's no occasion for humor, Mr. Mason."

Mason said to Perkins, "You saw Duncan spin the combination on that vault door?"

"Why, yes, Mr. Mason."

"He spun it through several revolutions without looking at numbers, didn't he?"

"I'm not certain. I remember he went over to the vault and said something about opening the door and spun the knob on the combination."

Mason grinned. "That's right, Perkins. He *said* he was going to open the vault door. As a matter of fact, the vault door was unlocked. What he was doing was *locking* it."

"You're crazy!" Duncan exclaimed. "What the hell are you trying to pull, anyway?"

Mason said simply, "That your accomplice, Arthur Manning, having killed Grieb by taking Grieb's gun from the drawer and shooting him through the head, was trapped in the inner office by Sylvia Oxman's arrival. There was no place for him to hide except in the vault. The murder had all been fixed up between you and Manning. You wanted Grieb out of the way. There was bad blood between you. Grieb was commencing to check up on you. You prepared an elaborate alibi by going to Los Angeles to file a case in the Federal Court. You knew Grieb would ring for Manning sometime during the evening. Manning was to grab Grieb's gun from the drawer, shoot him, leave the gun so it would look like a case of suicide, and then slip out and pull the door shut behind him.

"Grieb summoned Manning to perform some errand or other, but Manning couldn't close and lock the door without making Grieb suspicious, since Manning was supposed to go right out again. Manning grabbed the gun and shot Grieb just as the exhaust of a speed boat drowned the noise of the shot. But the roar of that exhaust also drowned out the sound the buzzer made when Sylvia Oxman came walking down the corridor. The first thing Manning knew, before he'd had a chance to drop the gun or plant any evidence, he heard Sylvia Oxman in the outer office calling, 'Yoo-hoo! May I come in?'

"There was only one thing for Manning to do. He slipped into the vault and pulled the door shut. But he couldn't lock the door from the inside. He sat there, holding the murder weapon, waiting either for a chance to escape or for a chance to shoot his way out.

"Naturally, when you came aboard, the first person you looked for was Manning. You didn't see him in the casino, so you went down to the offices, found me sitting there, were in a position where you had to open the door of the inner office and pretend surprise at finding Grieb's body. You naturally wanted it to appear as a suicide, and started looking for the gun. When you couldn't find it, you realized something had gone wrong.

"It didn't take you very long to find out what that something was. Manning had been interrupted before he'd had the opportunity to plant the gun. You did some fast thinking and figured he must be hidden in the vault. You thought that Perkins or I would make a move to open that vault, so, under the pretense of trying to open it, you spun the combination so we *couldn't* open it. Fortunately, Perkins played into your hands by suggesting you leave it alone; otherwise you'd have pretended you'd forgotten the combination.

"You were most anxious to get rid of us, so you accused me of having taken something from the room, persuaded Perkins to take me to your cabin to be searched, turned on the signal for Manning; then, as soon as you were alone in the room, opened the vault and let Manning out. You realized at once there was one vitally weak point in your story. In order to protect yourself, no one must ever suspect you and Manning of being accomplices. So you fixed things up with Manning so he'd tell the officers he'd found you snooping around the chair in which I'd been sitting when he entered the offices. That made *his* story sound a lot more plausible, made it seem less likely there was collusion between you, and put you in the *outer* office and away from the vault door. Later on, when Manning reported that Paul Drake had employed him, you worked out a story about the target practice which would enable Manning to lay a good foundation for a suicide theory. The bullets Manning dug out from the beam were fired this morning. But, while you were doing all this, you suddenly realized there was a much better chance to pin the crime on Sylvia Oxman. So you had Manning stress the suicide angle, but were ready to toss that theory overboard if it looked as though you could pin it on Sylvia."

Duncan laughed and said, *"That's* one of the greatest pipe dreams I've ever heard. I always knew you were an ingenious attorney, but I never thought you'd break out with such a wild story as that in order to save a guilty client."

The Federal District Attorney nodded. "Yes, Mr. Mason, I'm afraid your desperate attempt to free Mrs. Oxman will act as a boomerang and leave you convicted of complicity in the crime by your own statements, without . . ."

"Wait a minute," Mason said, "I'm not talking through my hat. I have proof."

"What proof?" Duncan asked.

"Simply this," Mason said. "Belgrade was watching the entrances to the office. He didn't see Manning go *in*. No one saw Manning go *in*. No one saw Manning in the casino. When Duncan and Perkins came aboard, Manning wasn't in the casino. Manning claims that he slipped down the passageway just as Perkins and I went out, but *I* didn't see him and *Perkins* didn't see him."

"You had your backs turned to me," Manning said.

"Then why didn't Belgrade see you?" Mason asked.

Manning shrugged his shoulders and said, "Belgrade's a crook. He sold Paul Drake out. I wouldn't take his word for anything."

The Federal District Attorney frowningly inspected Belgrade. "Did you see Mr. Manning go in those offices?" he asked.

Belgrade shook his head, his puzzled expression indicating his sincerity. "No," he said. "By God, I didn't!"

The Federal District Attorney thoughtfully regarded Duncan, Manning and Mason. "This," he said irritably, "is one of the damnedest things *I've* ever encountered. I simply can't believe that . . ."

Matilda Benson interrupted him to say, "Well, I may as well confess."

"You may as well *what?*" the district attorney demanded.

"Confess," she said. "You don't mind if I smoke, do you, Mr. Wilson?"

"No," he said. Duncan and Manning exchanged glances, then Manning looked away hastily.

Matilda Benson calmly pulled a cigar from her leather cigar case, cut off the end, and lit the cigar before the astonished eyes of the district attorney. "This shorthand reporter is going to take down everything I say?" she asked.

"Yes. He's taking down everything," the district attorney said.

"Very well," Mrs. Benson remarked, in a voice of complete resignation. "I don't know what the punishment will be for what I've done. Whatever it is, I'm willing to take my medicine. I'm not afraid to die. My life-expectancy is short, anyway. Sylvia and her daughter mean a lot more to me than my own life. Grieb and Duncan were blackmailing Sylvia. I felt they were both a couple of rats. I didn't think they deserved to live. I went aboard the ship with the deliberate intention of killing both Grieb and Duncan."

"Were you armed?" the district attorney asked.

"Certainly I was armed," she said. "I carried a .38 automatic in my handbag. What did you think I expected to kill them with, my hands?"

"Go ahead," the district attorney said hastily.

"I watched for a chance, waiting. I saw Sylvia go into the office. I waited. I saw Frank Oxman go into the office. I opened my bag and slipped the automatic down the front of my dress. I saw Oxman come out. I saw Mason go in, and Sylvia come out. I saw Duncan and Perkins go in. Then I saw Perkins and Mr. Mason come out. I said to myself, 'Now is my time. Both the men I want to kill are in there.' I gripped my gun in my right hand and tiptoed cautiously down the corridor. I slipped silently into the outer office. I could see the door of the vault in the inner office, but I couldn't see Grieb's desk. The door blocked my line of vision; but I supposed, of course, Grieb was sitting there at his desk. I saw Duncan bending over the vault door, opening it. I leveled my gun, and was just about to pull the trigger, when Duncan opened the door of the vault and I saw Manning come out. I didn't want to kill Duncan while Manning was there, so I slipped back into the corridor. I saw Duncan come out. I followed him down to the room where Perry Mason was being searched. I listened at the door. I heard voices and learned Grieb had been killed, so I ran up on deck and waited a few moments, wondering what to do. I saw Sylvia come up, and I thought Sylvia was going to speak to me. I realized then that I'd be searched, so I tossed my gun overboard. But Sylvia didn't see me. She ran down the landing-stairs and took a launch which was leaving for the shore. I tried to protect Sylvia, because I thought she might be implicated in Grieb's murder. So I had Mr. Mason get my coat, and I threw it overboard. I smuggled Sylvia's coat ashore and . . ."

"You're willing to swear to this?" the district attorney interrupted, his voice excited. "You're willing to swear that you actually *saw* Duncan open the vault and Manning step out?"

Slowly, impressively, Matilda Benson got to her feet and held up her right hand. "You show me the grand jury room, young man," she said, her eyes snapping, "and I'll go in and swear to it right now. I'm telling the truth and nothing but the truth."

Duncan met the district attorney's accusing eyes. His own eyes were slightly squinted as though he were making a rapid mental readjustment. Suddenly he said, "They're all wet. I wasn't Manning's accomplice. I *didn't* know Manning was in the vault. I didn't lock it, as Mason claims. I *did* open it after Mason had left the office. You could have knocked me over with a feather when I opened that vault and Manning walked out. He told me he'd gone into the vault to get some papers for Grieb, when he heard someone knock at the outer door and a woman's voice call out, 'This is Sylvia Oxman. Let me in.' Grieb yelled, 'You stay in there for a few minutes, Arthur,' and slammed the door of the vault shut.

"Arthur stayed inside and heard the muffled sound of a shot. He tried to get out and couldn't. He didn't hear anything more until I opened the door of the vault. It was Sylvia Oxman who shot Grieb, and she carried away the gun.

"I wanted to get rid of Mason and Perkins so I could get those I O U's out of the vault. I'm willing to admit I figured I could pull a fast one with them. I didn't see any reason why they should be a part of the partnership assets and be ruled uncollectable by a court. If I could have found them, I could have collected from Sylvia and pocketed the coin.

"Finding Manning in there gave me an awful shock. Manning told me what had happened. He said Sam had the I O U's under the blotter on his desk. I looked for them and they were gone. I knew I'd put myself in an awful spot. If I said anything about finding Arthur Manning in that vault, I knew someone would accuse me of having planned the whole business, with Manning as my accomplice. I figured Perry Mason was covering Sylvia Oxman.

"I realized no one knew Manning had been in the vault, so I figured the best thing to do was to let Arthur out, say nothing about what had happened, and let the police pin the murder on Sylvia Oxman. Of course, if I'd known Mrs. Benson had seen me. . ."

"You damn fool!" Manning screamed. *"She* didn't see you! She *couldn't* have seen you. She's lying. Belgrade was watching the corridor, and *he* didn't see her go down the corridor before you came out. What's more, she didn't ring the bell in the inner office. She'd have done that if what she says is true. You've walked into a trap!"

Perry Mason chuckled delightedly. "Keep right on talking, Arthur," he said.

16

PERRY MASON sat in his office and regarded Matilda Benson with respect in his eyes. "How the devil," he asked, "did you ever concoct such a beautiful lie on the spur of the moment?"

"Young man," she said, taking her cigar from her mouth and staring at him with snapping gray eyes, "I've lived sixty-eight years. I lived my girlhood in an age of universal hypocrisy. I found it was necessary for me to lie. I've had exactly fifty years of practice in extemporaneous prevarication. I'm not exactly a fool; and when I sized up the situation and saw how absolutely logical your theory was, I felt that it needed a damned good lie to bolster it up. And if you think it took any great amount of skill to think up as simple a lie as that, you should have heard some of the whoppers I've told in my time." She wrapped her lips about her cigar, puffed a couple of times, took the cigar from her mouth, nodded her head, and went on proudly, "And made them stick, too! Don't forget that."

Della Street opened the door from her secretarial office to bring in a filing jacket filled with papers.

"All there, Della?" Mason asked.

She nodded. "Everything's ready for Sylvia's signature."

Mason said to Matilda Benson, "Here are the papers in Sylvia's divorce action. She's alleging cruelty on the ground that her husband made a false statement to the officers, willfully, maliciously and falsely accusing her of the crime of murder."

"Can she get a divorce on that?" Matilda Benson asked.

"You bet she can," Mason said. "We've got Frank Oxman right where we want him. The minute Charlie Duncan thought there was a chance to save *his* bacon by trying to invent an explanation which would account for Manning's being in the vault, he gave us every trump card in the deck. Now, with those two crooks in separate cells and each one thinking the other is going to double-cross him, with Manning thinking that Duncan is going to make him the goat all the way through, it's a cinch something's bound to break."

Matilda Benson nodded, tucked the filing jacket of papers under her arm and said, "All right, I'll get Sylvia's signature to the complaint."

"And she'll have to sign the affidavit of verification

216

before a notary public," Mason said. "Then I'll be ready to file the case."

The white-haired woman's jeweled fingers gripped the lawyer's hand with a firmness which was almost masculine. "I knew you'd see me through," she said.

Case after case
Mystery, Suspense and Intrigue...

ERLE STANLEY GARDNER'S
PERRY MASON MYSTERIES